NATIONAL BE

YAHRAH ST JOHN

Untamed
Hearts

Dear Reader,

If you enjoyed Entangled Hearts Volume I and II, you'll love the 3rd edition in the Harts of Arizona series. The idea for the book came back in 2012 over dinner with friends in Washington DC. One of my friends mentioned that a friend's daughter had a rendezvous with a prince whose father was a sheikh. And so the idea for **Untamed Hearts** was formed. Rylee served as a great foil to Chynna's story, but she was due one of her own. I loved her feistiness and that she was an unconventional heroine working on her family's ranch.

Meeting playboy and sheikh's son Amar Bishop was the catalyst that would propel her away from the ranch to explore new adventures which was critical to the storyline and character development. More importantly I wanted their love story to be color-blind even though I knew the hero: Amar Bishop would be of mixed heritage. It was really exciting to research and write about the Kentucky Derby, sheikhs and palaces. It was so cool, I created a fake kingdom!

Stay tuned for the final book in the Harts of Arizona Series (Book IV) when I tell Caleb's story in **Restless Hearts** later in 2014. I would love to hear from you feel free to write me: **yahrah@yahrahstjohn.com.** Or visit my website: **www.yahrahstjohn.com**

Best Regards,
Yahrah St. John

Chapter 1

"RYLEE, I NEED YOU."

"Excuse me?" Rylee Hart stared in bewilderment at Jeremy Wright, her date and pseudo boyfriend, as they stood in her family's living room at their dude ranch, Golden Oaks in Tucson, Arizona. She'd known Jeremy for years. Had grown up with him. Even played in his family's kiddie pool. He was her father's choice of a mate for her — a trust fund baby who didn't seem to have any ambitions of his own, save for racing horses and pitching in to help his father run a cattle business on the family's ranch outside of Tucson.

Rylee had been humoring her father, Isaac Hart, by agreeing to see Jeremy, but bless his heart, Jeremy didn't light her fire. Sure, he was good-looking, with smooth cocoa-colored skin, big kind-hearted eyes and a well-kept physique, but without ambition and drive, he didn't stir her loins. To her father, however, Jeremy's riches, coupled with the fact that he was a sincere, honest man, were enough to make him the perfect marriage partner for his daughter.

Well, Rylee wasn't having it, and now Jeremy's declaration that he *needed her* was just too much.

"I need you to come with me to Louisville to look after Dreamer," Jeremy explained. "I wouldn't trust her health to anyone but the best vet in all of Tucson."

At his compliment, Rylee couldn't resist a smile. Dreamer was the beautiful thoroughbred racehorse Jeremy had bought two years ago and had been steadfastly training. He felt she had a surefire chance of winning the Kentucky Derby. Even though she was considered a long shot, Jeremy had absolute faith in the horse.

"Thank you, Jeremy. You're very kind to say that, but wouldn't Dreamer be better off with one of the vets from your stables?"

"I'd think you'd jump at the chance to get away from the ranch," her father interjected, having suddenly appeared. Isaac Hart was tall and imposing, with salt-and-pepper hair and a broad nose. He could be very intimidating when he wanted to be, and tonight was no different. "Especially when it's an all-expense paid trip. Not to mention you would get to visit your old stomping grounds, Pembroke Stables, where you completed your residency."

Her father reminding them all of that two-year residency made Rylee frown. It also made her remember how stupidly she'd behaved by falling for her mentor, Dr. Shelton Gray, a world-renowned veterinarian at Pembroke Stables who was also very married. Of course, Rylee hadn't known it at the time. Shelton had told her they were divorced, but apparently "separation" didn't mean the same thing to him as it did to the rest of the world.

Rylee had been mortified to be found on top of Shelton as they made love, riding him like there was no tomorrow in their marital bed by none other than his wife! And to be informed that they were still married on top of that had been the icing on the cake. The remaining year of her residency had been excruciating. She'd had to work with the man side by side after he'd lied to her, and to constantly fight his advances. He'd tasted some of Rylee, and he wanted more. But she was made of strong stock and managed to keep him at bay as she continued with her studies. She was going to become a vet, no matter what.

Looking back on the experience now, Rylee supposed it had made her stronger. Yet by the same token, it had made her wary of smooth-talking men and false promises. And today, with all this talk of accompanying Jeremy to the very place where her drama with Shelton had played out, she reflected on her sexual inadequacies. She'd never been able to have an orgasm except by way of oral sex. If a man as suave, fine and accomplished as Shelton Gray couldn't make her come alive in the bedroom, Jeremy certainly couldn't do it either.

"We could make it a girl's trip," her best friend, Camryn Sanders, chimed in beside Rylee, breaking her from her thoughts. "You know, hit all the big parties. It would be a chance to wear a fabulous dress and a fancy hat."

"When have you ever seen me in a fancy hat?" Rylee replied.

"Well ... never," Camryn admitted with a blush. "But it's time to give it a try. I promise. And when have I ever steered you wrong?"

Rylee was more comfortable in jeans and a cowboy hat than she'd ever been playing dress-up like other girls. Hell, even tonight, she couldn't wait to take off the spaghetti-strap dress and spiky sandals her sister-in-law, the top-selling pop singer and media best-dressed list favorite, Chynna James Hart, had insisted she wear. Camryn, on the other hand, although full-figured, was rocking a cocktail dress and stilettos along with impeccable makeup.

Rylee gave her friend's ensemble an admiring look, although it wouldn't be her own fashion choice.

"It would really mean a lot to me if you came along," Jeremy said, squeezing Rylee's shoulder.

Rylee looked down at his arm and then back across at her father, who she could see was silently pleading with her to say yes. "Okay. Okay, I'll go." What choice did she have? She'd been caged in not only by Jeremy and Camryn, but by wanting to please her father.

"You'll see, it'll be the time of our lives," Camryn replied.

Rylee highly doubted it, but she would give it the old college try.

"Hey, what's wrong?" Chynna Hart asked Rylee when she saw her later that night, nursing a glass of Shiraz. "I thought you'd be happy for Noah and me."

Rylee had been excited to hear her brother Noah and Chynna's big announcement that evening — they were going to become parents, which Rylee knew was a big deal for Noah. He'd lost his first love and wife, Maya, and their unborn child in a tragic car accident three years ago. Noah had endured a lot of pain, and she was thankful he'd found love with Chynna. Rylee adored her.

"I am happy for you two," Rylee said, squeezing Chynna's hand. "But I'm surprised Daddy hasn't filled everyone in on the news that I've agreed to go with Jeremy to Louisville."

Chynna's brow furrowed. She knew Rylee wasn't interested in Jeremy in a romantic sense. "How did that happen?"

Rylee shrugged. "You know, the usual — Daddy and Jeremy ganging up on and me. And did I happen to mention that my BFF" — glass still in hand, Rylee pointed to Camryn — "added fuel to the fire by telling them how much fun we'd have."

"You probably will," Chynna offered. "I sure had a blast the first time I went to the Derby. The clothes, the parties. It's all very sophisticated. Being invited to sing made me feel like I'd arrived."

"Easy for you to say," Rylee replied. "You don't have someone following you around like a puppy dog."

"He's easy on the eyes. You could do worse."

Rylee gave an exaggerated sigh. "Or I could do much better."

"What are you looking for, Rylee?" Chynna asked. She'd only known her sister-in-law for a year, but there were still parts of Rylee that were a secret.

"I don't know," Rylee said, shrugging. She'd always felt she'd know Mr. Right when the moment came, would feel it someplace deep in her belly, but she'd yet to meet him. "What I do know is, Jeremy isn't it."

"C'mon, Rylee, don't be such a spoilsport," Camryn said on their limo ride to the private airport where Jeremy's jet — actually his *father's* jet — awaited to whisk them away. Rylee was sure Jeremy was using it as a ploy to show off. It was too bad she wasn't interested in what he was selling.

"I won't be a spoilsport," Rylee replied. "I told you I would embrace the experience, and I will." She'd agreed to go shopping with Camryn in Louisville and update her wardrobe from her usual fare of plaid shirt and jeans to something more sophisticated for the Derby.

Camryn rubbed her hands in anticipation. This trip would be a colorful respite from her job answering letters for her relationship advice column at a small daily newspaper. "This is going to be so much fun. I get to dress you up."

Rylee rolled her eyes. She could imagine what she was in for and what Camryn would have her wearing for the myriad Derby events.

The limo came to a stop several minutes later, and the chauffeur came around to open the door for her and Camryn and assist them out. The jet waited on the tarmac.

"This is so awesome," Camryn gushed as they climbed the exterior staircase. "I've never been on a private jet before."

As for Rylee, it was only her second ride on one. Last year, Chynna had sent her jet to Tucson to pick up Noah and Rylee so they could fly out and meet her on a tour stop. There wouldn't be much of those for a while because Chynna planned on taking sabbatical from singing to enjoy being a newlywed and a new mom.

Rylee would enjoy being an aunt, because she could have her fill of babies as much as she wanted with her niece *or* nephew and then hand them back to their parents. Oddly enough, she'd never thought about having kids herself. She had always assumed she'd be Aunt Rylee to Noah's kids because her younger brother, Caleb, sure wasn't having any unless he happened to knock someone up. It wasn't that she didn't want kids, she just wasn't sure she'd ever meet Mr. Right. She'd certainly encountered her share of *Mr. Wrongs*.

"Thank you," Rylee said, accepting the hand offered her by the chauffeur, and ascended the stairs.

Jeremy was waiting for them. She had to admit that Chynna was right — he *was* an attractive man. His hair was clipped short, and he had a broad nose, full lips and a goatee that suited him. He was casually dressed in jeans, a crisp white shirt and a casual linen blazer. "Ladies," he said, rising to greet them. When he reached Rylee, he gave her a quick hug and a kiss and did the same to Camryn. "Have a seat." He gestured beside him.

"Thank you, Jeremy," Rylee said. "This is really lovely."

"Anything for you," Jeremy replied, holding her gaze. Undisguised adoration filled his eyes.

Rylee half-smiled to mask her distress.

"I'm so happy to have you on this trip, looking after Dreamer," Jeremy said. "I know everyone thinks I'm crazy and that she's a long shot to win the Derby, but I just have

6

a feeling, ya know" — he patted his stomach — "that's she's meant for greatness. I sent her trainer, Hank, ahead of us with her to Louisville."

"I don't think you're crazy," Rylee said. "Sometimes we have to listen to our gut, and usually it doesn't steer us wrong. And I'm here to help with Dreamer and ensure you have a healthy horse come Derby day."

"I know you will," Jeremy said, patting her knee. "When your father told me you interned at Pembroke, I knew asking you to come was the right thing. Why did you leave Golden Oaks, if you don't mind my asking, and go to Pembroke?"

Rylee shrugged. Speaking about her time in Louisville was her least favorite subject, but she knew Jeremy was just being sociable and even Camryn stopped reading the magazine she'd brought with her to hear the answer. Rylee had never even told Camryn what had happened between her and Dr. Gray. She'd been too embarrassed to say she'd been a sucker and fallen for a married man.

"Well ..." She paused, gathering her thoughts. "I just needed to get off the ranch, see another way of life. You know my father. He'd have been content if I stayed on the ranch and never left, but I wanted to explore the world and have new experiences. Not to mention Pembroke was world-renowned for their care of thoroughbreds and stallions."

"They sure are," Jeremy added.

"As long as she has a strong jockey and a good trainer, Dreamer will do great," Rylee assured.

"Enough about horses," Camryn said, "as I have little to add to this conversation. Tell us about all the parties."

Thankfully, Camryn's animated interest about Derby fashion and fetes had kept the flight from Tucson to Kentucky from being a bore, and Rylee arrived hopeful that her week in Louisville would be better than her last experience.

A limousine greeted them at the airport and whisked them to the historic Brown Hotel, which was less than fifteen minutes from Louisville's International Airport. A uniformed bellman opened the doors, and luxury and grandeur greeted and overwhelmed Rylee as she walked on the marble floors. She was a hick by no means, as Golden Oaks was an established and well-respected dude ranch, but she felt like a fish out of water wearing her cowboy boots.

"This is fabulous," Camryn gushed, squeezing her arm.

"You're telling me." Rylee admired the ornate two-story lobby, with its hand-painted ceilings, decorative crown mouldings, golden chandeliers, fine china and opulent paintings.

"I can't believe we'll be staying in a place like this," her friend said with open-mouthed glee.

"We're just as good as any of these fine people," Rylee whispered, trying to help Camryn regain her composure. She'd noticed several onlookers staring in their direction. She suspected not many people of color frequented the establishment, and she didn't want a spotlight on them. "C'mon," she said, tugging Camryn's arm, and together they met Jeremy at the front desk.

The attendant was handing Jeremy their room key cards when they arrived.

"Ladies," Jeremy said, handing each of them a key card, "your rooms are on the ninth floor. Unfortunately, we are on different floors since I booked my room several months ago, but I won't be far if you need me."

"We can take care of ourselves," Rylee said, "but thanks again." She quickly tugged Camryn's arm and began down the hall.

"Dinner at seven at the English Grill?" Jeremy called out after them.

Rylee turned back around long enough to say, "Sure! See you then."

"You really *aren't* interested in him, are you?" Camryn said when they stepped onto the elevator. "He's not all bad you know. He has a good heart."

"I know that, Camryn, really I do," Rylee said. "It's just that I'm not attracted to Jeremy in that way. And the more he tries, the more I retreat."

Camryn shrugged. "I wish I had a man that fine with money in the bank that was interested in me and willing to take me and my best friend to Louisville in the hopes he could charm the pants off me."

"Then *you* should go after him," Rylee encouraged.

"No can do. As much as I love you, girl, I don't want your sloppy seconds. And more importantly, it's against girlfriend code. I can't hook up with one of your men any more than you could hook up with one of mine."

Rylee leaned over and hugged Camryn. "And that's why I love you, because you're the best BFF ever!"

"You can say that again!"

Amar al' Mahmud arrived at the Brown Hotel several moments later and jumped out of the limousine, not waiting for the driver to open the door for him. Most of the business world and his colleagues knew Mahmud as Amar Bishop, self-made media tycoon with interests online and in publishing and television.

Amar looked around the hotel, assessing its décor.

"Will this do, sir?" Sharif Khoury, Amar's assistant, asked.

"This will do just fine."

Amar walked inside the hotel with a regal bearing that imitated that of his father, Sheikh Abdul al' Mahmud, King of Nasir, a small country outside of Dubai. His carriage and height were probably all that Amar would willingly agree that he'd taken from his father. As for his clothing, it was all Amar. He was immaculately dressed in a charcoal Armani suit made of the finest materials, and he wore Ferragamo shoes.

Amar took a phone call while Sharif checked them into the Muhammad Ali Suite that he'd prearranged to have for his boss for the week. Only the best would do.

Amar finished his call and noticed several onlookers staring at him. He should have been used to it by now, but he wasn't. He knew they were puzzling over his facial features —

dark eyes, bushy eyebrows, a broad nose and full lips — trying to figure out his heritage. *Is he African-American, Mediterranean or of Arab descent?* He was all of them. His mother, Camilla Bishop, an African-American professor of American Studies, had met and fallen in love with his father while he'd been in the U.S on a mission to become more cultured in the American way of life. His father had certainly done that when he'd met Camilla, sired Amar and begun an affair that would last nearly a decade, even after he'd married a suitable mate.

Amar nodded at several patrons as he walked over to Sharif. "Is the room ready?" If they couldn't figure out his heritage, they could most definitely ascertain Sharif's because he had the same olive-tone complexion and smooth jet-black hair of most men of Arabic descent, though he wore American clothing of a pullover and trousers.

"Yes, sir. Follow me." Sharif motioned for the bellman to follow him with their luggage.

They took the elevator in silence to the room, and when they arrived, Sharif instructed the bellman on where to put Amar's belongings while he surveyed the suite.

Amar appreciated Sharif's attention to detail, but he hadn't always been at his side. Before, Amar had been all alone, content with his solitary lifestyle, but that had not suited his father, the Sheikh. He'd wanted eyes on Amar.

His father had agreed to leave Amar be, if he agreed to have someone, i.e., Sharif, to look after him properly as benefitting the son of noble blood. Amar didn't see why, since everyone in Nasir considered him a bastard and only tolerated his presence during the summers when he was permitted to visit their precious kingdom. But eventually, he'd consented if only to get the Sheikh off his back.

The Muhammad Ali Suite was exactly what Amar had come to expect after cultivating a life of luxury the last five years after his company took off. The one-bedroom accommodations were masculine and richly decorated and nearly the size of an apartment. Memorabilia from Ali's heyday, including photos and boxing gloves, were sprinkled throughout the room. It had a king-sized poster bed and a marble Jacuzzi tub which Amar intended to take full advantage of with one of the ladies he would meet this weekend. It even had a dining room with hardwood floors, a wet bar and comfortable living area. It would suit his needs very well.

"If there isn't anything else, Amar, I'll get settled in my room," Sharif stated.

"That'll be all for now. Thank you, Sharif."

"You're welcome." As Sharif closed the door, it still surprised him that Amar actually thanked those under his employ, unlike some other important people of Nasir.

Now alone, Amar sunk into the plush couch and looked down at his iPhone. There were two missed calls from his father. *What does he want now?* Wasn't it enough that he'd agreed to watch over his horse during the Derby this week? Horses were about the one thing he and his father shared a love of. Otherwise, Amar would have no use for the man who he blamed for his mother's death.

After all they'd been through together, the Sheikh couldn't even be bothered to attend his mother's funeral. Sure, he'd seen to it that all her medical bills were paid, but that wasn't what had killed her at fifty-four. Truth be told, it was losing his father. Even though she remarried for a short time when he was older, Amar doubted she'd ever really forgotten his father. He remembered how she'd always been on hand whenever the Sheikh visited the U.S. for a quickie with his mother, his favorite mistress — the mistress his father couldn't be seen with in public for fear of his reputation.

Reputation, family and honor were everything in Nasir. It's why his father, Abdul, had married Saffron, because *Abdul's* father had prearranged the marriage long ago. It sounded so prehistoric to Amar, but that was the way of the world over there. And it would be that way with his younger half-brother, Khalid, next in line in the royal succession. In the eyes of Nasir, Khalid was the rightful heir to the throne because his mother was of noble descent, even though Amar was the oldest son and by all accounts should be King. But Amar didn't want their old ways and traditions — he scoffed at them. He was happy the duties fell to Khalid. He wanted to live his life on his own terms.

And Amar had done just that. Born and raised in the U.S., he had freedoms Khalid and Khalid's younger brother, Tariq, would never have, while still going to the best colleges and boarding schools that money could buy. He supposed that was Abdul's way of showing his love — by throwing his money at him.

Truth was, neither Amar nor his mother, Camilla, had wanted him to go to boarding school. Amar had once heard his parents arguing about it, but the Sheikh had been insistent that it would provide Amar the best structure and education, and his mother had acquiesced. She could never seem to say "no" to the man. Amar, on the other hand, had no problem doing so, and he was sure he would incur the Sheikh's displeasure sometime during this trip because they were like oil and water — always were and always would be.

Chapter 2

RYLEE'S ROOM WASN'T JUST A room. It was a suite. About a thousand square feet, the spacious living quarters held two luxury bedrooms and an adjoining separate parlor. The oversized parlor was furnished with plush seating, a 32-inch flat screen television, a grand dining table, a wet bar and two full baths. The generous windows throughout the suite provided Rylee and Camryn a beautiful view of Louisville and plenty of natural sunlight.

"You have to come and check out this view," Camryn yelled at Rylee from the balcony outside. Rylee immediately hurried over and saw that the parlor overlooked 4th Street and Theatre Square.

"Sweet!" Rylee glanced down at the bustling street.

"Do you think we have time to go exploring before dinner?"

Rylee peered at her watch. "Sure we do."

"Let me go change first," Camryn said, rushing into the room.

"Why?" Rylee asked.

Camryn put her hands on her hips. "Because ... you never know who you might see. It'll only take me a sec."

Rylee shrugged. She supposed her attire of plaid shirt, low-rise skinny jeans and an army jacket wasn't exactly the look of a fashionista, but she most certainly wasn't changing.

Fifteen minutes later, Camryn came out of the second bedroom in full makeup and wearing skintight leggings, a sequin T-shirt, a denim jacket and four-inch peep-toe booties.

"You do realize we're walking, right?" Rylee said, laughing as they exited the suite.

"I can walk in these," Camryn replied with a huff.

Several hours later, after visiting a couple of upscale boutiques, Rylee and Camryn returned to their room with an armload of purchases and Camryn was still upright in those shoes. During their shopping spree, Rylee had even allowed Camryn to talk her into nearly a half a dozen new outfits.

Glancing at her watch, Rylee realized they barely had time for a quick shower before Jeremy was due at seven o'clock to pick them up. "Girl, look at the time," Rylee said. "We have to get a move on it."

Camryn quickly made a beeline for her room while Rylee rushed into the master to get ready.

A half hour later, Rylee wiped the foggy mirror in the bathroom and glanced at her reflection. She had to admit she looked darn good. It wasn't like she didn't appreciate nice clothing; she did. She just didn't care for what it took to get there. Rylee spun around for a full view of her new ensemble.

The strapless emerald jersey jumpsuit, teamed with dangling gold necklaces, chandelier earrings and strappy sandals, was casually chic. And rather than try to tame her unruly spiral curls with a blow-dryer, she'd embraced them and wore her hair down, allowing it to cascade over her shoulders. Her warm brown skin shone with some light bronzer, mascara and glossy lipstick.

"You look great," Camryn said from the doorway as she snapped her earrings into place.

Rylee smiled. "Thanks, girlfriend. So do you." Camryn was wearing wide-legged pants and a one-shoulder embellished tunic showing her shapely bosom.

A knock sounded on their door. Rylee surmised it must be Jeremy. He was nothing else if not punctual. "I'll get it." She walked over to the door and opened it with a flourish. When she did, Jeremy's warm smile greeted her.

"Wow!" Jeremy exclaimed. His eyes roved, giving Rylee a lazy appraisal as he walked into the suite. "You look amazing."

"It is nice to get out of jeans every now and again," she said, closing the door. "Camryn isn't quite ready. Would you like a drink?" She noticed there was a full bar in the room.

"A shot of whiskey would be great, thanks," Jeremy said.

"Neat?"

"That'll do." Jeremy followed Rylee inside the parlor and sat down on a chair opposite the balcony to watch her. The jumpsuit suited her without being conspicuous, which is why he liked Rylee. She wasn't showy, just down-to-earth. She was exactly the kind of woman he could see having a future with, if only he could get her to see it too.

Rylee poured Jeremy a shot glass of the potent drink and decided to make one for herself. She'd been known to drink with the fellas on the ranch every now and again. She brought the glass over and handed one to Jeremy before sitting down with the other for herself on the plush sofa.

"You drink whiskey?" he asked, surprised.

Rylee laughed. "C'mon, Jeremy, I'm not some priss. I live on a ranch with a bunch of ranch hands. I can hold my liquor."

Jeremy raised an incredulous eyebrow as he threw the shot back. "Is that so?"

Mirth alighted in Rylee's eyes, and she did the same. "Yes, it is."

"Do I hear a challenge coming on?" Camryn said, entering the room and plopping down on the sofa. "Because if so, I want in. I would give good money to see Rylee tie one on."

"Thanks a lot." Rylee smiled at her frank friend as she turned her shot glass down on the table. "Do you want anything?"

"No, I'll wait for dinner, but you two go ahead."

Jeremy put down his glass and rose to his feet. "Truth be told, we don't have much time to spare if we want to make our dinner reservation. Would you ladies care to leave now?" He offered a hand to each lady to assist her to her feet.

"Let's go," Rylee said. "I'm ready to get this weekend started."

"Is there a problem?" Sharif asked, noticing Amar had barely touched his aperitif before the amuse-bouche arrived from the chef.

Amar looked up from his phone. "No, why would you ask?"

Sharif shrugged. "Usually you've had at least one glass of strong drink before dinner."

Amar laughed heartily at his assistant before reaching for his decanter. "You watch me entirely too much, Sharif. You need a hobby."

"It's my job to look after you."

"And as I've told you before, I can take care of myself. Despite what my father thinks, I don't need a babysitter."

"True, but he has enemies that might seek to harm you, and with you here alone in the Americas without any protection, you're a target because you're wide open."

"I doubt anyone from Nasir or its neighboring kingdoms give a rat's ass about the bastard son of a sheikh."

"Don't talk that way, Amar. You are the first-born son."

"A fact which bears no mention since it means absolutely nothing to me," Amar replied. "I could care less about a small desert kingdom thousands of miles away that has cast me off as if I were a pebble at the bottom of their shoe. I care about Bishop Enterprises and ensuring I continue to grow my media empire."

Amar was about to continue on with the same duplicative speech he'd given Sharif a million times before when the most lovely creature he'd ever seen entered the room in a vision of emerald. His heart stopped momentarily, and he was stunned into silence. At the abrupt end to his speech, Sharif followed his gaze. Amar looked like a tiger ready to pounce on its prey.

"Easy, Amar," Sharif whispered. "She's with someone."

"Maybe, maybe not," Amar said, having finally regained his speech. "There's two women. She could be available." His eyes followed her movements as she, her male companion and another woman sat at a table across the room from them. "I need to know."

"Need to know what?"

"Don't be dense, Sharif," Amar said, exasperated. "Find out who she is, and if she's single."

"I thought this trip was about business," Sharif said, imitating Amar's earlier words.

Amar picked up his drink and took a generous sip. "Who says it can't be about business *and* pleasure?" His gaze returned to the dazzling creature with the cascading curls. Something told him that she could bring him lots of pleasure if the stirring in his loins was any indication. One way or another, he had to find a way to make this woman's acquaintance.

"What have you found out about the dazzling female I saw last night," Amar asked Sharif the following morning over coffee in the Ali suite.

"Wow, you don't allow for very much time, do you?" Sharif said. Although he'd found the answer to the question Amar sought, he'd just been given the task last night. *What does Amar expect — miracles?*

"Well, that's what happens when you always exceed my expectations," Amar replied smartly. "I've come to rely on you."

Sharif laughed. "Smooth, Amar, very smooth." He sipped his coffee.

"So, are you going to keep me in suspense or what?" Amar peered into his confidant's eyes.

"It was really quite simple. She's a veterinarian and is here with Jeremy Wright, a friend from her hometown near Tucson, Arizona, and her best friend, a Camryn Sanders. I believe she's taking care of Dreamer, Mr. Jeremy's long shot here at the Derby."

Amar rubbed his chin thoughtfully. "Is that so? And what about her and Jeremy?"

Sharif shrugged. "That's the best I could come up with on short notice, as it's common knowledge. You'll have to give me more time to obtain a more thorough dossier."

Amar rose to his feet. "No need. Where is she now?"

"I would imagine she would be at the stables tending to the animal."

"Good, because I need to check on the Sheikh's horse for the race, and there's no better time than the present. Care to join me?"

Sharif put down his fork, signaling the end to his breakfast, which he'd barely touched. "Do I have a choice?"

"She's beautiful, Jeremy," Rylee said, stroking Dreamer, the horse she'd been tasked with taking care of for the weekend. It was the first time she'd laid eyes on the breathtaking animal with the chestnut coat and black mane and tail.

Rylee had gone to bed early last night, much to Camryn's chagrin. Camryn had wanted to stay up partying the night away, but Rylee had to get up at five AM to meet with the trainers and other vets to tend to the animals, so she wasn't having it.

The animals were at their best during their morning workouts, as they usually napped during the late morning and early afternoon. Rylee would be better able to assess Dreamer's health if she could see her fresh and in action.

She was wearing her normal attire of jeans, long-sleeve checkered shirt and worn boots as she worked in the stables. Not much had changed; it was the same as she'd remembered, except now Dr. Gray had moved on to another facility, so she would have no chance of running into him. Rylee was surprised to find Jeremy had beat her to the punch and was already onsite. He was wearing the same attire except he had on a denim shirt and cowboy hat.

He smiled unabashedly at her. "She is beautiful, isn't she?" he said, dangling a carrot to the horse, which she immediately took and began munching. "I know everyone thinks she'd never win this, but that's what they said about Secretariat and she won the Triple Crown."

Rylee turned around to face him. "You believe she's capable of that kind of feat, don't you?"

"If I don't believe, who will?" he said, glancing at Rylee. "I know my father thinks I'm out of my mind for spending all my time and energy on a horse he thought was worthless, but she's been with one of the best trainers in the world the last year. I know she has what it takes."

"I admire your conviction," Rylee said, leaning against a stable wall. She'd never seen Jeremy speak with such passion about anything before. Perhaps there was more to the man than she gave him credit for.

Jeremy walked over to her until he stood mere inches from her face. He looked at her intensely before saying, "Well, it's easy when you believe in something *or someone.*"

"So true," Rylee said, looking downward. It hadn't escaped her notice how close he'd move into her personal space — a little too close. *Is he going to make a move and try to kiss me?* She tried to lighten the charged moment between them by focusing back on the horse. "Dreamer did really well in her workouts this morning with the trainer."

"What's your assessment of her health?"

Rylee grinned. "She's in good health as you know or you wouldn't have entered her in the Derby."

"What do you mean?"

Rylee rolled her eyes; he was deliberately being obtuse. "You know what I mean. You don't need me here." She glanced at the thoroughbred. "Dreamer is in excellent condition."

"Yes, she is, but I need to ensure she stays that way until race day. And to address your comment, no, I don't need you here." He moved even closer to Rylee. "But I *want* you here."

Rylee used her hand to push against Jeremy's solid chest as he leaned in closer to her face. "Easy, Jeremy," Rylee warned. "I agreed to come here on a professional basis to help you."

"And what if I want more than that?"

Rylee sighed. "Jeremy ..." She never got to finish her sentence because Hank, Dreamer's trainer, called out to him.

"We'll talk later," Jeremy said, righting himself. "This conversation isn't finished." Jeremy walked away toward Hank.

Great, just great, Rylee thought. She'd be fending Jeremy off all weekend. Now there was an idea of a good time!

"You want to tell me that wasn't personal?" Amar asked Sharif from the opposite side of the stables.

"Yes, he stood very close in her personal space, but if you ask me, it was not a welcome advance."

"How can you tell?"

"Her body language was indicative of a woman who *did not* welcome his advances. I don't believe they are lovers."

"Good!" Amar said and strode off toward Rylee, leaving Sharif abruptly.

Amar walked purposely across the stables to where Rylee was now bending over. She was looking at Dreamer's hooves and was cooing words that Amar couldn't quite hear from the stable door but wished he was on the receiving end of. "Hello."

Startled, Rylee fell in the hay on the ground.

Amar rushed toward her. "I'm sorry, I didn't mean to startle you," he said, offering her his hand. She accepted it as she rose to her feet. When she was standing, their eyes connected and a lightning bolt went right through Amar as if he'd been struck. She had to have felt it too. It was as if a kinetic energy had passed between them and neither was quick to let the other's hand go.

Rylee's beauty stunned Amar. From afar, it hadn't nearly shown how glittering her light-brown eyes were, hadn't shown how gorgeous her hair was, so curly and sexy. He could picture his hands running through it as he brought the two of them to a satisfying climax.

"It's okay." She finally let go of his hand so she could brush the hay off her jeans.

Amar's eyes followed her hands, taking in her athletic figure attired in form-fitting jeans and her dainty feet, adorned in worn leather boots. When his eyes finally moved back up to her face, he found she was staring at him.

"Do you always look at ladies like a hungry tiger?"

"Only ladies as beautiful as you."

Rylee smiled half-heartedly, and her warmth shot through Amar like wildfire. He could feel his manhood throb. Lord, this woman was making him feel all kind of emotions. If he was back in Nasir, he would push her back in the stables and have his way with her, not caring who saw or heard them.

"Wow! That was a little cheesy," Rylee commented, jolting Amar out of his fantasy.

"Cheesy?" Amar asked with a questioning look.

Rylee's eyes rose. "You know, lame, unoriginal? C'mon, you must have better pick-up lines than that."

"Apparently not," Amar replied. "I will need to work on my charm."

"You do that." Rylee moved to step away, but Amar touched her arm again. And just as before, his body tingled from the contact. She must have felt it too, because she looked at him in alarm.

"I don't believe I caught your name," Amar said.

"That's because I didn't give it."

Amar grinned. "Whose manners are in need of work now?" he asked. "Amar Bishop." He offered her his hand.

She looked down at it for several moments. He wasn't sure what she expected to happen, but she finally shook his hand, and before she could withdraw, he brought her hand up to his mouth and brushed his lips across it.

She quickly snatched it back at the close contact.

Just then, Jeremy walked toward them. Amar did his best to retain his composure and stood up straight to his full six-foot-four height.

"Is everything okay over here, Rylee?" Jeremy eyed Amar suspiciously and came over to circle his arm around Rylee's waist.

Amar could see Jeremy was assessing his competition as most men do, but Amar knew he was far superior to this man in intelligence, looks and stature — by several inches — and in overall suaveness, not to mention he was rich as sin.

Amar watched Rylee remove Jeremy's arm from around her waist. "Everything is fine, Jeremy." She glared at her companion. "I was just making Mr. Bishop's acquaintance."

"Bishop?" Jeremy said. "You wouldn't be *the* Amar Bishop, would you? I'd heard you would have a horse in this year's Derby."

"The one and the same," Amar said, barely glancing at Jeremy before returning his gaze back to Rylee. "I'm here looking after Desert Storm, a joint venture between me and my father."

"Sheikh Abdul al' Mahmud, right?" Jeremy pressed.

Amar would have preferred his heritage not be revealed in such a careless manner. He would have preferred Rylee hear it from his lips. "That's correct."

"A sheikh?" Rylee's voice rose ever so slightly. "Well, that would explain it."

"Explain what?" Amar and Jeremy asked at the same time.

"Oh, nothing," Rylee said. "Listen, I'm going back to the room to go check on Camryn. I think we're done here until this afternoon's workouts."

She started to walk away, but Amar called, "Can I offer you a ride?"

"I don't take rides from strangers," Rylee responded. Seconds later she was gone, leaving Amar and Jeremy alone.

"Listen, Mr. Bishop," Jeremy began.

"Please, call me Amar."

"Amar, it is," Jeremy said, turning toward him. "Rylee is spoken for."

Amar glanced at Rylee's retreating figure. "Does the lady know that? Because if I'm not mistaken, she removed your hand from her waist mere moments ago. That leads me to believe that she is very much a *free* woman."

"Not for much longer, if I have anything to say about it," Jeremy replied.

"Then let the best man win," Amar said. He'd never walked away from a fight in his life, and he wasn't about to do it now. He wanted Rylee, and he wouldn't allow anyone, including Jeremy Wright, to get in his way.

"How were the stables?" Camryn asked when Rylee returned to the room shortly after her encounter with Amar Bishop.

"Fine," Rylee said absentmindedly as she walked over to the wet bar. She unscrewed a bottle of water and drank generously as she paced the floor.

Camryn eyed her suspiciously. "Is everything okay? You look a little tense."

"Why would you say that?" Rylee's voice rose an octave.

"Because you haven't sat since you got here. Come." She patted the couch where she was sitting. "Tell me all."

Rylee stopped pacing long enough to walk over to join Camryn. "There's nothing to tell, really. I went to the stables and watched the morning workouts. Jeremy tried to get a little close for comfort, as always, and then the son of a sheikh made a pass at me. See, nothing to it!"

"Whoa, whoa! Time-out." Camryn put up her hands in the shape of a "T". "Did you say the son of a sheikh made a pass at you?"

Rylee let out a deep breath. She couldn't believe it had happened herself. There she'd been, minding her own business, when Amar Bishop had come out of nowhere and interrupted her peaceful world.

When she'd glanced up, she'd seen his sexy-fine ass looking down at her, and she'd lost her footing. He thought he'd startled her, and she hadn't been about to correct him. The truth was, she'd been overcome by the mere sight of him. Amar Bishop was not like any other man she'd ever come across in Tucson. Not only was he fine and sexier than any man had a right to be, but he also had an air about him that *commanded* attention. She hadn't known he was of noble descent until Jeremy had spilled the beans, but that didn't explain why she'd had such a potent reaction to the man — didn't explain why she'd felt heat and electricity at his touch.

"Earth to Rylee." Camryn waved a hand in front of Rylee's face.

Rylee blinked and snapped out of her reverie. "Sorry. What did you say?"

"Wow, whoever he was must have put some spell on you, because I haven't seen you this glassy-eyed since, since ..." Camryn searched her memory for a time when she'd seen Rylee so infatuated and came up empty. "Well, since never. What the heck happened at those stables?"

"That's the thing, Camryn. Nothing." Rylee ran her fingers through her curly tresses. "Then this guy walked into the pen where I was tending to Dreamer, and I was literally knocked off balance. And when he offered me a hand, the sparks that flew between us were off the record books. It was crazy."

Camryn's eyes grew large with excitement. "So what happened next?"

"Jeremy found us and got all territorial by putting his arm around my waist like I was his girlfriend."

"Girl, men recognize when another wolf is sniffing around their catch."

Rylee stared at her friend in bewilderment. "Seriously, Camryn, you're calling me his catch?"

Camryn shrugged. "If the shoe fits. I bet Jeremy wanted to pee on you to ward him off."

Rylee fell backward onto the couch in a fit of giggles. "Girl, you are too much."

"I don't think *I'm* too much. Sounds like this sheikh's son was too much for you. What's his name again?"

"Amar Bishop."

"*The* Amar Bishop?"

"Yeah, what of it?

"Well, Amar Bishop happens to be the next Steve Jobs or Mark Zuckerberg. He's started up his own Internet company, and it's now making billions, like Facebook. He's diversified his portfolio with sound investments in publishing and television."

"How do you know all this?"

"I know some people think I'm a ditz, but I do watch and read the news," Camryn replied, snapping her fingers. "And as you said, the man is drop-dead sex on a stick."

"Yes, but I don't date men like Amar. He may be his own man, but he's too smooth, too slick. I bet he's used to women's panties just falling at his heels. I won't be another notch on his bedpost."

"Would that be so bad?"

"Camryn!"

Camryn shrugged. "What's wrong with a little vacation romance? Weren't you just saying that Jeremy doesn't light your fire? I bet Amar could. He's probably just the man to awaken the sexuality you like to keep so hidden."

"I do not."

"I call it like I see it," Camryn said. "And if one touch from him can get you this fired up, just imagine if you had all of him."

"That's what frightens me. There would be nothing but scorched earth."

"How's the Arabian looking?" Amar's father asked Amar over the phone later that morning after he'd returned to the hotel.

"He's looking well. The odds are five to two. Some have an unknown finishing in the top five."

"Second place is not good enough, Amar, as you very well know. I will settle for nothing but taking the top spot at the Derby."

Amar fumed. He did not appreciate his father's tone. "I recognize your need to win, Father, as it matches my own; but even I can't predict how a horse will run."

"Which is why I have ensured the very best trainers and jockeys. You were supposed to be overseeing this effort."

"I have, and I am." Amar tried to contain his fury.

"Make it happen," his father replied. "And what's this I hear that you've fallen prey to the fancies of yet another woman?"

Amar looked around the room for Sharif. *The little devil!* He was supposed to be keeping his confidence, not ratting him out at the first opportunity. "I haven't fallen prey. I am capable of keeping my desires in check and keeping my eye on the races. I just have a little competition."

"From whom? No one is more educated and sophisticated than you. I saw to that."

Trust the Sheikh to bring everything back to him and what *he'd* done for Amar, not what Amar had accomplished on his own.

"I don't want to discuss this."

"You might as well. I'll find out one way or another."

Amar wanted to tell his father to stay out of his business and keep his eye on the continent, but instead he answered honestly, in case Sharif said differently. "She's accompanying the owner of Dreamer, the long shot I mentioned."

"Then take him out!"

"Excuse me?"

"Not in the literal sense. But if you can neutralize him and get his focus off the Derby and on fighting for this woman, all could be yours."

Amar sat back in his seat. His father was ruthless, but why would that surprise him? "Well ... thanks for the advice ... Father." This was a rare, uncharacteristic fatherly moment. Usually the Sheikh acted like he could care less about what happened to Amar — at least, that's how Amar felt. Wonders never ceased.

"Heed it. Because I won't have a son who is a loser." The phone went silent. Bam! His father had shattered the moment.

"I'll remember that," Amar said to the dial tone.

Chapter 3

"I DON'T KNOW, CAMRYN. THIS DRESS is a bit revealing."

"If you mean eye-catching, then I see nothing wrong with it." Camryn smacked Rylee's hand away from touching the one-shoulder, red spandex mini-dress she'd talked her into wearing along with matching fire-engine red peep-toe heels and dangling earrings. "It's about time you caught someone's eye."

"If I wanted Amar to notice me, he definitely will in this dress," Rylee said somewhat self-consciously as she looked at herself in the mirrored reflection of the elevator cab. The dress barely reached her thighs. It was indecent.

"I doubt you will have to try," Camryn said. "You did just receive nearly an entire florist shop of roses this afternoon."

Rylee sighed. She hadn't forgotten that a dozen of the most beautiful roses in a variety of colors had been delivered to their suite with a note that said, "Dinner. Tonight." When she hadn't responded and called the number on the card within the hour as instructed, another dozen had been delivered. She'd thought it a fluke until a third dozen had arrived. She'd finally called the number listed and agreed to a drink, since she and Camryn already had dinner plans with Jeremy.

29

Rylee thought Amar would have answered, but instead it had been Sharif, who'd advised her that Amar would be less than pleased with her answer, but that he would relay the message. And so, she and Camryn were on their way to the lounge to meet Amar, who had no idea she was showing up with reinforcement; but Rylee needed to keep her cool, and Camryn would be a great buffer.

They exited the elevator and walked the marble floor to the hotel bar. It was filled with other cocktail goers. Amar and Sharif were in a secluded corner and stood when Rylee and Camryn entered the room. *So he's not alone either!* Rylee smiled.

Amar greeted them when Rylee stepped to the table. "I'm so glad you could join us." His eyes scanned every inch of her, from her hair to the length of her mini-dress. He missed nothing. When his eyes finally returned to her face, he gave her a quirky smile.

Rylee felt color rising to her cheeks, but she maintained her cool. "Did I have much choice? I believe my room would have become a florist shop if I hadn't agreed to your request."

Amar shrugged. "I know how to get what I want."

"And should I take it you want me?" Rylee asked.

Amar didn't answer. It wasn't polite to talk about such matters when they had guests, so instead, he pulled out a chair from the table. "Please, have a seat."

Rylee looked at Camryn, who shrugged and waited for Sharif to pull out her chair. They sat down simultaneously. Amar and Sharif soon joined them.

Amar signaled a uniformed waiter, who immediately came over to take their order. "What can I get for you, Mr. Bishop?"

"We'll have a bottle of your best Dom Perignon," Amar said.

Suddenly glancing at Rylee, Camryn's eyes widened. Clearly, Rylee didn't know how much a bottle like that cost, but it must be outrageous given Camryn's reaction.

"That's not really necessary," Rylee began.

"Of course it is," Amar said silkily. "We're celebrating getting better acquainted. And I've been remiss in introductions. You must be Rylee's beautiful friend, Camryn."

Camryn smiled. "Yes, I am." Then she paused. "But how do you know my name?"

"I make it my business to know everything about those close to me."

Rylee was most certainly *not* close to him and didn't appreciate him looking into her or her friends for that matter, but she also refused to let him think he had the upper hand. "I imagine it must be quiet difficult in your position, being the son of a sheikh." Rylee glanced around. "I'm surprised there aren't guards around you twenty-four-seven."

Amar smiled wryly. "Well, when you're the *bastard* son, not much interest is given to your comings and goings."

Rylee's throat hitched. Clearly she'd hit a nerve. "I-I'm sorry. I—"

Amar interrupted her and put up his hand.

"Rylee," he called her by her first name, and it was like a sensuous caress on his full lips. "It's fine. I accepted my position in my family decades ago. My brother Khalid is in line to the throne, and if anyone was at risk, it would be him, not me."

"Sounds like a tenuous position to be in," Rylee commented.

"Khalid has been training for this his entire life. He will do well."

"You sound like you have no animosity," Rylee said.

"I do not." Amar was glad that the waiter arrived with the bubbly so that they could move on to bigger things.

"Ah, our champagne is here." He waited for the waiter to pour glasses for everyone before raising his glass in toast. "To new acquaintances."

Rylee raised her glass, and Amar clicked his flute against hers. "To new acquaintances."

Amar sipped once and put down his glass. "So, how long are you ladies staying in Louisville?"

"I'm sure you already know the answer to that question," Rylee replied.

"Humor me."

"A few days," Camryn spoke for Rylee. "Rylee's a vet, and she's helping our friend Jeremy with his horse."

"Ah, yes, Dreamer," Amar added. "A long shot at best, yes, Sharif? Our horse, Desert Storm, is a sure thing."

"True," Sharif finally spoke after he'd been watching the back and forth tennis match of words between Amar and his new lady love.

"You shouldn't underestimate the underdog," Rylee said. "You never know when they might come and nip at your heels." Not thinking, she reached across to playfully run her fingers up Amar's arm, but before she could pull back, he'd grabbed her hand and their eyes connected. Amar's were dark and intense. *And passionate.*

An undeniable current sparked between them until Rylee snatched her hand away. She laughed, attempting to lighten the mood. "Looks like someone doesn't like to lose."

"Losing isn't in Amar's vocabulary," Sharif replied.

"I'd heard that." For good measure, Rylee added, "That you're ruthless." She wished Amar would stop looking at her like she was dessert. It unnerved her to be looked at with such raw, unabashed passion.

"In business you have to be to get ahead," he said, his voice husky with desire. He reached for his champagne flute and took another sip before continuing. "Starting out an Internet company like mine and competing against the likes of Facebook wasn't an easy task and was not for the faint of heart."

"You must have had a lot of opposition," Camryn added.

Amar nodded. "From my peers as well as my family. They thought I would amount to a rich playboy content to live on his father's riches by carousing women and driving fancy cars."

"But you wanted more than that," Rylee said. She liked how Amar was driven to find his own path, unlike Jeremy, who did what his family expected of him.

"I didn't *want* to ride on my father's coattails. Still don't."

Rylee's eyes narrowed. "So what brings you here to the Kentucky Derby, when, forgive me for saying this, it's all about the playboy lifestyle. I mean, isn't this event about rich men and their toys?" She coughed. "Er, I mean horses. This is a far cry from where Camryn" — she glanced at her best friend — "and I live. We have a simple life without all" — she motioned her hands around the room — "all this extravagance."

Amar watched her carefully. "You're interesting, Rylee. You snub the rich for their excesses, yet here you are this weekend appreciating all they have to offer."

Fury boiled in Rylee, and she saw red. "Are you calling me a hypocrite?" She couldn't believe his nerve. Her family and friends may not be poor, but they worked hard for the life they enjoyed.

"I'm merely pointing out the fact that you are enjoying all the excess."

Rylee glanced at her watch. "Oh, my, look at the time." She rose to her feet, pushing back her chair. "I believe it's time for our dinner date. Camryn?" She turned to her friend.

And as if on cue, Rylee saw Jeremy, outfitted in a black suit with a white shirt opened right above his chest, looking around the room for them at the door of the hotel bar.

When he spotted them at the table with Amar, he looked less than amused. Rylee had to admit Jeremy looked very dapper in his designer suit, and she wished she felt more for him than brotherly affection.

Rylee gave Jeremy a broader smile than normal when he arrived at the table she and Camryn had shared with Amar. "Jeremy, ready for dinner?"

"Yes. I was just looking for you ladies. I thought I had the time wrong."

"You didn't." Rylee glanced at Amar. "We're done here."

Jeremy glared at Amar before offering Rylee his arm and extending his other to Camryn. They walked away leaving Amar and Sharif staring after them.

"She's something, isn't she?" Amar turned to Sharif.

"I'll say," Sharif replied. "She doesn't hold her tongue like the women of Nasir."

Amar sat down and took a sip of his champagne. He liked how Rylee had stood up to him, returning his serves with a strong hand. He wasn't used to that in a woman. "I wouldn't want a yes-woman," he mused aloud. "What would be the fun in someone who did everything I asked?"

"Less drama." Sharif chuckled.

Amar inclined his head. "But that's what life is all about, and I intend to live life to the fullest. And Rylee Hart is part of that package."

"Rylee was not interested in your advances, Amar."

"I think the lady doth protest too much, and I intend to call her out on it later at the Taste of the Derby event."

Sharif shrugged. *It is Amar's funeral.*

"Why were you having drinks with Amar Bishop?" Jeremy asked once he, Rylee and Camryn were in the limousine being driven to Freedom Hall for the Taste of the Derby.

He was sitting directly across from Rylee and could gauge whether she was being truthful about her connection to the billionaire playboy.

It was a fair question, but Rylee didn't particularly want to have this discussion, especially with Jeremy, but she answered honestly, "Because he asked me."

"And I tagged along for moral support." Camryn patted Rylee's thigh.

Jeremy's eye immediately zeroed in on where Camryn's hand had landed. Rylee's thighs were sexily accentuated by her mini-dress. He was receiving a tantalizing expanse of leg as he sat back against the cushions of the leather seat. It was unusual for Rylee to wear something so revealing, and he could sense her uneasiness. *So why is she wearing it? No doubt for Amar's benefit and thanks to Camryn's coaxing.*

"Fair enough," Jeremy responded eventually. "But Amar *does* have a reputation as a ladies man. You would do well to steer clear of him."

"Duly noted," Rylee replied. "But I can assure you Amar isn't the first ladies man I've encountered. I can handle him." A mental picture of Shelton Gray instantly sprung to Rylee's mind, reminding her of what a supreme idiot she'd been falling for a married man. She wouldn't make the same mistake with Amar Bishop.

Jeremy smiled. "Glad to hear it. And it looks like we're here." The limo came to a stop, and he quickly jumped out of the vehicle and came around to open the door for Rylee and Camryn. "Ladies."

Rylee looked up at the Freedom Hall sign as Jeremy escorted them from the limo. The Taste of the Derby was already underway, and they walked toward a red-swagged tent with *Taste of the Derby* in bold letters across the top with a giant rose. They walked the red carpet, pausing long enough for photographers to snap photos. Jeremy stepped away when one of the photographers yelled he wanted a picture of the ladies in their cocktail dresses. As she and Camryn posed for the cameras, Rylee was glad she had listened to Camryn and bought a new dress. She had no idea there would be so much press.

Eventually, they rejoined Jeremy and walked into the Hall's north lobby, which had been transformed into a grand spectacle with multicolored lights and Chinese lanterns. A dozen food stations were on hand to accommodate the celebrity chefs cooking and lending their support to the event. "Where are the proceeds for tonight's Taste going?" Rylee asked.

"AIDS research," Camryn answered before Jeremy could get a word out.

"That's great." Rylee glanced around because the well-dressed, well-coifed and well-manicured people in this room could easily feed a small nation. Rylee came from a family that was one of the biggest supporters of its local community. Considering giving back was so close to her heart and experience, Rylee was glad the proceeds would benefit a charity.

"Well, let's dig in," Jeremy said. "Everything smells delicious."

It didn't take long for Rylee, Camryn and Jeremy to start tasting the sample entrées, appetizers and amuse-bouches the celebrity chefs had prepared. Rylee even saw a few chefs she recognized from *Top Chef*.

"This risotto cake with wild mushrooms and pancetta is wonderful," Rylee commented after they'd sampled several dishes.

"I'm trying not to moan in ecstasy," Camryn replied from beside her.

Jeremy laughed at Camryn's unabashed response. "That's what I like about you, Cam. You always speak your mind."

"No other way to be," Camryn said. "So how about you get us something to wash this down with?"

Jeremy grinned. "Absolutely. I'll be right back."

When he left, Camryn turned to Rylee. "C'mon, what's wrong with Jeremy? He's a good-looking, upstanding guy. You should be all over that."

Rylee shrugged as she popped the last of the risotto cake into her mouth and wiped it with her napkin. "I dunno. I just don't feel that way toward him."

"Alright then, there are plenty other fish in the sea," Camryn said. "And I see one that has just caught my interest." She inclined her head ninety degrees to a tall, dark-skinned man standing on the sidelines drinking a beer. "I'll be right back."

"Go get 'em." Rylee whistled.

"Finally, you're alone," a male voice said from behind her. "I thought I'd never get the opportunity."

Rylee knew the owner of that smooth-as-silk baritone. She spun on her heel to face Amar. "Were you watching me?"

Amar's dark eyes focused on hers. "Would it embarrass you to know that I was?"

"No," Rylee said and leaned past him to throw her small plate into a nearby trash can. When she did, she caught a whiff of his spicy cologne. It smelled exactly as she envisioned a man as dangerous as Amar would smell. She retreated backward. "No, it wouldn't. You're welcome to look."

Amar's brow rose at the implied reference. "But not touch?"

"Take it any way you like." She turned to walk away, but Amar's hand circled her waist and before she knew what was happening, he'd whisked her away from the crowd into a quiet area of the hall.

"Why do you persist in acting so unaffected by me," Amar whispered huskily, "when I know that's not the case?"

Rylee leaned against a nearby exposed column. "Amar, I'm not interested in being your next conquest. The only thing I can offer you is my friendship."

Amar leaned in closer toward her. Heat suffused throughout Rylee's body, and she tried her best to suppress it by lowering her eyes, but there was no use; Amar was right. There *was* something between them.

"What if I want more than friendship?" Amar's lips were inches from hers. "What if I want us to be lovers?"

Rylee made the mistake of looking up, and when she did, she got lost in Amar's magnetic dark eyes. He had her. She felt one of his hands encircle her waist seconds before his lips laid claim to hers. It wasn't a sweet, tender kiss like the one Jeremy might have planted on her. This was one of hunger and lust, balled into one.

Amar pushed her backward against the column and plundered her mouth. His tongue teased at its seams until she had no choice but to succumb. He didn't pause before delving inside and discovering every crevice. He devoured her as if he were trying to unleash everything she'd tried so long to keep under wraps.

When his tongue touched hers, a fire sparked deep within her belly, and when it dueled with hers for supremacy, she gave up the fight and let Amar take the lead. And he did, teasing, tasting and nibbling every inch of her lips. When he finally lifted his head, Rylee knew she'd been thoroughly kissed.

"Finally," Amar whispered, brushing his thumb back and forth on her sensitized lips. "I get to taste you, and you taste like the nectar from an orange."

Rylee tried to swallow to get air into her lungs, but her heart was beating so fast, she thought she might expire right then and there. The effect Amar had on her with *one* kiss had her weak at the knees and had robbed her of speech.

"And I want more," Amar said. "Much more." He reached for her again, but Rylee laid her hand on his chest. "Rylee, let's not play games. That kiss told me you want me."

Rylee couldn't think. She turned away and faced the column. She needed a few minutes to gather her wits about her, but Amar was relentless.

He brushed away the hair at her nape and placed feather-light kisses across the back of her neck as one of his hands wrapped around her to caress her stomach in the skintight red dress she wore. "Don't deny yourself. Don't deny us what comes naturally."

"St-stop, y-you're trying to seduce me, confuse me."

"Seduce you, yes, but I don't want you to be confused," Amar whispered, turning her around to face him and grasping her face with both his hands. He tipped her head, forcing her to look at him. "Make no mistake, I want to go to bed with you, Rylee, but I want you to be *sure*."

"This" — she pointed back and forth between them as she shook her head — "confuses me. This is not me. I don't make out with strange men I just met in public." She glanced around. Even though they were in the back of the hall, they were still in plain view of partygoers. Anyone could see them.

Amar smiled. "There's a first time for everything, and I'm glad I can bring out your passionate nature."

That's exactly what scared Rylee. She wasn't a virgin by any means. She'd had her share of lovers, but it was usually on her terms, and she hadn't felt this way since perhaps her experience with Dr. Gray. And maybe not even then. That didn't compare to the emotion she'd felt just now with Amar.

"I have to go." She started to move away, but Amar blocked her path.

"You can't just ignore what happened between us."

"Why not?" Rylee said. "Unlike you, I didn't come here to have a fling. I came here to help a friend go for a shot at a Derby win. You're a distraction."

"A distraction or a *complication* to the neat plan you'd laid out for yourself this weekend."

"Does it matter?" Rylee said. "I don't *need* or *want* either."

Amar chuckled. "Rylee, you're such a contradiction. Your words say one thing, but your body, your mouth say quite another."

"Well then, it's a good thing. I use my *brains* to direct my actions. Good night, Amar." Rylee sidestepped him and quickly walked back toward the crowd milling throughout the hall. She ran into Jeremy, who was holding a mint julep he'd bought for her.

"There you are," Jeremy said. "I was looking all over for you. I found Camryn sidelined next to a famous basketball star, but you were MIA."

"Sorry." Rylee smiled half-heartedly. "I had a slight distraction.

His brows drew together in a frown and searched her face. "Anything you need my help with?"

Rylee shook her head. "No, no. I handled it."

"Okay, well, then you have to come with me to try this mint julep. It's the best." He lightly touched her waist and led her toward the front of the lobby.

Rylee looked backward and when she did, she saw Amar staring hungrily after her.

Chapter 4

"WHAT'S NEXT?" CAMRYN ASKED AS the limo pulled away from Freedom Hall.

"Well, you ladies are headed back to the hotel," Jeremy replied.

"And where are you going after you drop us off?" asked Rylee.

"Male business."

"How sexist of you!" Rylee exclaimed with a smile.

"I doubt my activity would interest you."

"How would you know if you didn't ask us?" Rylee said, folding her arms across her chest with a feigned pout.

Jeremy hated for Rylee to be upset with him. "If you must know, I'm going to a poker game."

"We wanna come," Camryn said.

"The invitation said men only."

"So?" Rylee didn't see why that would be a problem. Men brought their women to those sorts of things all the time. "We'll be your backup to cheer you on."

"I don't know ..."

"C'mon, Jeremy," Camryn pleaded and gave her best puppy dog eyes.

"Alright, alright, you can come, but you have to be quiet," Jeremy replied. "No gesturing or talking, because it may tip my hand or be a tell. Not to mention it would be emasculating in front of the other men."

"What's a tell?" Camryn asked.

"That's when you show the other players how *strong* or *weak* your hand is, and I can't have that. So not a peep out of the two of you, ya hear?" He pointed his fingers at each of them.

"Promise." Both women crossed their hearts.

The poker game was held in a private room at a gentleman's club in Louisville. When they arrived, they were ushered past several uniformed waiters and were brought into the cellar of the club. The room was filled with several older Caucasian men, two distinguished looking African-American men and Amar. Several of the men were smoking cigars and drinking Scotch.

Rylee's heart started in her chest to see Amar so soon after their heated encounter at the Taste. She tried not to look at him, but she could feel his eyes on her.

She had been right in her assessment that she and Camryn wouldn't be the only women there, because several other women of various ages and sizes stood behind their respective men draped in jewels and furs. Rylee just knew PETA would have a field day here!

"Are you okay?" Camryn asked, noting Rylee's fidgeting.

"Not really," Rylee whispered at her side. "Amar is here."

Camryn glanced his way and noticed his eyes were firmly planted on Rylee. "I can see why. He's staring at you."

"I know," Rylee said, smiling at Jeremy as he made his way around the room making introductions.

Camryn glanced sideways at Rylee. "Something happened tonight, didn't it?"

42

"Men, take your places," the dealer said. "We'll get started in five minutes."

When Rylee didn't answer, Camryn said, "No need to confirm it. Your guilty expression and the way Amar is looking at you as if you're a bowl of soup he'd like to sop up tells me enough."

Across the room, Amar was pleased with the twists and turns the evening had taken. Earlier, he'd finally pierced through the wall Rylee had held up and forced her to confront their mutual attraction. Of course, she'd run away like a scared schoolgirl, but that wouldn't deter him. Then Sharif, who'd been keeping tabs on the illustrious Mr. Wright, had told him Jeremy would be attending a poker game after the event, so Sharif had gotten him a place at the table. How could Amar have known that Rylee would choose to accompany Jeremy and see his downfall? It would be the icing on the cake.

"Why are you grinning like a Cheshire cat?" Sharif whispered in Amar's ear.

"Because this evening couldn't have gone any better if I'd planned it."

Sharif glanced across at the object of Amar's affection. "A twist of fate she would attend this evening, that's for sure."

Amar nodded. "And the opportunity to show her once and for all that Wright is not the man for her."

Sharif knew Amar to be an excellent poker player. "You're going to annihilate him, aren't you?"

Amar shrugged. He was a take-no-prisoners kind of man, and he would bring Jeremy to his knees.

Rylee watched the dealer give Jeremy one hundred thousand in chips and was stunned that he would play with that kind of money, but given the company of the men he was with tonight, she supposed it was probably on the low side. She noticed that not to be outdone, Amar had a half a million in chips, five times what Jeremy had. the dealer distributes the cards face down starting with the player to his or her immediate left and continuing clockwise, one card at a time, until everyone has five cards. The deck is placed in the middle of the table. the dealer distributes the cards face down starting with the player to his or her immediate left and continuing clockwise, one card at a time, until everyone has five cards. The deck is placed in the middle of the table.

After shuffling, the dealer distributed the cards facedown and handed each player five cards and placed the deck in the middle of the table. Rylee noticed that one player started breathing a little heavier and another was avoiding eye contact. Were these the "tell" signs she'd heard of? Jeremy was stone-cold and was holding his poker face, as was Amar.

The Caucasian man to the dealer's left placed the first bet. "One thousand dollars."

Since Jeremy was immediately next to him, he saw his one thousand. Rylee took that as a good sign that Jeremy had a good hand. She watched as others around the table placed their bets. Then it was Amar's turn.

"I'll see your one thousand and raise you five thousand," Amar stated. He noticed Jeremy's brow furrow. He could see he only had one hundred thousand to play with. This was child's play with this group of bankers and CEOs, but if he wanted to play with the big boys, he was about to learn his lesson.

"I'll see your five thousand," Jeremy added when the dealer turned to him again. He threw a chip into the pot and looked at Amar as if challenging him to say something.

Amar was surprised he had the balls to increase his bet with such a pittance of chips in front of him. He felt sorry for the poor schmuck because he was about to be had tonight.

An hour later, Rylee watched in horror when the pot rose to fifty thousand dollars and Jeremy still hadn't folded. *What the hell is wrong with him?* He didn't have this kind of money to blow on a poker game. His father would kill Jeremy if he knew how shamefully he was throwing money around as if it grew on trees.

She wanted to stop Jeremy to prevent a travesty, but she'd promised him she wouldn't say a word. How could she stand by while he blew his future, his trust fund? The pot was steadily growing and was now up to one hundred thousand, the exact amount Jeremy had in chips. The last of two Caucasian men who'd been holding on folded until it was just Amar and Jeremy remaining.

Rylee knew the root cause of why Jeremy wouldn't fold: He refused to allow Amar to win. But it was a poker game, for Christ's sake. It wasn't like they were fighting over her. Or were they? *Is that what this is all about?* Jeremy refused to concede because he wouldn't let Amar win her? Didn't Jeremy get that there would never be anything between them except friendship. Probably not, because she'd given him mixed messages. Agreeing to date him to please her father and coming on this trip had been a mistake, but she couldn't change those things. She could only affect the here and now.

Amar raised the bet from one hundred thousand to two hundred thousand. The dealer turned to Jeremy to see if he would raise or fold.

Rylee couldn't help herself and coughed loudly. Everyone instantly looked up at her, annoyed by the interference.

The game was intense and exciting, and everyone wanted to see what Jeremy would do next.

Camryn merely held her head low, but it was Jeremy who turned around and gave her a "knock it off" look.

With her eyes, Rylee tried pleading to Jeremy one final time to stop the madness, but he quickly turned back to the game.

"So what's it going to be?" Amar stared at Jeremy, trying to figure him out. Players had already folded with Three of a Kind and a Full House, so Jeremy had to have something good. Amar had to hand it to him — he was going down swinging. But in the end, Amar would be victorious because he had the best hand of all.

Jeremy stared at Amar. He knew Amar Bishop wanted to win and usually he would have folded, but Rylee was here. How would she feel seeing him cop out like a punk? He had to go the distance. "I don't have any more chips."

Amar looked at the empty spot on the table in front of him. "I can see that. So you're folding?"

Jeremy stared down at his hand. It wasn't the best hand he'd ever had, but he'd won on a bluff on far less.

Amar motioned Sharif over to his side and whispered something in his ear. Sharif nodded his consent. "You need collateral to raise your bet."

Jeremy stared back, dumbfounded. "Collateral. Like what?"

"I'm willing to accept Dreamer as collateral against your bet," Amar said. He would make Jeremy put up his prized possession and make his father proud by following through on his request to destroy their Derby competition.

This time the crowd began talking in loud yet hushed tones. Most of them knew why Jeremy was at the Derby — so Dreamer could take a run at the title.

Rylee rushed to Jeremy's side. "Stop this lunacy now, Jeremy. You can't bet Dreamer away. Please don't do this."

"Back off, Rylee," Jeremy warned, glaring at her. He didn't appreciate her interference in front of Amar of all people. It was disrespectful. She needed to let him handle this, handle Amar.

"What's it going to be?" Amar asked. "Make a bet or fold."

Jeremy paused for several beats as everyone in the room, including Rylee, waited for his answer. She couldn't believe he was willing to gamble away his horse — a horse he'd been training for years — to prove a point to Amar that he was worthy of her. She shook her head in frustration. "What's he doing, Camryn?"

"I don't know," Camryn whispered. "Stop him."

"He won't listen to me. It's like he's in some old world duel with Amar in which neither of them will blink."

"Oh, Lord!" Camryn rolled her eyes. "Then he'll have to lie in the bed he makes."

And lie in it he did, because when it was time to reveal their hands, Jeremy had a Four of a Kind, but Amar had a Royal Flush.

Rylee watched agony cross Jeremy's face when Amar said, "So, I'll have my attorney draw up the papers for Dreamer and have them delivered to your suite in the morning." Amar held out his hand to Jeremy.

Jeremy looked at it for several moments and Rylee thought he was going to slug Amar, but he shook his hand instead. Amar had won the hand fair and square. It wasn't his fault that Jeremy had gambled carelessly with his most prized possession.

Amar walked over to where Rylee stood in stunned disbelief behind Jeremy while Camryn walked out of the room in disgust.

Rylee didn't want to look at Amar, but his commanding presence made it impossible for her to ignore him.

"You didn't have to do that," she said tersely, glancing up at him. "It was cruel."

"No, I didn't, but perhaps someone should tell him not to gamble away something so priceless," Amar said. "As I told you before, I always get what I want. I look forward to seeing you tomorrow." He grasped her hand, brushed his lips across it and then sauntered out of the cellar.

Rylee stared at his retreating figure.

If he was this ruthless when it came to winning at poker, what was he capable of when it came to going after her?

"You're looking rather smug this morning," Sharif commented. They'd had to rise early to take care of some overseas business that required their attention and were now in the hotel gym for a workout. Amar was lying on his back completing weight reps while Sharif spotted him.

"If you're commenting on my winning hand last night," Amar replied, lifting the two-hundred-pound weight, "then you know I'm a master poker player and I don't like to lose."

"You annihilated that poor man, and he didn't even see it coming," Sharif said, looking down at his boss. "Couldn't you have left him some dignity without taking his horse?"

"He wanted to play in a high-stakes game." Amar lifted the weight again and sat up on the bench. "Casualties happen."

"I've seen you ruthless before," Sharif said, taking the weight and placing it back on the holder. "But last night it was personal."

Amar turned around to face him and inclined his head, conceding the point. "I suppose you're right, Sharif. This Jeremy fellow was acting as if he were above me, as if he were the better man for Rylee than me, and it stuck in my craw."

"Clearly," Sharif said and handed Amar some free weights. "But how's your father going to feel when he hears you have a horse running against his horse in the Derby. He won't be pleased."

Amar shrugged and accepted the weights to begin his bicycle curls. It was a risk he was willing to take. "Won't matter. The horse is a long shot at best. Plus, I had to show Rylee that any man willing to gamble away his horse shows a total lack of self-control and confidence. How could Rylee want a man like that?"

"And you think she wants someone like you?" Sharif asked, lifting up the dumbbell to help Amar complete his shoulder presses. "If you ask me, she was sickened by both your behaviors."

"But it's me that she craves," Amar responded smugly, putting down the weight.

"You're that sure of yourself?"

"I know when a woman is attracted to me, and the kiss Rylee and I shared at the Taste of the Derby was just the start. We're not over, not by a long shot."

"Last night was a travesty," Rylee heard Hank, the trainer, tell a stable hand the following morning as she gave Dreamer the once-over. "How could Jeremy gamble her away?"

Rylee couldn't understand it either. *How could he have been so careless?* It was upsetting to know that she might be the reason Jeremy hadn't used good judgment. She supposed that's why she'd come to the stables so early to check on his horse. Or she should say, his *former* horse. She'd tossed and turned all night long and finally, at four AM, had given up the pretense of sleep. She'd showered, dressed in her jeans and a plaid shirt and headed to the stables. She knew her job here was over now that Jeremy had signed Dreamer away, but she'd kind of had an affinity for the large animal.

"Who knows how this Amar Bishop will take care of her," she heard one of the men say. "He's used to Arabians, not a gentle breed like Dreamer."

"I heard his father's a sheikh," Hank said.

"How can that be? Isn't he part black?" another asked.

"Father must have had a thing for dark meat," one of them said, laughing.

Rylee didn't like hearing the men and Amar's potential employees talking ill of him, so she walked out of the stall with her hands on her hips and said, "Perhaps you shouldn't gossip about a man you know nothing about until you've actually had the chance to meet him."

The men replied with an exaggerated "Humph!" and stalked away.

Clapping sounded from behind her, and Rylee rounded to find Amar standing within inches. "I should have you as my defender more often."

Amar was wearing a polo shirt, riding britches and boots. He looked freshly shaven, equestrian and super sexy, but Rylee was furious with him. She rolled her eyes and went back into the stall to finish her final check of Dreamer.

Amar followed her. "Wow! I don't think I've had an eye roll since I was in boarding school," he said, watching her and laughing as he leaned against the stall door.

"What do you want, Amar?" Rylee asked. "Did you come to gloat over your winnings?"

Amar straightened at Rylee's harsh tone. She was *truly* upset with him. "No, I came to check on the horse I won fair and square."

Rylee rolled her eyes again. "Gambling!" She said the word with such distaste that Amar hung his head low.

"Rylee, I didn't make Jeremy bet his horse away."

"But you sure as hell didn't stop him, did you?" she said, spinning around to face him. "You were determined to one-up him. And why? Because he was spending the evening with me? It was juvenile!"

Amar's blood began to boil. He did not appreciate Rylee's tone nor her condescending manner. "If you're looking for an apology for my actions, you won't get one."

"As arrogant as you are, I wasn't expecting one," Rylee returned. When she'd completed her check, she softly brushed Dreamer's chestnut coat and whispered words of good luck to her as if the horse could understand.

Rylee picked up her medical bag from the stall floor and tried to push past Amar, but he wouldn't budge. "Where do you think you're going?"

"To my hotel room to pack."

"Pack?" Panic started to set in Amar's belly, but he tried his best to belie it by responding in a cool tone. "What do you mean?"

"My job here is over," Rylee said matter-of-factly. "The only reason I came to the Derby was to help Jeremy win. Now that he no longer has a horse, I'm sure he'll be charting his jet back to Tucson with as much steam as humanly possible, and Camryn and I will be right there beside him."

She tried again to push past Amar, but all she did was connect with a solid expanse of his rock-hard chest and breathe in that spicy cologne he wore that was so masculine and intensely him.

"You can't leave," Amar said quietly.

"I can, and I will."

"But Dreamer is in the Derby tomorrow."

"And?"

"And you've been taking care of her all of this time. You can't just abandon her." Amar knew it was a feeble attempt to get her to stay, but he was grasping at straws.

"I came here to help a friend, and you've succeeded in making that no longer necessary. There's no reason for me to stay."

"Isn't there?" Amar said, tilting her chin upward to look into her piercing eyes. "The only reason you're leaving is because you want to run away from what's happening between us."

"I'm not running. I'm walking."

Amar smiled. "Semantics. You're running scared and ready to bolt right when things are heating up between us."

"I told you before, Amar, I wasn't going to be your weekend plaything."

"How do you know it couldn't be more? You're so quick to rush off. So why don't you stay? Not just to take care of the horse, which I think is your ethical responsibility, but stay because you want to be with *me*. Because you want to explore the chemistry between us as much as I do."

Rylee shook her head. "I can't."

"Why not?"

"Jeremy's my ride. He brought me here to Louisville."

"He's not the only one with a private jet, Rylee," Amar responded. "I'll take you back home. Stay here with *me*. What other excuses do you have?"

Rylee spun away from Amar and the powerful energy he exuded and began pacing the stall. She couldn't think straight if she was standing that close to him, and he knew it, sensed it. "I just can't," she said with her back to him. She couldn't face Amar because if she did, she knew her resolve would break.

"I think you want to," he said softly, spinning her around and forcing her to look at him. He lightly touched her cheek. "You just have to allow yourself to," he said, leaning down, planting a kiss on her shoulder, neck and face, "enjoy the moment."

Rylee tried to lean backward and wiggle away from Amar, but he just pulled her more tightly against him until they were hip to hip and she could *feel* him. He pinned her with the weight of his body and that's when he lowered his head and gave her a feather-light kiss.

"Say yes," he murmured as his mouth moved upward to graze her earlobe with tantalizing persuasion.

"I-I ..."

Rylee felt her resolve weaken when his damp tongue circled her ear and then slid in. She clutched his biceps through his shirt to prevent herself from falling, but Amar had a tight hold on her. He left her ear long enough so his mouth could return to her lips and coax a response. She succumbed to the domination of his tongue and circled her arms around his neck, greedily kissing him back.

Amar was an excellent kisser. He was confident, skillful and totally delicious. A rush of desire coursed through her right to the apex of her thighs. She wiggled herself against his growing erection, and he groaned a sigh of pleasure. She wanted to reach down and touch him, but she resisted the urge. Instead, she mated her tongue with his, and he answered by deepening the kiss and swirling his wicked tongue. He probed deeper and deeper until she met him stroke for beautiful stroke.

Rylee could feel her nipples pucker into pebbles. Before she could react, Amar began freeing the buttons on her shirt and sweeping his hands over her. He unfolded a bra cup and took a hardened nipple, rolling it between his fingers. He dipped his head, ready to take a nipple in his mouth, when they heard a loud crash and footsteps retreating.

Startled, they jumped away, and Rylee noticed a rake had fallen to the floor. She was panting uncontrollably, her breasts heaving, but she recovered long enough to rush from the stall and see Jeremy striding down the stables. "Jeremy, wait!" she said from the doorway as she buttoned her shirt, but he kept walking.

Rylee went to run to him, but Amar caught her arm. "What's it going to be, Rylee?"

She glanced down the hall at Jeremy's retreating figure and then back up at Amar, with whom she'd shared the most amazing passionate kisses she'd ever had in her life. She'd been bold and brazen with the intimacies she'd allowed Amar after only knowing him for a short time. She hadn't behaved this way with any other man. Should she stay with Amar to find out what passion truly meant? Or should she go with Jeremy?

"I'll stay," Rylee replied, jerking her arm away, "but I have to talk to Jeremy, so you're just going to have to trust that I'll be back."

"Go!" Amar said. "I'll be waiting."

Chapter 5

RYLEE CAUGHT UP TO JEREMY just as he was getting into the limousine waiting for him outside the stables. "Jeremy, wait!" She grabbed the door just as he was about to close it in her face. "Don't leave like this."

"Like what? Humiliated," he said, his lips a thin line of anger. "That, that bastard" — he pointed toward the stables — "made a fool of me, and I allowed myself to get caught up."

"Jeremy, calm down!"

"Why should I, Rylee?" he asked, stepping out of the limo to face her. "You've known for years how I felt about you, yet you continued to lead me on. This weekend was my chance to show you that I could be the man for you, but clearly I failed."

"Jeremy, it was never a competition between you and Amar."

"No?"

"No." Rylee touched his arm. "I simply don't feel that way about you."

"Like you feel about him?" Jeremy asked, his nostrils flaring. "I saw you back there." He pointed to the stables. "You have *never* kissed me the way you kissed him."

Rylee lifted her chin and boldly met his gaze. "And I never will, because I just see you as a big brother. I always have and despite how much my father and your parents tried to push us together, it was never going to work. C'mon, you must have realized something wasn't right when I wouldn't sleep with you."

"And you think it'll work with him?" Jeremy scoffed with cold sarcasm. "It won't, Rylee. Amar's a user and opportunist. Once he's gotten what he wants, he'll be on to the next woman. I don't want to see you get hurt, Rylee. I love you."

"And I you."

"But like a brother?" he added.

Rylee nodded, bleakly.

"Then I wish you the best of luck, because I promise you that Amar will leave you when he's had his fill of you." He slid back into the limo.

"Then I guess it's my mistake to make, and if I get hurt, then it's on me. It's not on you to protect me."

"No, it's not, not anymore," Jeremy said. "Take care, Rylee. I'll see you back in Tucson when Amar has returned to his playboy ways." He closed the door behind him. Seconds later, the limo drove off leaving Rylee staring at its rear window. But she wasn't alone for long.

"Are you okay?" Amar asked as he came up beside her.

Rylee glanced at him sideways. "What do you think? I just had to hurt a friend I care deeply about. I've been friends with him since childhood."

"Better you set him straight than allow him to continue to believe he has a chance with you."

Rylee frowned because Amar was right. She should have had that conversation with Jeremy long before now. Had she told him before, maybe none of this would have happened. But then again, would she have ever met Amar?

"How about a ride?" Amar asked. "The stables have a great trail, or so I've heard. I'd love to share it with you. Spend some time together. Just you and me."

56

Rylee let out a tortured sigh. What a morning she'd had, and it wasn't even nine AM. "Yes they do, but I've got to call my girlfriend first. Tell her what happened."

"Oh, yes, Camryn." He was so eager to get Rylee alone and get his hands on her, he had momentarily forgotten she hadn't come alone.

Rylee nodded. "Go ahead and arrange the ride. I'll be inside shortly."

"Sure thing."

As soon as Amar had walked back into the stables, Rylee pulled her cell phone out of her jeans pocket and dialed the hotel. Camryn answered on the third ring. "Hello." She sounded out of breath.

"Camryn, it's Rylee."

"Oh, you're in deep trouble, missy," her friend replied.

"Why?"

"Well, Jeremy called to tell me he's leaving and going back to Tucson and that it might be best if I come back with him since you might be otherwise engaged."

"Oh!"

"Don't start backsliding now, Miss Hot to Trot. You made your decision, or should I say your bed, and now you have to lie in it. And" — she threw several pieces of clothing into the bag while she cradled the cordless phone in the other — "and you better come back with some juicy stories to tell me since you're cutting short my first Derby trip."

"You don't have to leave, Cam."

"Bullshit! Do you think I wanna be the third wheel while I watch you and Amar make doe eyes at each other? No thank you. I'll go back now and see if I can't calm Jeremy down. He's seeing red now. He said he saw you two making out like rabbits."

Rylee laughed. *We were going at it like sex-crazed teenagers,* she thought. "I'm so sorry, Cam. I know how much you were looking forward to this trip and showing off your new hat."

Camryn shrugged. "The Derby comes every year. There will be another time for me and my fabulous hat. But you ..." She stopped packing long enough to say, "You need to enjoy yourself and just live in the moment."

"That's what I'm doing."

"And I'm proud of you. Just be safe, okay? I'm going to leave you a box of condoms in your lingerie drawer. That way I know you won't forget about 'em."

Rylee chuckled again at her dear friend. "Thank you, and you know I love you."

"And I you. Now get off this phone and go have some fun. You only live life once!"

Amar procured an Arabian stallion to ride and a beautiful palomino with a gold coat and white mane and tail for Rylee. The horses were waiting for her as soon as she returned back to the stables from her call.

"Everything all taken care of?" Amar asked as she walked toward him. As he lifted her onto the horse, he enjoyed the view of her curvy backside as she swung her leg over. His mind instantly wandered to what it would be like when she swung her leg on each side of him and rode him like there was no tomorrow.

"Yes," she said as he walked over and joined her by jumping astride the Arabian. "Camryn is on her way back to Tucson with Jeremy."

Amar smiled. It was impossible not to hide his relief as he'd been contemplating his way out of the scenario, but clearly Rylee understood their need for it to be just the two of them. "I hope they have safe travels."

"I just bet you do," Rylee said as she gave a little hitch and the palomino heard the cue and took off walking.

Amar followed behind her, and several minutes later they'd left the stable grounds and were headed onto the horseback riding trail.

It was a beautiful sunny day with a few puffy clouds on the horizon, but that didn't dull Amar's spirits. He and Rylee were finally alone with no interruptions. He'd wanted this since the first night in the hotel when he'd spotted her in the restaurant and then again at the stables. He'd never had such a strong reaction to a woman before and even though it scared him, he wasn't walking away. Instead, he'd done everything in his power to ensure their fate.

"What are you thinking?" Rylee asked when she looked up and found they'd stopped and he was staring at her.

"I'm sorry?"

"What were you thinking about just now?"

"Honestly?"

"That would be preferred."

"I was thinking about you," Amar replied.

"Oh!"

"I was thinking how beautiful you are and how lucky I am that you've agreed to spend the remainder of your weekend with me."

A wide smile took over Rylee's face. "How else could I get to know you beyond the charming persona?"

"Do you think me insincere?"

She shook her head. "No, not at all, or I wouldn't be here. But I would like to know what moves you, what's important to you, beyond our mutual attraction for each other."

"Fair enough." Amar gave his Arabian a kick and they took off again as he mused over her question. They had several quiet moments looking over the lush landscape and trees before Amar finally spoke. "I'm moved by how people still value what I and my company bring to the table. And what's important to me is loyalty, honesty and trust. It's been difficult to find people who have all those qualities."

His answer must have given Rylee pause because she was introspective before she asked, "Is that why you don't have a large entourage? My impression, or what I've seen, is that sheikhs' sons always have lots of people around them."

"Usually that's the case, but I have found that I can only trust a few in my inner circle."

"You mean one — Sharif."

"I agreed to Sharif for my father, but make no mistake about it, he's got bodyguards looking after me. They are just in the shadows."

Rylee stopped her horse. "Seriously?" She looked around her. "I don't see anyone."

"My father is a stubborn man. He only allows me to *think* that I have freedom."

"You're taking it all in stride."

"What can I do? It comes with being his son, even if I am a bastard."

Rylee stopped her horse at a small clearing, and before he knew it, she'd jumped down, still holding the reins to her palomino. "Don't talk about yourself like that!"

Rylee seemed appalled by his choice of words, so Amar slowly dismounted his horse. He grasped her reins and after he'd tied both horses to a nearby tree, he joined Rylee in the clearing that overlooked several mountains and valleys.

"Why? It's what I am." He tucked several curly strands of her hair behind her ear that had blown free from her cowboy hat. "My father was not married to my mother when she had me."

"That may be so, Amar," she said, looking up at him with big brown eyes, "but it's so negative to talk that way."

Amar shrugged and walked back to the horses to pull out a blanket and several canteens of water before walking back over to her. "It's what I've been called my whole life. I guess it doesn't affect me like most Americans."

"You're American?"

"Yes." He smiled and grabbed her hand as he walked her to a spot underneath a shady tree. He shook out the blanket and kneeled down on it. He held his hand out to her and she grasped it and joined him on the blanket. "Anyway, what moves you?" he asked, still holding her hand as he lay down. "What's important to *you*?"

"Well, that's easy," Rylee answered as she sat. "Horses move me, and I don't mean that in the literal sense. I've always been curious about big, beautiful animals, even though I had to learn how to treat other animals, and I do, on my family's ranch. But horses have a special place in my heart, and that's why I specialized as a horse surgeon."

"Not an easy field for a woman to get into."

Rylee nodded her agreement. "Not at all, but I was determined, despite my father's objections."

"Sounds oddly familiar." Amar knew what it was like to go against his father's ideas of what he should be doing with his life. Owning an Internet publishing company and several television and radio stations seemed trivial to the Sheikh, who was used to oil and big business.

"And family is *everything* to me," Rylee finished. "I love them all dearly."

"You have brothers, yes?"

Rylee glared at him. She knew he'd done his research, so the question was moot, but she humored him. "Yes, I have two brothers — Noah and Caleb. Noah's the eldest and Caleb is the youngest and a hell-raiser."

Amar laughed. "I can commiserate. My youngest brother, Tariq, is a handful, but I think it's because he knows all the responsibility falls to the eldest, so he can live life as he pleases."

Rylee smiled. "My brother Noah, being the eldest, is very focused on the family. He's loyal to a fault. You couldn't find a more honest or trustworthy man. He's someone I can count on, always has been."

"And Caleb?"

"Caleb's all heart. He cares about family too, and I know if push came to shove, he'd protect me against anyone; but he can be a bit unreliable at times."

"And your parents?"

"Isaac and Madelyn," Rylee said, "have been married for thirty-six years and are as in love with each other as they were on the day they married."

"I can see the love you have for them in your eyes. It's admirable."

"You don't feel that way about your family?" Rylee said, staring directly at him.

"Afraid not," Amar said truthfully. "I'm only close to Tariq, I guess because he doesn't see me as a threat or competition. But my other brother ..."

"Is he the oldest?"

"The oldest that the Kingdom of Nasir recognizes."

"So you're older than him?" Rylee surmised correctly.

Amar nodded. "But because I'm a half-breed and conceived outside of marriage, I'm not of noble blood."

"Has it been hard for you being American and black in that culture?"

Amar leaned down on the blanket and rested his head on his forearm. "You have no idea, but let's talk about a more pleasant topic." He grasped one of her arms and pulled her down on the blanket beside him.

"Like what?" She turned on her side to look into his midnight eyes.

"Like if you'll be my date this evening to the Julep Ball."

"I remember Camryn mentioning it, but I really hadn't thought about it."

"Meaning you don't wish to attend?"

Rylee smiled. "No, it just means I don't have anything to wear. Camryn and I had started shopping, but we hadn't found a gown yet."

"Don't worry. I'll take care of it."

"And how will you do that?"

Amar wrapped a hand behind Rylee's neck and pulled her closer until their lips were inches apart. "Well, first, I have to become acquainted with your lips." He kissed her softly on the mouth. "And then ..." — his other hand slid down her curves — "I need to become acquainted with every inch of you so I can ensure your dress has the proper fit."

"Is that so?" Rylee was breathless as he leaned down to nuzzle her neck.

"Oh, yes," he said, returning to her mouth. He kissed her as he'd always wanted — unrushed and unhurried. He wanted time to fully explore her lips and tongue. He wanted to melt under her heat, hear her heartbeat, smell the fragrance that was uniquely hers, sweet and floral.

Rylee pressed her lips against his as he gently covered her mouth with exploratory kisses. When she had kissed him earlier, Amar sensed she'd been holding back, but not now. Her kisses were tantalizingly slow and sweet and ever so satisfying that Amar let out a low moan. The lower half of him sprung to life, and he pressed himself against her middle. Rylee responded by grinding against him.

He grasped both sides of her face and dove his tongue inside her mouth, and she met him greedy kiss for greedy kiss. She began pulling his shirt from his britches so she could stretch her hot hands over the expanse of his back. This simply fueled Amar into action, and he reached down to lift his shirt over his head until he was bare-chested.

Rylee looked up at him through passion-glazed eyes, and Amar reached for the buttons on her blouse and began undoing them with trembling fingers. When he'd freed the last one, her shirt fell open and revealed a lacy bra. Amar fondled one full globe and felt a chocolate nipple harden underneath in response. He knew he shouldn't, but he had to have a taste and lowered his head to lick the nipple through the lace bra.

"Ah," Rylee moaned, and that was Amar's undoing. He pushed aside the fabric and with his tongue tantalized the bud which had swollen at his earliest touch. He laved it with his wet tongue and then moved to the other breast and loved it with equal attention. Rylee's moans grew louder as he teased and licked each nipple. She became so loud that Amar lost all thread of time and space and reached to take off her jeans. He unzipped them far enough so he could reach his hands inside past the matching lace panty until he touched the core of her womanhood. His finger slid inside her warmth and found she was already moist for him. But he wanted her wetter. He slid a finger inside her and searched.

"Oh!"

Rylee began to pant and squirm, but he didn't stop, couldn't stop. He began to stroke her using his fingers. Slow at first, then in and out, then faster and faster until Rylee began to buck on the blanket. Amar covered her cries of pleasure with his mouth; he wanted to taste every inch of her. He would like nothing better than to pull her jeans down her legs and plant his mouth at the apex of her femininity until she came again, but the time wasn't right.

He couldn't just take her out in the middle of the pasture without any romance, not to mention he didn't have any protection on him. He hadn't planned on making her come, but he did. The sound of her sweet release was calling to everything male in him to bury himself in her sweet heat. But she deserved better than a quick roll in the hay. Or should he say *grass*?

"Dear God, Rylee, I want you so bad," Amar whispered, pulling his hands out of her jeans and sitting up on the blanket.

Rylee was silent for several long minutes, no doubt catching her breath, before she said, "And I hear a 'but' in there."

"You do," he answered, looking down at her. She looked so beautiful and sexy, having just had an orgasm, that it pleased him as much as it had her. "But I want our first time to be right, to be special."

"Who knew you were such a romantic." Rylee sat up. She pushed her bra back into place and began buttoning her shirt.

"I am," Amar said. "Plus, I want more than a quickie. I want all night with you, Rylee. Can you handle that?"

She turned to look at him. "The question is *can you?*"

Rylee stared down at the box that was just delivered to her hotel room. She'd returned several hours ago to prepare for the Julep Ball that evening. She'd gone to a nearby salon and had her hair and nails done because she wanted everything to be perfect. At the last minute, she'd thrown in a bikini wax in preparation for the night she would spend with Amar.

After nearly making love with Amar out in the open this afternoon, there was no doubt in Rylee's mind that she and Amar would combust tonight. She was both excited and somewhat nervous. She was sure Amar had many lovers, and she wondered if she would live up to his playboy expectations.

Rylee snapped out of her anxiety and looked down at the Robert Cavalli designer gown that had been delivered to her door. It was a gorgeous gold-metallic gown that would show off her brown skin, which she'd dusted with bronzer.

She picked up her cell phone and dialed Camryn. Her best friend was sure to have landed in Tucson by now, and Rylee needed her advice.

"Hello?" Camryn answered.

"Hey there." Rylee tried to sound unfazed even though she was far from feeling that way. "How was the flight? How's Jeremy?"

"Oh, just fine. I kept to myself mostly as Jeremy was in a foul mood and wasn't much company. He spent most of his time on the phone on ranch business. He barely spoke when he dropped me off. I'm back at my apartment now." She walked to her refrigerator and removed a can of Diet Coke.

"I'm sorry about that, Cam. It's not you. It's me he's upset with. I hurt him badly."

Camryn popped open the can and took a swig. "That's life, and he's going to have to get over it. So what's new?"

"Nothing!" Her voice sounded high-pitched even to her, and sure enough, Camryn picked up on her anxiety.

"You're a bad liar, Rylee. Something obviously happened after I left, so what gives?"

"If you call nearly having sex with Amar outside in an open pasture, then I would say something happened."

"Omigod!" Soda sputtered out of Camryn's mouth, spraying everywhere. "Wow! I can't leave you for a few hours, and you're at it like rabbits, just like Jeremy said!" Camryn laughed as she walked over to the counter and grabbed a paper towel. "I'm glad I got out of there when I did, otherwise I would have been collateral damage in Amar's quest to take you to bed."

"Cam, I don't know what came over me. First, we're talking and the next minute, he has his hands down my jeans."

"Oh!" Camryn's hand came to her mouth as she wiped it with the paper towel.

"I know, it was completely impulsive."

"Did you guys—"

"No, *Amar* stopped," Rylee said. "Can you believe that? He was the clear-headed and romantic one telling me he wants our first time together to be special."

"Well, I'm glad clearer heads prevailed. So I assume you're calling because you're going to the Julep Ball this evening and have nothing to wear."

"Amar took care of it," Rylee said. "I'm holding a Robert Cavalli gown in my hands."

"Get out of here!"

"It's true."

"Send me a picture. Damn you, Rylee, you get all the fun. First you catch the eye of a sheikh's son *and* he sends you designer gowns. I'm starting to get a bit jealous."

"Don't get jealous, Camryn. Your time will come."

"But you're still nervous about tonight, aren't you?" Camryn sensed her friend's uneasiness even over the phone.

"Am I that obvious?"

"Only to me, 'cause I know you. What are you nervous about? This isn't your first rodeo."

Rylee laughed at Camryn's bluntness. "No, but as you just said, he's a sheikh's son. He's probably had tons of women, maybe even a harem. How can I compete with that?"

"You can't, and you don't," Camryn said. "Amar obviously sees something in you that attracts him. Just focus on that and let nature take its course."

"Thank you, Cam. I guess I just needed some reassurance."

"I'm always here if you need me," Camryn replied. "And I want details tomorrow — lots and lots of details."

"As soon as I come up for air, you'll be my first call," Rylee said.

Chapter 6

AMAR MET RYLEE AT HER door, holding a medium-sized black box. He looked dashing and handsome in a white tuxedo and bowtie. The tux was made for him and fit his wide shoulders and bulging biceps, which Rylee had seen for herself earlier that afternoon when he'd thrown off his shirt.

"Come in." She motioned for him to join her, but before she could move, he spun her around so he could see her fully in the gown. His eyes took in every inch, from the lattice detail on the bodice of her gown to the mini tulle train that whisked behind her.

"You're breathtaking."

"Thank you. You don't look too bad yourself."

Amar grinned. "Thanks, but I think you are missing something."

"Really, I think you thought of everything." Along with the dress box, there'd been another containing the most obscene pair of designer heels, a wrap and a clutch purse.

"Almost," Amar said, "but you need this." He opened the black box he'd been carrying and revealed a stunning diamond necklace and matching earrings.

Rylee's eyes widened. "Amar, it's stunning, but I couldn't possibly wear that."

"You can, and you will." He removed the necklace from the box. He turned her around until her back was facing him so he could put it around her neck.

"Amar, please tell me this is a loaner," she said as he swept her hair aside. She'd chosen to wear it straight rather than her usual curls.

He smiled. "Yes, so long as we mention the designer, it's yours for the night."

Rylee exhaled as she donned the matching earrings. "Thank God. I'll have to guard these with my life."

"You won't have to, you're with me. And now you're ready. Let's go."

Rylee reached for the wrap and the gold-sequined clutch that had arrived with the dress and walked out the door with Amar.

Everyone in the hotel noticed them, from the staff to the patrons to the bellmen. With Amar's six-foot-four stature, he was impressive to begin with, but add the tux and Rylee's eye-catching gown, which made her look like a golden goddess, and the two of them were showstoppers.

The doorman opened the passenger side door for them, and they slid inside the waiting limo. Butterflies swarmed inside Rylee's belly at the thought of not only being Amar's date but at what would happen after the ball. This afternoon they'd nearly gotten carried away in the moment, just enough so that Rylee had felt the package Amar was working with. She suspected he would be a demanding yet giving lover, and she was secretly thrilled that he was determined to romance her tonight, rather than do a *wham-bam thank you ma'am*, which he could have easily attained this afternoon.

"Are you okay?" he asked from beside her.

"Absolutely."

Most of the night was a blur for Rylee. She wouldn't remember where the Julep Ball was held or the elaborate decorations adorning the room. She wouldn't remember the champagne that flowed or the endless people Amar introduced her to, many of whom only wanted a photo with the successful businessman that they could tweet or Instagram, or the other couples eager to party hop to the Unbridled Eve or Barnstable and Brown Party.

She *would* recall the moment Amar took her into his arms for a slow dance that was more like a slow burn of what was to come later that night. Rylee allowed herself to live in the moment, breathing in his male scent by wrapping her arms around his neck.

"I'm so glad you stayed, Rylee," Amar said huskily as he hugged her close to his broad frame.

"So am I." She looked up into his dark eyes, which smoldered with passion and heat.

"Are you ready to get out of here?" he asked quietly as he looked at her intently.

She understood, and was she ready to take the next step in their relationship? She answered with one word: "Yes."

Once in the car, Rylee thought Amar would be raring to go, but instead he held her hand, circling her palm with his thumb as the limo pulled off. It was a tiny but intimate action that had Rylee up in arms as if he'd kissed her passionately.

The ride back to the hotel took longer than before, but eventually the limo came to a stop and the driver opened the car door. Amar exited first and held out his hand as Rylee stepped out of the vehicle. She was surprised to find they weren't going back to the hotel for a night of unbridled lovemaking, as she'd thought, but instead had arrived at a country cottage in the woods. Even more, dozens of rose petals adorned the path up to the cottage door.

Rylee turned to look up at Amar questioningly.

"I didn't want prying eyes," he said. "I wanted tonight to be about us and nothing more. Come." He led the way.

Rylee swallowed the frog in her throat and followed him up the rose-strewn path.

When he opened the door, allowing Rylee to precede him, she saw that the cottage was bathed in candlelight, and she heard soft music playing. A fire blazed from the fireplace and a bucket of champagne was chilling in a stand nearby. He'd thought of everything.

"Do you do this for all your women?" Rylee asked, turning around to face him.

Amar closed the door behind him, and Rylee heard it lock. "No, I don't." His eyes smoldered, and Rylee felt her lips chap. She licked them and watched Amar catch the action. Before she had time to react, he swept her in his arms. His lips came down over hers hungrily and moved to explore the shape and surface of her mouth. His kisses were soft but intent, with a purpose. His tongue coaxed apart her lips, invaded her mouth and quickly tangled with hers. It was electrifying and sent spirals of ecstasy swirling through them both. Before Rylee had time to recover, Amar was pulling her down onto the bearskin rug and pillows that had been strategically placed in front of the roaring fire. His hands splayed across her bare back and lowered even further to cup her butt as he held her securely in the safety of his arms. His touch made her skin tingle, and she wanted more, much more.

But just as quickly as he started, he pulled away from their embrace. "I'm sorry."

"For what?" Rylee stared up at him from his lap, where she was still nestled, and tried to catch her breath.

"I'm not usually so forward, but from the moment I saw you tonight, I've wanted to kiss you."

"You have?"

"Couldn't you tell?"

Rylee thought about several instances in which she'd caught him staring at her that evening, but then just as quickly he'd looked away and she'd wondered if she'd imagined it. "I suppose."

"I had this evening all planned out in my head," Amar said. "How smooth I was going to be when I took you to bed, and now I've ruined it all by behaving like a clumsy teenager."

Rylee touched Amar's cheek. "This" — she motioned around the room to all the trappings of a night of lovemaking as she rose to her feet — "and the dress and jewels are wonderful, and I'm sure it's what women have come to expect from a man like you, with your reputation." Amar lowered his eyes. "But" — she tilted his chin down to look at her — "I don't need all this or have to be made to feel like I'm in *Pretty Woman*. I'm here because I want to be with *you*."

Amar stared at her in disbelief as he rose to sit on his haunches. "You really mean that, don't you?"

"Yes, I do." She reached behind her to the zipper of the designer dress and tugged it down, letting it fall in a whoosh to the floor.

She could see Amar was stunned by her boldness, but he didn't say a word. He just let her continue.

The strapless bra she wore was next. She reached behind her, unhooked it and it slid down until she was standing before him in nothing but her bikini panties, garter belt and heels. She stepped out of the dress, knocking it away. She'd never been this bold before, but there was something about Amar that made her feel that she could be carefree with him and comfortable with her sexuality.

"I love the getup," Amar said, "but it's gotta go. I want you naked, Rylee. I want to be inside you."

She knelt down to Amar, and this time it was *she* who kissed him and opened her mouth to deepen the kiss. This time she took the lead. Amar was shell-shocked at Rylee's boldness. Every stroke of her tongue against his stoked a desire that had been building inside him for days, and now it was at a fever pitch. He combed his fingers through her hair. He liked it straight but preferred her natural, unruly curls. Wanting more, he pressed his thigh between hers, and when he did, they lost their balance and tumbled onto the pillows.

Her head tipped backward, and he used the opportunity to nuzzle a tantalizing spot where her pulse beat rapidly. Then his hands lazily moved all over her so he could devour her whole. But it was her breasts that he found first, breasts he'd only begun to really explore out in the pasture earlier that day. But this time he would not be rushed. This time, he could take all the time he wanted.

He took one of her already engorged nipples in his mouth, and he sucked and licked and teased it with his tongue. Rylee whimpered her pleasure as he continued to suckle one breast while teasing the other with his fingertips, bringing it to a rocky hard pebble.

"You have on too many clothes," she murmured.

Amar realized he'd been remiss in not providing her the same luxury he'd had of touching her soft, scented skin. He rose long enough to remove his tuxedo jacket and unbutton his shirt. But Rylee wasn't wasting any time. She reached for the zipper on his trousers and undid it. His erection was obvious and jutted out as she relieved him of his pants. He kicked them off in a huff. Soon he was bare-chested and wearing only his boxer briefs and socks.

"That's much better," she cooed, batting her eyelashes at him.

"You think? Because I think you're still wearing entirely too much." Amar returned to the rug, and this time he was the aggressor, pushing her backward on the pillows. He unlatched each of her garters one at a time, watched Rylee's eyes become more hooded as he hooked his thumbs under the side of the sexy knickers and gently drew the material down her legs. Rylee lifted her bottom to help remove them, and then she was completely naked to his adoring eyes. And adore her he did, but now she seemed slightly embarrassed.

"You're so beautiful," Amar whispered, stroking her inner thighs. He wanted her to know how much he loved her body. "I'm going to enjoy exploring you, Rylee, tasting all of you." There would be time for his own needs later. Right now, he wanted to please her, pleasure her and make her scream his name.

"That sounds like an intriguing promise."

"And I plan on delivering." Amar lowered his head to her feet. He started at her ankle with one kiss, working his way up with teasing flicks of his tongue to the underside of one knee and then the other. His mouth idly played with the soft folds of her inner thighs. He felt Rylee begin to quiver as his mouth made its way higher.

"Amar, please ..."

He gave her exactly what she craved, with a long stroke of his tongue at her sex. Rylee jumped, but he held her down with his hands and swirled his tongue across her clitoris, teasing her, blowing on her.

Rylee moaned as he went deeper with his tongue first and then his fingers. He could feel her arousal coiling tightly around him and it excited him to no end. He wanted nothing more than to bury himself inside her and end the torture, but this was her moment. He did figure eights with his tongue, circling, delving, teasing until she climaxed, calling out his name.

"Amar!" She fell backward against the pillows.

Pleased, he looked down at her and saw a small sheen of perspiration across her brow and chest. "This was just the beginning, baby. There's more to come, so prepare yourself."

Rylee glanced down at his rock-hard penis. "I can see that. So bring it on. I'm ready for you."

Amar grinned devilishly and swiftly removed his boxers, freeing his penis and showing Rylee exactly what she'd *felt* earlier that day. He was magnificent, and Rylee licked her lips in eager anticipation, but it was Amar who was quick to react, and, on his haunches, reached for some strategically placed condoms near the fireplace. *When he said he'd thought of everything, he meant it,* Rylee thought.

"Allow me." She rose, reached for the foil packet and took it out of his hands. She was about to rip open the foil when she had a better idea and lowered her head instead to take him full and deep in her mouth.

"Oh!" Amar seemed shocked yet pleasantly surprised at her double cross. She bobbed her head, taking him in and out, circling her tongue around his shaft and then out to tease the head with quick flicks of her tongue. Amar fisted handfuls of her hair in his hands as she loved him with her mouth.

His moans of "Yes, Rylee, yes, babe," moved her. Rylee nearly had him at the brink when he swiftly turned her on her back. His fingers found the damp place between her legs, and she was just as wet as she'd been before if not more. Amar spread her wide with his thighs, and she lifted her knees in response, allowing Amar to ease inside her. He worked his way in until she was able to take all of him.

"Amar ..." She clutched at his back with his fingernails.

"Yes, love." He looked down at her with passion-glazed eyes.

Her eyes said, "more" and he gave it to her by rising slightly and moving slowly but deeply inside her. Rylee could feel herself opening up to him unlike she had to any

76

other man. She arched her pelvis against him, creating the perfect friction as he thrust deeper and deeper inside.

"Oh, yes!" she screamed, but Amar covered his mouth with hers and began to pump wildly into her. Rylee surrendered herself to the moment, to Amar, to the reaction he could cause within her. She exploded.

"Rylee!" Amar gave one final thrust, and she heard his release as he joined her in a peaceful bliss.

Amar stared down at Rylee as she slept. She looked beautiful, peaceful and very satisfied. He'd ensured that. Last night, they'd made love, and she'd climaxed again and again. When she had, she'd seemed surprised by it. That's when she'd shared with him that she'd never been able to reach orgasm with her prior lovers unless by way of oral sex.

Her admission had been like a test for him, one in which he had to score high marks. So he'd been determined to make sure she'd come each time they'd been joined together. And she had. As a man, that was immensely rewarding, knowing he could please his woman. And Rylee Hart was certainly his right now.

He hadn't exactly played fair. He'd used all his charm, romantic skills and prowess as a lover to make sure she'd eventually succumb. It hadn't hurt that Jeremy was no match for him. Sure, he was a nice guy, but he wasn't who Rylee needed. She needed a take-charge man, and Amar knew that he *himself* fit the bill.

A buzzing came from the nightstand, and Amar looked at his cell phone. It was his father. He would have to take the call.

"Hello," Amar whispered as he slowly slid out of the bed while Rylee continued to sleep.

"So, are we ready for the Derby today?" his father asked. "Did you neutralize your opponent? What are the odds now?"

Amar looked back at Rylee. He didn't want her to know he hadn't just gone after the horse because she was Jeremy's but also to increase his father's odds. "Yes. And our chances are improved," Amar replied softly.

"Why are you whispering?"

"I, uh, have company," Amar said. He sighed in relief as he entered the safety of the hall away from Rylee's ears.

"So you prevailed?" his father said. "I should have known. Enjoy the piece while you can."

"She's not a piece," Amar responded forcefully.

"Whatever," his father said dismissively. "You just ensure we have a win. I have some friends hoping to win big today."

"Dreamer is a long shot, but Desert Storm will certainly place." Amar took a seat at the small pedestal table in the dining room.

"Placing means nothing. I want a win."

Of course he did. His father wasn't used to losing.

"I don't ask much of you, Amar. I allow you to do your own thing in the U.S., but *you* said you wanted this part of the business."

"You don't need to remind me," Amar replied. Years ago, he'd thought agreeing to oversee his father's horses would bring them closer. Now he knew he'd been wrong. He knew his father just saw it as a way to try and control him. "And you don't *allow* me to do anything. I'm in control of my own life."

"You think so? If I wanted you back here, you would be."

"Why would you even want it, Father? So your favorite son and country people can mock or degrade me? No thank you. My home is in the States, and I'm happy here. You're just going to have to accept that."

"That godforsaken country is not your home. Nasir is."

"Nasir has never been my home."

Amar heard his father's long audible sigh. Why must they have this same argument? Wasn't it just a bit repetitious?

"I don't want to argue with you, son."

"And I don't want to argue with you. I'll call you after the race is over."

"Agreed."

Before Amar could press the End button to terminate the call, he heard a dial tone. His father had hung up on him. *Again!*

"Everything okay here?" Rylee asked from behind him as she swung her arms around his shoulders.

When had she awakened? He hadn't even heard her footsteps. He turned around in the chair and swung her into his lap.

"Everything's fine," he said, holding her. "I was hoping to rejoin you in the bed before you woke up so we could pick up where we left off."

"Hmm ..." Rylee trailed light kisses up his neck. "We don't have much time to get to the racetrack."

"Then we'll have to make it a quickie." Amar rose to his feet, and, with her still in his arms, carried her back to the bedroom.

They eventually separated to shower, but even that had dragged on for an additional thirty minutes because he hadn't been able to resist making love to her again when she'd been all soapy and wet. He'd backed her up against the tile of the shower stall, lifted her off her feet and surged inside her moist heat. Their tongues had mated just as their lower bodies had, and he waited for Rylee to come before he'd finally allowed himself his own release.

Amar and Rylee may have never made it out of the cabin save for Sharif's quick thinking and having clothes delivered to the cottage. Once dressed, they'd hightailed it to Churchill Downs. Amar knew he should have been there earlier instead of making sweet love to Rylee at the cabin he'd procured for the weekend, but he hadn't wanted to leave her side. Rylee was a special lady that he could envision himself spending more time with, but duty called first.

When they arrived to Churchill Downs, they went directly to the Paddock, where the trainers and jockeys were already prepping for the Derby's events.

Sharif was already there waiting for him at Dreamer's stall. Amar went to talk to him, but Rylee didn't stand idly by his side. Instead, she went to work and did a quick evaluation of Dreamer's condition after the morning workouts.

"So nice of you to join us," she heard Hank say.

Amar liked that she wasn't one of those ladies who lunched or sat in the stands with the pretty dresses and big hats. Today she'd worn exactly what she'd worn every other time he'd seen her in Pembroke Stables — worn boots and jeans — but this time she'd added a crisp white shirt. Rylee wasn't afraid to get her hands dirty or deal with tough guys like Hank.

"I take it everything was to your satisfaction last evening," Sharif whispered to Amar.

Amar glanced sideways at him. "Everything was great! You did a fine job of setting the mood."

"Thank you, sir."

"I'd like you to arrange something similar for tonight," Amar said and turned to whisper instructions in Sharif's ear. He didn't know how much time he would have with Rylee or when she would have to get back to her family's ranch, so he had to make every moment count.

"I will take care of it."

"Good. Let's go about seeing Desert Storm." Amar left Rylee to her own devices while he went to check on his father's investment.

Rylee glanced up long enough to see Amar walk away with Sharif. Last night, after she'd boldly stood up and undressed in front of Amar, she'd enjoyed the best lovemaking of her entire life. Amar had been romantic and gentle when he needed to be and aggressive when she wanted more. They'd made love several times.

Rylee blushed as she remembered when Amar had flipped her on her stomach and taken her from behind. He'd tugged on her hair as he'd brought her to another mind-blowing climax. She hadn't known those existed before. She'd heard how some women never enjoyed them, and she'd thought she'd be one of them until last night. Until Amar.

He'd brought out something in her that she couldn't explain. She'd behaved out of character from the moment she'd met him. Agreeing to a casual affair for the weekend was definitely not her M.O., but she'd wanted to experience the pleasure of being with Amar, and she had — on the floor, on the sofa when she'd sat in his lap and rode him wildly and this morning in the shower. She looked forward to riding him again tonight.

"Hello." The trainer waved his hand in front of her face. "Earth to Rylee, or are you so captured by the prince that you can't think straight."

"You know, Hank," she said, rising to her feet, "I've had enough of your comments. Knock it off."

"Why should I?" Hank replied. "You're a traitor. You turned on Jeremy and stayed with Bishop. Where's your loyalty?"

"My loyalty," she said, standing up straight, "is to this beautiful animal and ensuring she's in the best health.

Jeremy gambled away his horse, so don't blame me for his shortcomings. I signed on to take care of Dreamer, same as you."

"Coulda fooled me," he said under his breath as he walked away.

Rylee glared at him. She turned and looked at the stable hand and the jockey, who were all standing nearby staring at her. Did they all think her disloyal for not leaving with Jeremy? Loyalty was one of the things she prided herself on most, and she didn't like the folks thinking less of her, but what could she do? She would just have to tough it out as she'd always done in this predominantly male field.

"What are you looking at?" she asked, causing both men to turn away.

Chapter 7

ONCE RYLEE COMPLETED HER ROUTINE check of Dreamer, she went in search of Amar, who she'd learned was looking over Desert Storm. She found him and Sharif in the Infield by the fences, where horses were brought to be shown off to spectators. The sky was blue and clear, with not a rain cloud in sight. It would be a great day for the races.

Amar smiled when he saw her approach. "Come here," he said, motioning her over. "You have to meet this beautiful creature. Now this is a man's horse. This is Desert Storm."

Rylee walked over to the jet-as-midnight thoroughbred and brushed his black mane with her hands. "He's beautiful."

"Like someone else I know." Amar seared her with an intensely sexual gaze. She read his mind and knew he was thinking lascivious thoughts.

She was surprised that he could still have such lustful eyes after he'd tasted, touched and caressed every inch of her. Not to mention, her usual cowgirl outfit and infamous riding boots were not the least bit stylish or showed any skin. She was a far cry from the overdressed socialites standing around ogling him right now and wishing they were her.

He was about to respond when a reporter came his way. "Mr. Bishop, how are you feeling about Desert Storm's odds?"

"He's done well in the other stake races," Amar said, "so I can only imagine he'll do well today."

"Rumor is you're the new owner of Dreamer, the underdog in this race. If you were a betting man, would you bet on Desert Storm or Dreamer?"

Amar smiled, revealing straight white teeth, and it made Rylee warm as the memory of those teeth nipping and tugging at her nipples came roaring back. She felt them harden underneath her shirt in response. "We'll have to wait and see."

"Either way, you're a winner," the reporter said. "But that's your M.O., right? You never lose."

She noticed Amar frown as the man walked away. "Are you okay?"

Amar's conciliatory smile returned. "Of course. I am just surprised how much my reputation precedes me as a ruthless businessman."

Rylee leaned backward on the fence to study him. "It's what you've cultivated, yes?"

"Ruthless? No. But do I have a singular focus when I want something? Yes. I think ruthless is how you Americans perceive someone who is determined to achieve a certain result. And I don't like it. It has a negative connotation."

She stared back at him. Amar was an enigma. At moments, he was ruthless, though he didn't want to appear that way, but by the same token, he could be immensely charming and romantic. She wondered what more lay underneath the smooth exterior he portrayed.

"Let's go upstairs to the box." Amar took her hand and led her up the steps so they could head to the Finish Line Suites. "These are private for owners and serious equestrian lovers."

Sharif followed them quietly at their heels. It always surprised Rylee how he stood on the sidelines and knew when to speak or when to act.

When they arrived, Rylee could see that the private box gave them a bird's-eye view of the races and was an excellent vantage point. She walked over to the windows and peered out. "This is great, Amar." She was sure this box was better than even the VIP seats Jeremy had procured.

She noticed the platters of cold meats, cheeses, pâtés, crackers, fruits and beverages aligning the table in the box, along with a bucket of champagne chilling.

"Hungry?" Amar asked when he noticed Rylee eyeing the table.

"I did work up an appetite," she said coyly, underneath flirty lashes, "and we had no time to eat before we came to Churchill Downs."

"By all means enjoy," Amar said as he pulled out his buzzing phone.

Amar watched Rylee indulge in a large plate of food as he looked down at the text from his father. *Are you confident, we'll win? You'd better be.*

Amar didn't want the added stress of worrying about his father's reaction to the races from across the ocean, but it was impossible not to. The man had a way of getting under his skin despite Amar's best efforts to keep him at bay.

As the races began and "My Old Kentucky Home" rang out in song across the stadium, Amar maintained his focus and folded his arms across his chest. A few times, he couldn't help but smile as he watched Rylee animatedly get into the action of the Derby. The announcers had a way of reeling you into the excitement and feeling the buzz.

Eventually, when it was time for Dreamer and Storm's event, he pulled Rylee outside onto the balcony for a better view of the finish line.

"This is exciting," Rylee said, looking up at him.

"You have no idea."

The horses came to the gates, and Amar's stomach clenched. The gun sounded, and he held his breath. Desert Storm came out of the gate for the lead. He appeared to keep the top position and stayed on the far outside as they headed into the first turn. Then slowly but surely, Dreamer began to move into the clear. Next thing he knew, Dreamer was near the front of the pack. Then, to the announcer's surprise, she surged forward.

Dreamer was in the lead.

"She's in the lead. She's in the lead!" Rylee shouted, squeezing Amar's arm.

Sharif turned to Amar, and he could see his friend's mind spinning just as his was. They both knew he'd come there to ensure Desert Storm won the Derby, but now he was conflicted as he witnessed Dreamer continuing to pull away from the pack and head toward the finish line. Just as the clock ran out, Amar envisioned the rage that would be on his father's face.

"Dreamer won! Dreamer won!" Rylee jumped up and down excitedly and then hugged Amar. When he didn't return her hug, she looked up at him. "Isn't that great?"

"Of course it is," he said, plastering a smile on his face even though his head was reeling. "It's fantastic. Who would have imagined." He sure hadn't. The only reason he'd bought the damn horse was because he'd wanted to teach Jeremy a lesson, but had he secretly wanted to teach his father one too?

He hadn't known a long shot would beat a prized well-bred Arabian thoroughbred like Desert Storm, who'd been sired for this very thing. His father would be furious to learn that his horse hadn't won, and Amar was sure he and his friends had gambled on Desert Strom winning and had probably lost a fortune.

"You sure don't look happy. This is great news. Dreamer won."

"I am."

"You could have fooled me."

"Rylee, you must realize that when there's a winner, there's also a loser, and my father spent northward of a million dollars on Storm. He will not be happy."

Rylee frowned as realization dawned on her. "Oh, I'm sorry, Amar. I guess I was so happy. I hadn't thought about what this meant to your family, but no one could have predicted this. Dreamer was a long shot." She looked back at the racetrack.

"You and I know that, but my father will still be furious. Horses are about the one thing we have in common and now ..." His voice trailed off.

Rylee touched his arm. "It'll be okay. You'll see. Let's go celebrate." She tugged him toward the door, where press and excited patrons were already swarming outside the suite.

Amar followed reluctantly behind her. When he got to the tracks, he did what was expected. He posed with the jockey and accepted the cup as the press snapped photos. As much as he appreciated Rylee's optimism, he knew there would be hell to pay with the Sheikh.

And he was right. It wasn't long after they'd gone down to the tracks where the winning jockey sat on Dreamer and was bestowed with champagne and praise that Amar's cell phone began to ring. He didn't have to look at the display to know who it was.

He stepped away from Rylee, who was caught up in the momentum, and took the call.

"What the hell is going on over there, Amar?" his father yelled. "You assured me that I had nothing to worry about, and now I and some of my associates have lost thousands and, in some cases, millions."

"It's not my fault."

"Like hell it isn't. I told you to neutralize the threat. But what do you do? You go off and buy the damn horse. And now you're sitting pretty, and I'm out of millions."

How could his father have known about the purchase from overseas? He should have known the man had spies. "I'm sorry you're upset, but I really had no idea Dreamer would win. I only bought her to teach the owner a lesson."

"Don't you mean to show off and take his woman?"

Damn him! Who is feeding him information? It couldn't be Sharif, could it? Amar had always thought him a loyal and trustworthy friend. "Watch it, Father. You have no idea what you're talking about."

"Oh, I know what I'm talking about," his father said. "You let some twit that you've known all of five minutes" — he could hear the snap of his father's fingers — "come in and sabotage my plan. I paid a pretty penny for that horse and have been training him for this moment. I don't ask much of you, Amar. I just ask that you look over my horses in the States. I thought that was the one love we shared, but instead you took your eye off the prize because you wanted a piece of ass."

Fury boiled within Amar at his father's harsh reprimand, and he lashed out. "Well, I'm sorry that again I've lived up to the image you have of me as a worthless son," Amar hissed.

"I've never said that, Amar!"

"Bullshit!" Amar yelled into the phone. He saw several folks look at him because of his foul language, so he moved farther away from the crowd. "It's what you and your people think of me. I'm the bastard son that you couldn't be bothered with. Hell, you couldn't even be bothered to come to my mother's funeral after she'd died a slow death from lupus even after she spent a lifetime waiting on you to come back to her."

"I never asked her to wait."

"You didn't have to. She loved you. And she died loving only you, but you were too selfish to see that. Instead, you would just stop in when it was convenient for you, take what you wanted and then leave her alone again. And that's how she died —

alone."

"You're hitting below the belt, Amar. You should stop while you're ahead."

"Since you already think so highly of me, Abdul al' Mahmud, King of Nasir, why don't you forget I exist, because I'm done trying to live up to your expectations or trying to please you, because it's a never-ending battle that I won't win. Goodbye."

Amar ended the call and then threw the phone down on the concrete, smashing it into a hundred tiny pieces.

From across the way out of the corner of her eye, Rylee had seen Amar getting more and more upset with whoever had been on the opposite end of that call. It had to have been his father, she thought, and she had rushed over when Amar smashed the phone.

"Amar?"

When he looked up at her, pain and anguish sprang from his eyes, and Rylee pulled him close. He gripped her so tightly, she could barely breathe.

"It's okay," she whispered, and eventually, he eased his death grip on her but didn't let her go. "What's wrong?" She hazarded a glance up at him. She had never seen this side to him before, and it made her a little uneasy. He was always so cool and polished.

Amar was silent for several long beats, so Rylee wondered if he'd heard her. Eventually, he spoke. "Not anything you can help with. These wounds go deep."

She grasped each side of his face. "I understand."

"I'm not sure you can."

"I may not have experienced them myself, but I helped my brother Noah grieve over losing his first wife and unborn child in a car accident. So I know a little bit about loss and pain."

"That's horrible," Amar said, coming out of his fog. "How did he get through something like that?"

"Time," Rylee answered softly, "and lots and lots of love from my family and eventually Chynna, my sister-in-law."

"He's lucky to have all of you, especially you." He squeezed her tighter again and tucked a curly strand of hair behind her ear.

Rylee sensed his mood changing from one of anger to calm. She could also feel a certain member slightly swelling at her mid-section from their close proximity. "Easy boy," she whispered, glancing down. "There will be time for that later."

"Promise?"

"Promise."

The celebration of Dreamer's win continued from the afternoon into the evening, with a big party at the Galt House Hotel. Sharif had planned and anticipated Desert Storm's win. Who would have known it would be for Dreamer and not his father's Arabian?

The soiree was attended by politicians, businessmen and socialites, but none of them mattered to Rylee. As she stood on the rooftop terrace overlooking the heart of Louisville and waterfront, she was only interested in one man that evening: Amar. But her thoughts momentarily lapsed to her phone call from earlier that day. She'd gone back to the hotel to shower, but first she'd called Jeremy. She was sure he'd heard about the win, and she'd wanted to see if he was okay. He hadn't been happy to hear from her.

"What do you want, Rylee?" he'd asked tartly.

Rylee hadn't prepared for such a chilly response, and it took her several moments to recover before she said, "I was calling to check on you. I'm sure you've heard that Dreamer won."

"Did you call to rub salt in my wound that your prince just made a killing off my horse?"

Rylee was taken aback. "Of course not. I would never do that Jeremy. I just—I just—"

"You just what?" he asked. "You wanted to see if I was licking my wounds? Well, if you must know, I am. I'm kicking myself for having let my emotions get in the way of business. I worked hard day and night with Dreamer to make sure she'd qualify for the Derby. And for what? To lose her in a pissing match I was never going to win? So as much as I appreciate the sentiment behind the call, I'm not interested, Rylee."

"I can see that you're upset with me, Jeremy, and I'm sorry I wasn't straightforward with you about where we stood — that's on me. And I guess I just wanted to say that ... your instincts were dead-on. I hope you don't let this moment define you as you're very talented. That's all I wanted to say."

There was silence on the other end of the phone, and Rylee thought Jeremy had hung up on her, but instead he said, "Thank you. And Rylee?"

"Yes."

"Amar has gotten everything he wanted this weekend: You and my horse. Take care of yourself, okay?"

Rylee didn't want to get into another argument with Jeremy about Amar because they were never going to see eye to eye, so all she said was, "I will," and ended the call.

"Penny for your thoughts," Amar said as his strong arms encircled her waist and brought her back to the present.

Rylee cocked her head to one side to look at him. "Nothing I want to discuss," she said. "Can we enjoy the moment, just you and me?"

"Absolutely," Amar replied as she rested her head on his shoulder. She suspected he wasn't eager to get into a serious discussion either. Otherwise he might have to share with her what had occurred with him and his father at the Derby after Dreamer's win.

"We've had one rollercoaster of a week," Rylee said.

"Is that a good thing or bad thing?"

Rylee turned around to face him and touched his cheek gingerly. "It's been a great thing."

"Oh, just great?" Amar asked. "I was shooting for amazing, spectacular. I guess I'm going to have to step up my game."

She laughed. "A jokester. I like this side to you. You should show it more often."

"You bring it out in me," Amar said honestly.

"I can say the same for you," Rylee said, smiling. "I usually don't act this impulsively."

"No? Then we must change that." He grabbed her hand, slid into a dark corner of the terrace shrouded by local flora and shrubbery and backed her up against the building.

Before she could react, Amar was on his knees reaching up underneath her dress and pulling down the thong she wore, pocketing it in the breast pocket of his tuxedo jacket. His hands slid alongside the outside of her thigh until they came to her bare bottom, and he cupped it in his hands. Rylee knew what was coming next and was mortified.

"Amar, what are you doing? Get up. Anyone can come out here." Rylee tried to swat his hands away, but Amar wasn't moving a muscle. He had her pinned against the wall.

"That's what makes it fun and *impulsive,*" he replied as he slid his head under her dress. She tried to close her legs, but she heard him command, "Open your legs."

She complied and parted them. That's when she felt his tongue at the triangle between her thighs. He slid inside her. Rylee gasped.

"Easy," he murmured from his knees and made the same action again. His tongue slowly slid in and out of her vagina while his hands caressed her backside. Rylee could feel herself becoming more and more turned on that Amar was giving her head in public when anyone could walk out on the terrace and catch them.

"Oh ..." She tried to suppress a moan.

But that didn't stop Amar. He continued to deliberately tease her clit, the center of her pleasure, with his tongue. In and out. In and out. She clutched at his shoulders for support, but that only spurred him on and caused him to put one of her legs over his shoulder while the other remained on the ground. And he didn't just use his tongue. Soon, she felt his fingers and his tongue play with her as they stroked her clitoris gently.

"Oooh, yes ..." Her moans were coming involuntarily now as his tongue and fingers continued to work their magic, bringing her pleasure to a feverish pitch. In and out. In and out.

"Amar! Oh, God!" It was such delicious torture that Rylee thought she would turn into a puddle, but Amar kept her upright. She clutched at his head, spurring him on, and he complied.

When his tongue dove inside her and hit *the spot,* her climax hit her with full strength, and Rylee's entire body began to contract and convulse. Amar steadied her as her knees began to liquefy. As her contractions subsided, he licked her until he'd gotten all her juices before he rose to his feet.

He licked his lips in delight. "You tasted so good."

Rylee blushed several shades of red as her heartbeat raced at what had just happened between them in the middle of a party!

"But that was just an appetizer. I want the whole entrée," he whispered just as two partygoers crashed the terrace, interrupting their heated encounter.

"Oh, we didn't know anyone was out here," the woman said.

"No worries," Amar said, pulling Rylee toward the door. "We're finished here."

"Is everything ready for tonight at the cottage?" Amar asked Sharif when Rylee went to the ladies room to freshen up.

Sharif stared at him.

"What?" Amar asked.

"Why do you look so flushed?"

"No reason," Amar said. "Must be warm in here." He loosened his tie.

"No, I don't think that's it. You have a look." Sharif eyed him suspiciously. "A look that says you just had sex. Did you and Rylee just do it on the balcony?"

"Lower your voice," Amar ordered.

"Well, did you?"

"Mind your own business."

Sharif shook his head. "You just answered my question. And to answer yours, yes the cottage is ready as you instructed."

"Good. 'Cause I'm ready to get out of here."

"It's a party celebrating your horse's win."

"No one cares about that anymore. They just care about the free food and drink. I don't want to miss a moment with Rylee. You make my apologies," Amar said and headed for the door.

Sharif grabbed his arm. "Wait! You forgot your new phone." He handed Amar an iPhone. "Try not to smash this one."

Amar rolled his eyes and snatched the phone as he went in search of Rylee. They hadn't talked about when she would return home, but he suspected it would be soon and he didn't want to waste another minute. He had a surprise waiting for her that would show Rylee just how special she was to him.

The cottage was again lit with candles and rose petals when Rylee and Amar arrived back later that evening, but as Rylee opened the door, she was shocked to hear someone singing. LIVE.

Rylee looked up at Amar questioningly.

"Should we look for the source?" he asked.

She nodded and he took her hand, leading her outside onto the patio. The backyard was lit up like the Eiffel Tower at night and there in the moonlight was John Legend on a piano singing "All of Me."

"May I have this dance?"

"You may," Rylee said, completely blown away that Amar had gone through the trouble to romance her in such a fashion. She knew it was all a fairytale and would soon come to an end, but she would enjoy it for as long as it lasted.

Amar pulled her into his embrace, and they swayed to the love ballad. She lay her head on his chest, and he held one of her hands while the other rested on the curve of her lower back.

When Amar gazed down at her, radiating magnetism and vitality and maybe just a little bit of danger, Rylee's breath caught. She could hear her heart throbbing loudly in her ears and not just there, but lower in her nether regions. Her body ached for his touch.

When the song was over, they thanked John and moved back inside. The riveting climax Amar had given her earlier had her insides clamoring with excitement for what was to come next. As soon as he'd closed the patio door, they moved toward each other, propelled by their mutual passion. They began ripping at each other's clothes, desperate to be free of them. Her dress hit the floor, followed by his shirt, then his trousers. A trail of clothes were behind them as they made their way to the bedroom.

They joined together on the bed, Rylee in her bra and panties and Amar in his boxer briefs. "Let's slow this down," he said. "I don't want to rush." He bent down to place a kiss on her shoulder and then another on the opposite shoulder. "I want to savor you like a fine wine."

He slid his hands behind her back to unclasp her bra and bring her breasts into his full view as he laid her backward against the pillows. He took an exorbitant amount of time paying homage to each breast, suckling each, teasing them with his tongue, molding them with his hands. She whimpered, wanting more.

He licked his way from her breasts down to her flat stomach, teasing her belly button. But he didn't stop there. He went lower until he found her wet and throbbing center. He'd been right that the balcony was just the appetizer. She knew he would be even more diligent in his efforts to make her come.

"Please, Amar, don't make me wait."

Rylee wrapped her legs around his waist and tried to bring him forward so she could reach for his boxers, but he grasped both of her hands with one of his and then he lowered his head to her womanhood. And that's where he stayed.

Her breathing became hard. She couldn't focus. She felt feverish, but Amar wouldn't stop tasting and teasing her with his masterful tongue and pliant fingers. He didn't stop until she had two shattering orgasms and pleaded with him to take her.

"You want me now?" he asked.

"Yes, now! Please!"

He pushed down his briefs in an instant and donned a condom. His rock-hard arousal pressed against the V of her thighs demanding entry. "I want to be inside you." He clasped her ankle, skimming her thigh and the curve of her breasts.

"And I want you to be," she murmured. Their lips met and a spark ignited, hotter and brighter as he slowly eased inside her, inch by beautiful inch, and Rylee moaned in ecstasy.

"Yes, oh God, yes!"

Her sighs and moans of pleasure spurred Amar on, and he began to thrust, slowly at first, allowing them to find a rhythm. Then he quickened the pace. Faster and faster. Harder and deeper. All thoughts in Rylee's head went away, and she was lost. Her only thoughts were of Amar and this time, this place and how it couldn't get any better than this. Her fingers stroked his skin, and she dragged them down his back as she clutched him to her and circled her ankles across his backside. She buried her face in his neck, and when he found the *perfect* spot, she cried out his name, "Amar!"

Amar was awakened from his sleep again by the buzzing of his cell phone on the nightstand. The clock read four AM, but the display on his phone caused him concern. It was his youngest brother, Tariq. Careful not to wake up Rylee, Amar quickly pressed the answer button and slid from the bed.

"Hello?"

"Amar?"

"Yes, what's wrong, Tariq?" He knew it couldn't be good if Tariq was calling now, as Tariq knew what time of day it was in the States.

"It's Father."

"Yeah, what about him?"

"He-he's had a heart attack." His brother's voice trembled.

"Heart attack?" Amar's voice rose, and he glanced at the bed, but Rylee still slept peacefully.

"Several hours ago."

"Why am I just hearing of this now?" Amar asked as he searched the room for his pants. When he didn't find them, he crept out and found them in the hallway. He struggled to pull them on as he cradled the phone in one ear.

"Your phone just rang and rang."

That's when Amar remembered he'd smashed his phone earlier that day after he and his father had quarreled.

"No one knew your new phone number," he heard Tariq say. "We had to chase you down to the hotel and finally Sharif before we got your new number."

"How is he?"

"His condition is critical."

"As soon as I call Sharif, I'll be on my way."

"No need. I already contacted Sharif, and a limo is waiting to take you to the airport. Your jet is fueled and has clearance to leave within the hour. All you have to do is go straight there and be ready for immediate takeoff."

"I'm on it." Amar said. "And Tariq?"

"Yeah ... don't worry. The old man is as strong as an ox. He'll pull through this."

"Thanks. I'll see you soon."

Amar ended the call and looked toward the bedroom where Rylee lay sleeping. He wished he could wake her up and tell her everything that had happened, but he had no time to spare. He glanced down at his watch as he pulled on the shirt he'd been wearing last night. He barely had enough time to get to the airport, and if he woke her, there would be questions and she'd be upset. Better he let her sleep and call her in the morning.

Chapter 8

RYLEE FELT THE MORNING SUN on her face as it peeked through the windows. She didn't want to open her eyes. Last night with Amar had been just as amazing as the night before. Each kiss, each touch, each caress was more feverish and passionate than the last. He hadn't been able to get enough of her, and the feeling had been mutual. She wanted Amar like she hadn't wanted another man. Not even Shelton could come close to what she felt for Amar. He'd awakened a desire that had lain dormant for some time, but now that he had, she couldn't wait for another round.

Languorously, she stretched across the bed and reached for Amar, but all she found was emptiness. Her eyes popped open.

"Amar?" she called out.

No response.

Rylee sat up. He was probably in the kitchen making coffee or something. She slid from the bed, pulling at the sheet and wrapping it around her. Her dress from last night was nowhere to be found and was most likely in the living room or on the floor of the hall, where she and Amar had left their clothes in their haste to be naked.

She padded on the floor in bare feet and found no clothing. "Amar?" she called out again until she made it to the living room.

"Good morning." Sharif rose from his seat at the kitchen table.

"Omigod!" Startled, Rylee hugged the sheet closer around her body. "Where's Amar?"

"I'm sorry, Ms. Hart, but Amar has been called back suddenly to our country of Nasir to deal with an urgent family matter. He wanted me to send you his regrets that he was unable to relay this information to you this morning, but it was most pressing he return home to the kingdom at once."

"Really?" Rylee asked as the cold realization that she'd just been played by a rich playboy flooded through her.

"Yes, ma'am. He was most upset to have to leave you."

"I highly doubt that!" Rylee spat as she searched the room for her clothes. Instead of the dress she'd been wearing last night, which lay over a chair, she found an outfit had been laid out for her on the table beside it: jeans, a shirt and lingerie, along with her boots. She stormed over to grab them.

Sharif began to walk toward her, but Rylee warded him off with her hand. "Stay back," she warned. "I need to get dressed."

"Of course." Sharif turned away. "My apologies if I have offended you. That wasn't my intention or Amar's, I'm sure."

"I could give a rat's ass about your boss's intentions," Rylee hissed as she spun on her heel and rushed out of the room.

She made it to the bedroom before the tears that had been behind the anger flooded down her cheeks. How could she have been so foolish to believe she would be any different from the countless other women Amar had taken to bed? But at the very least, she thought he would have had the guts to face her and not have his assistant give her the kiss-off. Had she really believed they might spend a couple of more days together before she had to go back to Tucson because they'd had great sex?

Rylee stormed into the bathroom adjacent to the master bedroom and turned on the taps to the shower as hot as she could take it, but she doubted it would wash off the misery that was slowly starting to overtake her. She stepped into the walk-in shower and under the spray, allowing the water to flow through her hair and over her naked body. She wanted to wash away the night — hell, the entire weekend — as if it had never happened.

Jeremy had been right. He'd warned her that Amar would use her and after he'd gotten what he wanted, he would discard her and be onto the next woman. And that's exactly what he'd done. As soon as the thrill and chase were over and he'd taken her to bed, he'd hightailed it out before sunrise. He'd actually had the nerve to use a family emergency as an excuse when just a couple of days ago he'd shared that he was estranged from his family in Nasir. *Does he honestly expect me to believe he would rush out in the wee hours of the morning to go back home?* He must have thought she just fell off the turnip truck.

After she'd showered, Rylee wrapped a fluffy towel around her bosom. She wiped the mirror that had fogged from the heat and stared at her reflection. She'd been played the fool and now she was forced to look at herself, a woman bamboozled. It was not a pretty picture.

Rylee used the feminine toiletries and combs and brushes in a drawer under the sink that Sharif had so graciously thought of. She was dressed in under ten minutes and eager to get out of Amar's love shack. She wondered if he'd used his technique on other women.

When she walked back into the living room, Sharif stood up. "I take it everything was satisfactory?" he asked softly.

Rylee stared back at him. She could sense he was afraid to say anything that might set her off. She took a deep breath. It wasn't his fault that Amar had discarded her as if she were the gum on the bottom of his shoe. "Yes, Sharif. Everything is fine. I'm ready to go. I assume you're here to give me a ride back to the hotel?"

He nodded.

"Well, then let's go." Rylee headed toward the door.

"What about your dress?" Sharif asked, looking at last night's garment that he'd folded and was lying on the chair.

"I don't want it."

"But Amar bought it specifically for you."

"I don't care," Rylee said, opening the door. "Leave it for the next girl." She walked down the path and toward the limousine that was waiting to take them back to the hotel. At least she could thank Amar for his good taste as he'd made sure she would ride back in style.

The drive back to the hotel was fraught with silence. Sharif worked on his iPad while Rylee stared blankly out of the window. All she wanted to do was get back to Tucson where everything and everyone made sense. She didn't want to think about Amar Bishop ever again.

"How is he?" Amar asked once he'd landed on Nasir soil in the United Arab Emirates. Thankfully, the private jet had a shower, and he'd been able to change into clean clothes.

Tariq was waiting for him at the airport and gave him a long hug on the tarmac.

Tariq was a younger version of Amar. He had similar facial features, except his were more Arabian. He had straight jet-black hair, trimmed short. He had broad shoulders and a slim, athletic build, but they both had inherited their father's stature.

"He was airlifted to Dubai early this morning to ensure he got the best treatment possible."

"And?"

"He's holding his own," Tariq said as he walked him toward the town car that waited for them. "How was your flight?" he asked, getting into the vehicle.

"Long," Amar replied, following behind him. The day-long flight to Dubai was less than enjoyable. Amar had been anxious from the moment they'd taken off because he'd left Rylee without a word. His intention had been to call her from the plane, but neither his phone nor the jet phone had international cell phone coverage, so Amar had been unable to call Rylee and explain further. He could only hope that she wouldn't be too upset with the abrupt way he had departed.

"Something on your mind?" Tariq asked.

"You mean other than Father?"

"I would."

Amar shook his head. "Nothing I wish to discuss. Do you know what brought on the heart attack?"

Tariq shrugged and turned to look out the window, not answering him.

"What is it, brother?" Amar asked, keenly aware that Tariq was avoiding looking at him.

"The attack occurred right after you and Father argued."

The explanation was like a gut punch to Amar. "Are you sure?"

"His assistant said that he was visibly upset after the call, was pacing his study and wringing his hands. What were you discussing that could have caused him such anxiety?"

Amar thought back to the upsetting conversation he'd shared with his father yesterday. He remembered the accusations he'd made, the words he'd said. Words he might not ever get to take back. "We said a lot of things, Tariq. We quarreled. I don't know what else to tell you."

"Well, you might as well know that Khalid is furious. He blames you for Father's attack."

"What's new? He blames me for everything wrong in his life. You would think it would be the reverse, considering he's next in line to be King."

"Not this again."

"I'm not beating a dead horse, Tariq. I'm just stating the facts. This just gives Khalid another reason to hate me."

"He doesn't hate you."

"Like hell he doesn't. He's tolerated me with Father around because he had to. With Father laid up, he won't have to put on any pretenses."

Tariq eyed him warily. "I hate when you talk like this. We're brothers."

"You and I, yes." Amar reached over with one arm to pull Tariq into a one-armed hug. "And we always will be. But Khalid and I will never be on the same page."

Amar's comment couldn't have hit the nail on the head better, because as soon as they made it to the hospital in Dubai, Khalid was waiting outside their father's room alongside Saffron, the Queen, and Freya, Khalid's wife. Both women were dressed conservatively. As soon as Khalid saw Amar, he laid into him.

"So, the prodigal son has returned," Khalid snarled. "Did you come to finish the job since your little hissy fit with Father didn't do the trick?"

"Back off, Khalid," Amar said, glaring down at him. He was a few inches taller than Khalid, which probably bothered his younger brother to no end. Amar had always felt like his brother had a Napoleon complex since he was just shy of six feet.

"Why? What are you going to do?" Khalid replied. "Yell and scream at me until *I* keel over."

"Khalid!" his mother reprimanded him.

"That's a low blow," Tariq said, jumping in between the two men. He pushed at Amar's chest to stop a fight.

"Why are you taking up for him, Tariq, when he's the reason our father is in the hospital?"

"We don't know that, Khalid," Tariq answered.

"Don't we?" Khalid said. "Farouk said he heard Father arguing with him." He pointed to Amar. "Didn't he, Mother?" He looked to his mother, and she nodded in affirmation.

"Even if they were arguing," Tariq responded, "it's not Amar's fault if Father has some heart problems."

Khalid rolled his eyes. "That's right. Always take his side, Tariq." He walked away from them in a huff.

"God, why must he be like that?" Tariq ran his fingers through his dark hair.

"He doesn't know any other way to be," Amar replied, watching Khalid as he stormed off. He returned his gaze to Tariq. "I would like to see him."

"I don't think that's a good idea," said Saffron, holding a handkerchief. Amar suspected she'd never liked him much and had only tolerated his presence as a child. This was only another reason for her to dislike him. "Khalid may be wrong with his accusations, but I don't want to take a chance that your father could become agitated."

"By seeing me?" Amar asked. "I was his son before you became his wife."

"That's enough," Tariq warned, giving Amar a dirty look. He would not let Amar disrespect his mother.

"I'm sorry," Amar apologized. He was a little testy from everyone's insistence that he was at fault for the Sheikh's heart attack.

"Listen," Tariq said, pulling Amar by the arm to the side, "why don't you go in for a few minutes and see him."

"I don't think that's wise, Tariq," his mother responded.

"He needs to do this, Mother. Please step aside."

She stepped out of Amar's path and allowed him to enter his father's hospital room. The room was not only sterile but silent, save for the beeping of the machines monitoring his father's condition.

Slowly, Amar walked over to the bed where his father lay very still. Amar was used to the King coming from a place of strength, but looking down at him, he looked frail, nothing like the man he was used to, and it unnerved Amar. He moved closer and then took a seat at his father's bedside.

What could he say to him? Khalid had been right. They'd argued as they always do. For as long as he could remember, they'd been like oil and water. They didn't mix. The only thing they'd loved was horses, and Amar thought it would have been a tentative link between them, but he felt his father had turned it into business rather than something a father and son could share.

Yet, despite the animosity between them, Amar loved the old man. Lord knows, he wasn't an easy man to love, but he was the only father he had.

Tears threatened, but Amar blinked them back. He would never allow anyone to see them. They would consider it a sign of weakness, especially his father.

His father's eyes tentatively opened, and he blinked, trying to bring the world into focus. He slowly turned his head, and when he saw Amar, a surprised smile formed. "Amar, is that you, son? Or am I hallucinating?"

"No, it's me," Amar replied. He realized he hadn't been to Nasir, let alone Dubai, for nearly five years since he and his father had had one of their epic battles.

"I really must be dying if you're here." His father attempted to laugh, but the laughing caused a wheezing fit, prompting several monitors to go off.

Minutes later, a nurse rushed into the room, followed by Saffron and Tariq on her heels.

"What happened?" Tariq asked, looking alarmed.

"Nothing," Amar said, standing up. "I was just sitting here, and Father woke up."

"Thank God." Saffron rushed to her husband's side, pushing Amar away so she could get closer and hold the Sheikh's hand.

"Enough, Saffron. I'm okay."

"I'm so happy," she cried, touching his cheek.

"Me too, Father." Tariq beamed.

Seconds later, Khalid rushed into the room with Freya. "What's going on? Is Father okay?" he asked, looking at everyone. When his eyes rested on Amar, he hissed. "What's *he* doing in here?"

Amar glared. "I'm here to check on my father, same as you."

"He woke up while Amar was here," the Queen added, looking up from her husband's side.

"Is that so?" Khalid replied. "So, it took Amar coming for Dad to wake up. Wow!"

Amar ignored the dig even though Khalid's anger came off him in droves; but he didn't say anything else to upset their father. He would never understand his brother's irrational jealousy toward him. Khalid had everything laid at his feet, and he was still unhappy.

"Now that he's awake, I'm going to page the doctor," the nurse said after she'd finished taking his vitals and wrote them on his chart. Several minutes later, she exited, leaving the family in the room alone.

"I'm so happy you're conscious, Father," Khalid said, moving toward him.

"You mean you weren't getting ready for your coronation based on my impending demise?" he joked.

Khalid was visibly offended and stepped back from the bed. His face was a stone-cold mask. "Of course not."

His father patted the bed beside him. "Khalid, it's okay. It was a joke. Don't take everything so literal. You need to loosen up."

"Oh." Khalid sighed in relief.

"Where's Amar?" his father asked, lifting his head slightly to look at the family, who'd gathered around his bed. His eyes laid hold of Amar, who was leaning back against the wall at the far side of the hospital room.

"I'm here."

"For how long?" his father whispered.

Several pairs of eyes turned to Amar, eager to know the answer to that question as well. He could only guess Khalid wanted him on the first plane out, with steam.

"Until you're out of the woods."

"But no more?" his father surmised.

Amar didn't say anything. They both knew the answer to that question. Nasir was not his home. He'd never felt welcome and had always been an outsider, not just because the color of his skin was different from his brothers, but because he would never be one of them. He'd made his peace with that a long time ago.   "Excuse me," Amar said, nodding to his father before leaving the room.

He walked to the nurse's station. "How can I make an international call?"

"I'm sorry, we don't have that capability. Only local calls, sir."

"Thank you." Amar turned away, defeated. He hadn't been able to make contact with Rylee in twenty-four hours. He didn't know if Sharif had explained everything to her and if she understood why he had to leave her so suddenly. He just prayed that she would forgive him.

Chapter 9

R YLEE WAS QUIET ON THE way from the airport back to
Golden Oaks Ranch. Noah had come to pick her
up, and she'd been silent ever since. She was sure
he was wondering what had happened, but she wasn't in
the talking mood. She didn't want to have to explain why
she'd stayed on after Jeremy and Camryn had returned
to Tucson. How could she admit that she'd allowed a rich
playboy to talk her out of her panties?

She felt like such a fool for thinking there was something
more between them than intense physical attraction. Amar
clearly had his fill of her and was moving on. She still
couldn't believe that he'd crept out of bed in the middle of
the night and then had sent his assistant to deal with the
fallout. *What a coward!*

"Rylee!" Noah called her name.

"What?" she asked, annoyed.

"We're home," Noah said quietly as he exited his pickup
truck.

Rylee glanced up and saw her two-story family home.
She sighed in relief and a bit of regret. It was good to be
home with familiar surroundings, but she couldn't help
but feel a little wistful of what might have been. "Sorry,
Noah," she said, opening the passenger door and jumping
out. "Thanks for coming to get me."

"Of course," Noah replied, looking over the cab at her. "You know, I'd do anything for you, sis."

His words brought a smile to Rylee's face. "I know." Family — that was one thing she was sure of and could count on. "Are Mama and Daddy inside?"

Noah shook his head as he walked to the rear of the truck and removed her suitcase and overnight bag. "Naw, they're out for a ride."

Rylee nodded. Better she have some quiet time to herself to come up with a plausible story before she was twenty-questioned over the evening meal.

They walked in silence up the front steps of the house and into the foyer. She glanced around, taking in her surroundings. It was funny that she'd been gone barely a week, but it seemed like she'd lived a lifetime in the few days she'd spent with Amar.

"Are you okay?" Noah asked. "You've been quiet since I picked you up and—"

"If you don't mind," Rylee interrupted, "I don't want to talk about it, Noah." She reached for her suitcase to head for the stairs, but he shook his head.

"I've got this." He snatched up her luggage and walked up the stairs, leaving Rylee to follow behind him. When they reached the second floor, he took her things to the east side of the house, her wing and private escape.

Once he'd set down her luggage in her bedroom, Noah turned to her. "If you want to talk, I'm here."

"Thank you," she said, touching his shoulder. "That means a lot."

Noah started for the door, but then turned back around. "Chynna will be back tomorrow, if you want to talk to someone other than your big brother."

Rylee smiled and nodded. When he left, she fell backward on the bed in relief.

Later that evening, as dinner approached with her family, Rylee's trepidation increased. She hadn't left her room and had stared at the ceiling for most of the afternoon, beating herself up over her bad judgment. She'd even ignored Camryn's call in favor of moping, but her time had run out.

It was five thirty PM, and considering she'd been gone for nearly a week, her parents would be expecting her to join the family for dinner. She had no choice but to go downstairs and put on a happy face, even though she seethed inside.

After a quick shower and change of clothes, Rylee went downstairs. Her parents were sitting in the living room as were Noah and Caleb. Rylee rolled her eyes. *What the heck is Caleb doing home?* He was usually off gallivanting somewhere with a woman. She'd hoped to avoid him as he loved to needle her.

"Well, look who finally decided to come home," Caleb said, reminding her that they'd all said the very same thing about him last year when he'd disappeared for a couple of weeks and returned on the ranch's thirty-fifth anniversary party. He'd come back in just enough time to blow Chynna's ruse, exposing her as a pop singer hiding from the press by posing as her then-little-known twin sister, Kenya James.

"I haven't been gone that long," Rylee said as she came forward and leaned down to give her mother a kiss and her father a quick hug.

"If you say so," Caleb replied.

"Would you like a drink?" Noah asked.

"Love one," Rylee said, and she sat opposite her parents in the adjacent loveseat.

Noah walked over to the bar and began fixing her signature drink, a Cosmopolitan. He poured equal amounts of cranberry and Ketel One Vodka into a tumbler and added a few ice cubes.

"We're so glad to have you back home, baby girl," her father said. "We missed you."

"Especially your father," her mother said, glancing in his direction.

"It was pretty quiet around here without you," Noah admitted as he walked over and handed her the Cosmopolitan.

"How was the trip?" her mother asked, sipping a glass of wine, but before Rylee could answer, her mother continued speaking. "We heard that Jeremy gambled away his horse to some sheikh's son."

"I never knew Jeremy to be much of a gambler," her father commented. "He's always had such a level head on his shoulders, until now."

"Yeah, sis," Caleb said, smiling knowingly at her from behind the sofa. "So what's up with that?"

"Dinner is ready," Peggy, their housekeeper, advised from the living room door in the nick of time, but Rylee knew it was a short reprieve. Her family would want an answer at the dinner table. And hours after she'd arrived back in Tucson, she didn't have a plausible reason why, other than the truth.

They rose from their respective couches and made their way to the formal dining room. As was the custom, her parents sat at opposite heads of the table, while she, Noah and Caleb filtered in the center. Noah sat next to her, allowing Caleb to sit across from her. She knew Caleb had done it purposely to gauge her reactions. Ever since they were little kids, her younger brother always seemed to know when she was outright lying or wasn't being completely truthful.

They all began digging into the roast chicken, mashed potatoes and green beans that Peggy had made and passed the dinner rolls around. Rylee immediately dug into her plate to avoid conversation, but once everyone had settled in, as she'd suspected, Caleb began to stir things up.

"So, do you know why Jeremy gambled his horse away?" Caleb asked, buttering a dinner roll.

Rylee swallowed a forkful of mashed potatoes. "Quite simply, he was trying to impress me." She looked Caleb directly in the eye, daring him to say otherwise.

"You don't say?" Caleb said, laughing.

"What's so funny?" their mother asked.

"C'mon, Mama, don't tell me you haven't noticed the poor schmuck following Rylee around like a puppy dog when she could care less."

Her father's head sprung up. "Is that true, Rylee? I thought you liked Jeremy."

Rylee put down her fork. "I do. As a *friend.* Nothing more. You and Jeremy have always wanted there to be something more between us, and there's not. This weekend, it all came to a head."

"And he lost," Noah added.

Rylee glanced sideways at her older brother. "Much to his chagrin, yes. I warned him not to gamble with Dreamer, but he wouldn't listen to me." Her voice broke slightly. She didn't know how long she could keep up this line of questioning without breaking down in front of her family.

"And it cost him," Caleb said. He glanced at Rylee and, as if sensing her discomfort, he made a self-deprecating joke. "See, if it were me, there would be no way I'd let a female come between me and my money."

They all laughed. "Well, that's the difference between you and Jeremy," Noah replied. "He wears his heart on his sleeve."

"And he's got an empty pocket to show for it," Caleb responded.

"I just feel so bad that he lost a horse he'd been nurturing the last couple of years," her mother said. "All that hard work down the drain."

And he never would have if it hadn't been for me, thought Rylee. She felt terribly guilty. If she'd never gone with him to Louisville, he would have been a winner and she wouldn't feel like such a loser. Suddenly, she rose from the table. She couldn't take another minute and wanted to be alone.

"If you'll excuse me, I'm going to head back to my room. I'm feeling a little bit queasy," Rylee lied. "You know, jet lag and all."

Her mother rose and came over to feel her forehead as if she were a child. "Of course, baby doll, you feel better, okay?"

Rylee avoided looking at Caleb, as he would know she was lying, and she quickly fled from the dinner table.

Rylee's room was a welcome respite. She turned on some blues and pulled a bottle of whiskey and a plastic cup from her nightstand. She poured a glass to drown her sorrows.

She was on her second drink, listening to Nina Simone, when a knock sounded on her door. Rylee sat up on her bed and fluffed her curls before yelling, "Come in."

Rylee rolled her eyes when she saw who stood at the door. "Not now, Caleb."

"Yes, now." He closed the door and came toward her. He sat on the edge of the king-sized bed. "You have another cup?"

Rylee smiled, then reached for the drawer on the nightstand and pulled out another. She handed it to her brother, and he helped himself to the whiskey sitting on the nightstand.

"Bottoms up!" He held up his cup until she did the same. They clicked rims before taking a drink. "So, you wanna tell me what really went down between you and Jeremy?"

"Not really," Rylee said, eyeing him warily. "You might be my brother, but there's some things I can't talk to you about."

"Then just give me the highlights." He sipped his whiskey and stared at her.

Rylee sighed dramatically. She wasn't going to get out of this without spilling some of her guts. "Fine!" She took a huge gulp of whiskey and subsequently began to cough uncontrollably. Caleb patted her back. "Easy, love. Whiskey is meant to be sipped, not chugged."

"Whatever!" She rolled her eyes.

"Stop stalling, and start talking."

"Where do you want me to start?" Rylee asked. "Should I start with the fact that thanks to me, Jeremy felt the need to showboat to a rich playboy to win my affection? Or how about when he lost his horse to said playboy? Or how about when your dumb-ass sister spent the weekend with said playboy only to have him creep away in the middle of the night and send his assistant the next morning to come fetch her? Which of those should we talk about?"

"Damn!" Caleb reached for the bottle on the nightstand and poured more into his cup. "Could you have at least warned a brother that he was in for a major shitfest?"

"I told you I didn't want to talk about it," Rylee said, sipping her drink again, "but you persisted."

"That I did," Caleb said and leaned back, resting one forearm on the bed so he could look up at Rylee. "And because I did, I can tell you that you didn't do anything wrong."

"Didn't I? If you think about it, I'm the reason Jeremy lost his horse."

"Jeremy lost his horse because of *him*. Did he do it to impress you as you stated at dinner? Yes. But that's on him. He shouldn't have gambled away something that important. This will teach him a lesson to value what he has."

"I know that here," Rylee said, pointing to her head, "but tell that to my heart. I don't know how I can even face Jeremy. And did I tell you he warned me away from the playboy? But no, I had to play with fire, and what always happens? I got burned."

"Yeah, but didn't you have the best time of your life playing with it?" Caleb responded with a smile.

Through the drunken haze that was starting to form around her, Rylee blinked Caleb into focus. "What did you say?"

"There's nothing wrong with taking a chance or a risk," Caleb continued. "That's the best and most exciting part of life. Without risk, there's no reward."

Rylee chuckled. Trust Caleb to put a positive spin on the situation.

"Listen, listen." Caleb reached for her hand. "I'm not saying I don't wanna kill the bastard for hurting my sister, okay? If he were here, he would have me to contend with, but he's not and be that as it may — *you* chose to spend the weekend with him. And although I don't want to hear the details — you can tell Camryn those — you had a good time or you wouldn't have stayed, right?"

Rylee thought about his question for a long moment before answering, "Yes."

"Then call a spade a spade." Caleb shrugged. "Look at the experience for what it was: a chance to try something new, to take a risk. But it's over now, and it's back to the real world."

"That's easier said than done."

Caleb stared at her, searching her eyes. He stared so long, Rylee thought something might be on her face, and she began to rub a hand over it.

"Ah, there's the rub. The trick is not to care, but—"

"But what?" Rylee interrupted Caleb.

"But you fell for him, didn't you?"

Rylee looked away, reaching for the quickly dissipating whiskey bottle, and poured herself another generous drink. She didn't answer Caleb.

"That's where I can't help you. I don't do feelings and that yucky love stuff."

"It's not love," Rylee stated firmly, "but I *felt* something. And now it's over with no explanation. Not even a goodbye."

Caleb nodded. "That's the problem with taking a risk. It's fun as hell while you're doing it, and sometimes there's a big payoff, but sometimes you lose."

Rylee could understand that because that's how she felt. She'd thought she and Amar had something, but instead he'd only been along for the ride and the ride was over. Now, it was time for her to get off and move on with her life.

Chapter 10

"YOUR FATHER'S CONDITION IS IMPROVING," the doctor told Amar, Tariq and Khalid several days later. "We'll be releasing him today."

"Are you sure that's advisable?" Khalid replied.

"All tests indicate your father is stable and ready to continue his recovery at home. We could have released him a couple of days ago but kept him at your request to monitor his vitals to alleviate any concerns you may have."

"A heart attack seems pretty serious to me," Amar said, "and should warrant further testing. Could he suffer another setback?"

"Anything is possible," the doctor replied. "I can't predict that, but all indications suggest he's on the road to recovery."

"I have to begrudgingly agree with my brother on this one," Khalid said. "We are counting on your expertise to assure us."

"I have been in communication with your father's cardiologist in Nasir. He will be completing some additional testing such as cardiograms, stress tests, etcetera. In the meantime, you need to keep him calm and stress free."

Khalid looked at Amar. "That can be done."

"Good. I've signed the release papers and will have a wheelchair sent up to him shortly."

"Thank you, doctor," the brothers said in unison.

"Great news, yes?" Tariq glanced at Amar, who appeared preoccupied.

"Yes, it's great," Amar said, looking down at his phone again. No call from Rylee. There hadn't been one in *four* days. Not that he should expect any. When he'd finally been able to make an international call and had gotten a hold of Sharif, who was on his way to the airport to Dubai to meet Amar, he'd learned exactly how Rylee had taken the news of his early morning departure. She'd asked Sharif to relay a message to him: "Drop dead."

He'd telephoned her several times since then, but each time the call had gone unanswered. He'd left her several voice messages and sent multiple texts. No response.

It was driving Amar crazy to have no communication with the beautiful, sexy, amazing woman he'd only had the pleasure of spending the weekend with in Kentucky. He hadn't gotten his fill of her. He'd wanted more, but dammit, she wouldn't answer his calls or give him a chance to explain what had happened.

"Is something wrong?" Tariq asked. "You've been preoccupied for days. Father's release is great news. You should be jumping for joy like the rest of us."

Amar looked up and smiled half-heartedly. "Yes, of course it is. And I am happy."

"But?"

"But nothing." Amar pocketed his phone in his blazer.

"What is it, Amar? I've never seen you this way before. Usually you're so focused and sure of yourself."

Amar knew that was the problem. He'd lost focus thanks to Rylee Hart, with her wayward spiral curls, and he hadn't been the same since.

"Sorry, bro," Amar said, blinking back his thoughts. "Just have a lot on my mind." He wasn't ready to share his feelings with anyone yet because he didn't understand what they were. He just knew he had to see Rylee again. Make things right.

He needed to say his goodbyes and get back on a plane to the States. "Excuse me for a moment, Tariq." He left his brother in the hall to walk back into the room.

His father was already upright and dressed in plain clothes, ready for his wheelchair ride. Saffron and Khalid were at his bedside.

"If you don't mind, I'd like a few moments alone with Father," Amar said from the doorway.

Saffron began to speak, but her husband raised a hand, silencing her instantly. Showing their respect for his authority, both she and Khalid left the room without speaking or looking at Amar. "It's alright. Come here, Amar." The Sheikh motioned him toward the bed.

Reluctantly, Amar walked forward.

"I take it you've come to say goodbye?"

A small smile formed on Amar's lips. His father knew him well.

"I have," Amar said when he reached his bedside.

"I appreciate you coming all this way, considering we haven't had the best relationship."

"That may be so, but you're my father. Where else would I be?"

His father nodded, and the room was silent for several beats before he said, "And you're my son." Amar glanced up into his father's dark eyes. "And you will always be. Nothing can change that."

Amar nodded, unable to speak. He wasn't used to the King having a moment of genuine feeling.

"Take care of yourself, Father," Amar managed to say.

"I will, son."

Amar turned to leave, but his father said, "And that lady love you're pining over — you make her yours."

"How did you ...," Amar started to ask, but he needn't have bothered. His father had eyes and ears on him at all times. "I'll do that, sir," he said a second before opening the door and walking out.

He found Tariq in the hall, waiting for him. "Are you coming back on the plane with us to Nasir?"

Amar shook his head.

"C'mon, Amar. Father just suffered a heart attack. He needs all of us around him."

"And he had all of us," Amar responded. "I came here, didn't I?"

"Yes, but—"

"But nothing. You know how I feel about Nasir. I'm not welcome there, and I'm not coming back."

"Thank Allah for small miracles," Khalid said from behind them.

Amar turned around to glare at him. It was clear how Khalid felt about him, and now was no different. "I see nothing has changed," Amar replied.

"C'mon, you two," Tariq said, trying to stop a fight before it started.

"Tariq, there's no need to be a mediator here," Khalid responded. "Amar made a dutiful visit as expected and is going back to the States where he belongs."

Amar shook his head in disbelief. Khalid had never been one to mince words. "Agreed, which is why my jet is already here and fueled up." He walked toward Tariq and pulled him into a quick embrace. "I'll be taking my leave now. Call me if anything changes."

Tariq nodded. "I will."

Amar nodded at Khalid before leaving the hospital.

An hour later, Amar was on his private jet, where Sharif had been waiting for him. "Long time, no see," Sharif said.

"You're picking up Western colloquialisms quite nicely," Amar said as he took his seat and buckled himself in.

"I have to learn to assimilate," Sharif replied. "How's the King?"

"On the road to recovery," Amar answered, "and heading back to Nasir."

"Great news," Sharif responded. "Must be a relief to you and the Royal Family."

"It is. But I suspect it would take a lot more than one heart attack to break my father," Amar said. "Any messages for me?"

"Would there be any in particular that you would like?"

"Don't mess about with me, Sharif," Amar said with an edge to his voice. "You know who I'm referring to."

Sharif smiled. He knew Amar wanted to know about Rylee Hart, but he couldn't resist teasing him a bit. "No messages."

"Has our flight been chartered to Arizona?"

"Yes, as instructed earlier today."

"Good."

Amar couldn't wait to see Rylee again. He wanted to wrap her in his arms and make her remember everything they'd shared in Kentucky, just as he did. Rylee Hart was impossible to forget.

Chapter 11

"**L**OOK WHO FINALLY DECIDED TO come out to play,"
Camryn said when Rylee walked into a fine dining
restaurant later that week to meet her for dinner.
"I'm sorry, Cam," Rylee said as she came toward the
booth, "but at least I brought gifts." She held up the gift
bag and birthday card. "Happy birthday, girlfriend." She
bent down to give her best friend a kiss on the cheek.

"Thank you." Camryn accepted the bag as Rylee slid
into the booth opposite her. "But you have been MIA since
you returned from Louisville."

"And I'm sorry about that," Rylee said, taking a seat. "I
had a lot to deal with."

"Care to tell me about it?"

"After lots of cocktails."

Several hours later, after they'd shared a bottle of
wine, a seafood dinner of crab claws and a gigantic piece
of chocolate cake to celebrate Camryn's twenty-eighth
birthday, they took a cab over to a new nightclub that was
the latest hotspot for dancing and singles in Tucson.

Rylee tipped the host a hundred dollars, and they were
seated in the VIP section away from the crowd, but not too
far away to hear the music.

"This is awesome, Rylee. Thanks," Camryn said when
they sat down on a plush silver sofa.

"It's your birthday," Rylee said. "We have to live it up!"

When the waitress came over, Rylee ordered them two Pomegranate martinis.

"Easy, Rylee," Camryn warned. "We did just kill a bottle of wine earlier."

"And your point?" Rylee raised a brow. "You said you wanted to know what happened after you left the Derby. Well, that requires a lot of liquid courage."

Camryn eyed her warily. "Amar Bishop must have really done a number on you after I left."

Rylee shrugged. "No worse than he did to Jeremy."

"Speaking of ..."

Rylee followed Camryn's gaze and saw Jeremy approaching them. He paused for several beats, and Rylee thought he was about to turn on his heel, but he must have thought better of it because he continued toward them.

"Ladies." Jeremy nodded when he made it to the VIP area.

Rylee's throat suddenly became parched, and she sorely wished that that martini had arrived. "Jeremy, how are you?" She offered a small smile.

"Well. And you?" he asked, but before she could reply, he looked around then returned his gaze back to her. "Are you alone?"

His question was like a dagger to the heart because Rylee knew what Jeremy was implying. Although she was with Camryn, Amar was not present. "We're here celebrating Cam's birthday." Rylee reached across the couch and wrapped one arm around Camryn's shoulder. "Would you like to join us?"

"No, thanks," Jeremy said. "I'm not alone." He inclined his head toward a statuesque woman who was standing several feet behind him. "I just came over to say hello." He came forward and offered Cam a hug. "Happy birthday. Enjoy your evening."

Seconds later, he was gone, leaving a thick cloud of tension. "Wow! Talk about the hidden hostility," Camryn said. "If you looked up the word in the dictionary, you would see Jeremy's face."

"Can you blame him?" Rylee asked as she stared at his retreating figure. "I broke his heart."

"Looks like he's recovering just fine, but I wish the same could be said about you."

"What do you mean?" Rylee asked. At that moment, the waitress came back with their drinks and set them on the table. "Thank you," they said in unison. The waitress nodded and walked away.

"You know what I mean, Rylee. You've been back for over a week, and I've barely seen you. You haven't called or barely returned my texts."

"Listen, Cam, I'm sorry."

"Enough of the 'I'm sorries,' okay? I'm your best friend. And if you can't tell me, who can you tell?"

"My brother." Rylee offered a dry laugh.

"You talked to Noah about Amar?"

Just hearing Amar's name brought tension to her belly, but Rylee pushed it down. "No. I meant Caleb. And in his profound wisdom, he told me that I had to chalk up the moment to taking a risk and move on, but that's easier said than done."

"Why don't you take it from the top? What happened after we left?"

Rylee reached for her martini and took a generous sip. It was sweet yet potent, and she could feel the liquor spreading through her veins along with the wine she'd consumed earlier. "We had a great time," Rylee answered. "Amar pulled out all the stops to romance me, from a couture gown for the Julep Ball to a private cabin in the woods."

"I'm intrigued," Camryn said, grabbing her martini glass. "Do continue."

"He went all out. There was a path of rose petals to the cabin, chilled champagne and a roaring fireplace. I don't need to tell you what happened. I'm sure your imagination can take it from there. The only difference was I *felt something.* Amar brought out a passion in me that I didn't know existed, and girl ... I had my first orgasm being with him."

"That's big." Camryn eyes grew large, and she took another drink of her martini. "As I recall, you'd never had one ... *the typical way.*"

Rylee nodded. "No. And I did over and over with him. It was thrilling and exciting, and the two nights we were together were the most amazing passionate nights of my life, but then it was over."

"What happened?"

"I woke up the night after Dreamer won the Derby and Amar was gone. No note or phone call. I found Sharif in the living room, and he informed me Amar had to leave on an urgent family matter." Rylee sipped her martini. "None of it makes any sense, Camryn. Amar shared with me he wasn't close with his family, yet I'm expected to believe he had to leave on an urgent family matter?"

"Does sound a little shady, but has he called since then?"

"Yes, but why should I take his calls?"

"Because ..." Camryn's voice grew loud thanks to the music that began to blare. "Because you want answers. You'll never know why he left if you don't give him a chance to explain."

"I don't want to hear some lie he's concocted," Rylee replied. "He got what he wanted, and then he left."

"Hmm ... if that's the case," Camryn said, pausing to drink her martini, "why would he call you again?"

Rylee frowned. She hadn't figured out the answer to that question, and she wasn't sure she wanted to. The truth of the matter was, like Caleb had said, they'd shared a fling, nothing more. "I don't know, and I don't care."

"Bullshit!" Camryn eyed her friend suspiciously. "I think you care more than you're willing to acknowledge. Otherwise you wouldn't be carrying this big weight on your shoulders and letting it affect you this way."

"I'm over Amar Bishop," Rylee stated, putting on a brave front. Deep down, she knew it to be a lie. She was far from over Amar, and that scared her even more, because if he could cause this much damage to her equilibrium after just a few days, she could only imagine the damage if she let him further into her heart.

Chapter 12

"HELLO, HELLO," CHYNNA CALLED OUT as she walked into the stables of the Golden Oaks Ranch. It was a day after Camryn's birthday, and Chynna had just returned from her tour.

"Chynna?" Rylee poked her head out of a stall to see her sister-in-law sashaying down the hall in her latest designer duds. Rylee had missed Chynna while she was away. She'd come to look forward to having her around. Even at three months pregnant, Chynna looked just as chic as she pleased while Rylee was dressed in her usual fare of jeans and a plaid shirt.

"Girlfriend." Chynna hugged her when she approached. "So good to see you. How was the Derby? Did you love the fashion and the hats?"

Rylee smiled. "It was good. How was your concert tour?"

Chynna frowned as she searched Rylee's face, finding dark circles: signs of stress and lack of sleep. "Just good? What's going on? I expected way more than that, especially with Camryn going to the Derby too. Dish!"

"There's nothing to dish," Rylee said, returning to her task of checking one of the horse's vitals that had been ill.

Chynna leaned against the stall door. "C'mon, Rylee, it's me. I can tell when something's wrong with you. And something's definitely off. What gives?"

"There's nothing wrong, Chynna. I've made my peace with what happened, and there's no use in rehashing it." Rylee came out of the stall and began putting away her supplies.

"What could have happened to you in a week's time for this kind of reaction?" Chynna folded her arms across her chest. "There's only one thing that I know of that can cause this: a man. So who broke your heart?"

"Amar Bishop," Rylee said. "And I want nothing to do with him."

"Is there no way I change your mind?" a masculine voice asked from the door of the stables.

Amar stood staring at Rylee and another woman who he figured could only be her sister-in-law. She was dressed in flashy attire and stilettos. He'd read the dossier on Rylee and that her brother Noah had married America's sweetheart after she'd caused a big uproar by switching places with her twin, Kenya.

He'd come straight to the ranch from the airport after nearly twenty-four hours of flying. After he'd showered on the plane, he'd sent Sharif back to Palo Alto, California, to look after Bishop Enterprises, and rented a four-wheel drive to get himself out to Golden Oaks. Something had told him that Rylee wouldn't appreciate all the pomp and circumstance if he arrived in a limo, so he'd decided to come solo in the hopes that he could get through to her on his own. He'd parked outside the family estate and followed his instincts that Rylee would be in her favorite spot. He'd been right.

"Well?" he asked when both women were silent. "Should I turn around and go?"

Chynna glanced at Rylee's angry face. "That would be a good idea."

"Stay or go, I really don't care," Rylee said. She turned away to continue putting away her supplies.

Chynna looked at Amar's resolute expression and began moving toward the stable exit. "I'm thinking you two need some time alone, so I'm just going back up to the main house and unpack. I'll see you later."

Rylee didn't look up at Chynna as she left.

Amar walked toward Rylee, whose back was to him. He noticed her stiffen as she heard his footsteps. "Rylee, can we talk?"

She didn't answer and continued to ignore him. Finally, he couldn't take the deafening silence and reached across and grabbed her arm.

"Let me go!" Rylee's eyes blazed fury, and Amar quickly released her.

"I'm sorry." Amar held up his hands in defense. He hadn't known how Rylee was going to react to his sudden appearance, but he hadn't expected the absolute anger that emanated from her every pore.

"What exactly are you sorry for?" Rylee said, turning to face him.

Amar swallowed. The speech he'd recited in his head half a dozen times over the last week when he'd been in Dubai suddenly faded from his memory. He'd never been one at a loss for words, but when faced with such hostility from Rylee, he felt completely out of his element. Perhaps coming here had been a bad move. What if he couldn't get through to her?

"What do you want, Amar? I don't have all day," Rylee said, folding her arms across her chest.

He would just have to plow ahead and pray that he reached her. "I'm sorry for how I left you in Louisville," he began, "but it was unavoidable."

"Unavoidable?" Rylee's voice rose. "Are you kidding me? Please tell me you didn't fly all this way to tell me it was unavoidable, because if so, you could have saved your fuel and your breath." She began walking toward the door.

Amar caught up to her before she could exit. "It's the truth," Amar explained. "My father had a heart attack."

At his blunt admission, Rylee turned around to face him. "What did you say?"

"My father suffered a heart attack in Nasir. He was air-lifted to Dubai to see a specialist. As soon as my brother Tariq called me, I left for the airport, where he had a plane fueled and waiting for me."

Rylee stared up at him with her big brown eyes, and all Amar wanted to do was take her in his arms and lose himself in her, but she was looking at him with cautious disbelief. "Are you telling me the truth? Or is this a lie you've concocted to try and win me over."

"It's the truth," Amar answered. "You can look it up online. We did our best to try and cover it up for fear it would reach one of Nasir's enemies, but as soon as we left the hospital, someone leaked the story."

Shock registered on Rylee's face as she interpreted this new piece of information. "So he's okay?"

"Yes." Amar nodded. "He's been released and is back home safely in Nasir."

"And why aren't you there?"

"Because," Amar said, staring at her, "I needed to make things right between us. I couldn't continue to allow you to believe I'd discarded you after the nights we'd shared together, without a thought or care."

"Then why did you?" Rylee asked with a shaky voice. "I understand about your father, but you told me you'd never been close to your family. Can't you see how that must have looked?"

Amar nodded. "Yes, I do. It probably looked like I was lying and using my family as an excuse to break away from you when that couldn't be further from the truth."

"What's the truth now?"

Amar smiled as he reached for her arm and pulled her into his own. "The truth is this." He lowered his head to capture her lips. It was an open-mouthed kiss that sought her tongue and a desperate need to remember just how good Rylee tasted. She responded with a deep, throaty groan and wrapped her arms around his neck.

He deepened the kiss, tasting and exploring her recesses. After waiting so long for another hit of Rylee, he didn't rush the kiss. He savored it. Savored her. He kissed her with all the pent-up longing he'd been harboring for the last week in Dubai when he'd dreamed of having her in his arms, in his bed again. His hands cupped her bottom, and she tilted her head, giving him yet another angle to explore her mouth. His lips didn't stop there. They seared a path down to her neck and her shoulders, and she whimpered a soft moan, causing him to return to her mouth for yet another taste.

She splayed her hands across his back and buttocks, and soon he felt his erection swelling near her middle. His lower half ground against her, eager to be closer to her while his hands moved all over her body. When they found her breasts, he flicked one thumb pad across her nipple until he felt it pucker underneath his touch.

"Uh, excuse me." A cough sounded behind them, and they immediately broke the kiss. Rylee spun in front of Amar, giving him a few moments to pull himself together.

"Noah!" he heard her say. "What are you doing here?"

"Well, uh, I, uh, heard Chynna was down here." Noah fumbled for words. He was clearly not used to seeing his little sister make out with a man.

"Sh-she's back out at the house," Rylee replied, coming toward Noah and trying to usher him out.

"Okay, guess I'll go find her," Noah said. "But before I do, I don't believe I've made your *friend's* acquaintance."

Amar had no time to react as a fist came toward him and sent him flying to the floor on his butt, landing him in a pile of hay. He looked up at Rylee's brother, who towered over him in a cowboy hat.

"Noah! What the hell has gotten into you?" Rylee yelled and rushed to Amar's side. "Are you okay, Amar?"

Amar nodded and held his jaw as he tried to right himself.

"Is this the guy who had you so upset for the last week?" Noah asked, pointing at Amar. "If so, he should know you have brothers, and we have no problem kicking his ass up and down this ranch if he ever hurts you again. You got that?" He glared down at Amar.

"Oh, yes, I got that," Amar said as he rose to his feet with a little help from Rylee.

"That was really unnecessary, Noah," Rylee said as she took Amar's face in her hands and surveyed the damage.

"It's okay," Amar said as he brushed the straw from his jeans and long-sleeve shirt. "He was defending your honor, and I respect that."

"You just ensure you respect my sister." Noah pointed a finger in Amar's face. "Otherwise, you'll have me and my brother, Caleb, to deal with."

Amar nodded. And several seconds later, Noah left the stables, leaving him and Rylee alone. Amar moved his jaw back and forth several times. It wasn't broken, and that was a good thing. But his ego was bruised. He hadn't seen that coming.

"Your brother has one serious left hook."

"You should be thankful it was Noah," Rylee replied, "and not my younger brother, Caleb. He's a wild card and may have beaten you to a bloody pulp for making his big sis cry."

Amar peered into her brown eyes. "Did I make you cry?" he asked. "If I did, I'm sorry. I would never want to hurt you in any way." He searched her face for some sign that she believed him, and when he saw her blinking back tears as she nodded, he knew that he'd made the right decision in flying back home to the States. There was no place he would rather be than right here with the woman who was quickly stealing his heart.

Rylee was so taken aback having Amar in her world. He'd caught her completely off guard by coming to Golden Oaks Ranch and explaining why he'd left so suddenly from Louisville after the nights they'd spent lying in each other's arms. And now here he was in her home, in her room, telling her all the things she wanted to hear, that he hadn't meant to leave and that he wanted to stay with her. *But what does it all mean?*

She was wondering that as she stood in her bedroom getting ready for dinner with her family *and Amar.* They hadn't yet had time to figure out what they meant to each other before he would be forced to face the family juggernaut. He'd arrived so late in the afternoon that they'd barely had time to talk before she'd been called by radio to the field to check on an ailing steer.

She'd thought she was going alone, but Amar had refused to leave her side. He'd accompanied her on horseback. She supposed he wanted to show her that he wasn't going anywhere and that he would stay until they'd sorted things out. After she'd tended to the steer, they'd returned in just enough time to wash up before dinner at six.

Rylee had only a short time to tell Peggy to set another place for dinner before she'd rushed Amar up the stairs to her wing of the house to wash up for supper in one of the guest bedrooms. That's where he was this very minute as she stood surveying herself in front of the gilded pedestal mirror in her bedroom. She'd dressed tonight in a peasant shirt and flowing skirt and cinched it all with a belt. She was trying to look dressed up, but not like she'd tried too hard. She was just spraying on some of her favorite perfume at her earlobes and wrists when a knock sounded on her door.

"Come in."

Amar entered, and his six-foot-four frame filled her entire bedroom. He looked deliciously sexy and rugged in a pair of faded jeans and a grey pullover long-sleeve sweater that hugged his ripped arms.

When he walked toward her, she swallowed hard and had to remind herself to breathe. "Hey, beautiful." He brushed his lips across her cheek.

"Hello." Rylee looked at Amar through the mirror and wrapped his arms around her waist.

"What's wrong?" he asked as if sensing her uneasiness.

"Nothing."

"Rylee." Amar turned her around and took her face in his hands. "What's wrong?"

Rylee shook her head. "It's silly really. It's just so strange to have you *here* in my space. That's all."

"Strange in a good way or a bad way?" Amar asked in a husky tone. His eyes were dark with desire as they traveled over hers.

"A good way." Rylee looked into those dark depths and to prove it, she stood on her tippy toes to kiss him. His lips parted, and he kissed her hungrily. His tongue dove inside her mouth, past her teeth and tangled with hers. She suppressed a moan, pushing Amar back. "You'd better stop that, or we'll end up there." She inclined her head toward the bed.

"That's where I want you tonight," Amar murmured huskily.

"First you have to make it past dinner with my family." Rylee slipped out of his embrace and went back to her vanity to touch up her lipstick. She couldn't go down to dinner looking flushed and like she'd been thoroughly kissed.

"I'm sure your family will love me." Amar smiled.

Rylee could only hope.

Rylee and Amar entered the living room shortly thereafter and found her family had already gathered as if sensing fresh meat was near. Her parents were in their usual spot on the sofa. Her mother nursed a glass of wine while her father sipped whiskey. Noah and Chynna sat cuddled on the adjacent loveseat like the newlyweds they were. Caleb stood by the fireplace mantel, clutching a bottle of beer. He straightened as soon as Rylee and Amar walked in the room. She could see Caleb knew who Amar was — Caleb looked like he was ready to spring on Amar any minute.

Rylee ignored his glares. "Everyone, I'd like to introduce you to Amar Bishop. Amar," she said, turning to him, "this is my family." She walked toward her parents. "My parents: Isaac and Madelyn. My brother Noah and his wife, Chynna, and my brother Caleb, at the mantel."

"Good evening." Amar inclined his head toward each of them.

"No need to be so formal here," Caleb sniffed. "We're just a bunch of country folks."

"Caleb!" Their mother rose from the sofa. "It's a pleasure to meet you, Amar." She offered her hand, and Amar kissed it.

"The pleasure is all mine, Mrs. Hart. Now I see where Rylee gets all her good looks."

Her mother blushed. "Oh, my," she said, and touched her chest before sitting back down.

"Bishop?" her father questioned. "Name sounds familiar. You don't happen to be the *Bishop* in *Bishop Enterprises,* the multimedia corporation."

"Yes, I am," Amar said. "That's my company."

Her father's brow rose. "I see. And where did you meet my baby girl?"

"At the Derby," Amar answered.

"Rylee came back from the Derby out of sorts," her father returned. "Did you have something to do with that?"

"Now, now," her mother said, patting her father's lap, "there's no need to get into Rylee's personal business. Mr. Bishop is our guest."

"For how long?" Noah uttered from the loveseat.

Amar turned to Rylee with such warmth that she felt it radiate throughout her whole being. "For as long as necessary to see the smile back in Rylee's eyes."

"Might take a while, considering you were the reason it was snuffed out to begin with," Caleb muttered.

"Caleb!" their mother warned. "Mr. Bishop, would you like anything to drink before supper?"

"No, thank you. I'll just have wine with dinner, if that's alright with you."

"Sounds splendid," she replied. "Why don't we all retire to the dining room?"

Rylee glanced at her mother and thanked her with her eyes for stopping her father and brothers from ripping Amar to shreds ... but the night was still young.

Dinner fared slightly better with Rylee, Chynna and her mother keeping the conversation afloat with anecdotes about the ranch, Chynna's concert and the startup of Bishop Enterprises, all while the Hart men sized Amar up. Rylee's parents were at the head of the table as always, while Amar and Rylee sat together, with Chynna, Noah and Caleb sitting across from them.

When dessert arrived, Rylee thought they'd made it through the tough part until her father began questioning Amar about the Derby.

"So, how did you meet my daughter again?" Isaac Hart asked, returning to his earlier question.

"Saw her in the stables." Amar glanced sideways at Rylee and gave her a warm smile. "She was tending to a horse, and she stole my breath away."

"Would that be Dreamer, Jeremy Wright's horse?"

Rylee's heart sunk. She knew where this line of questioning was going, and she didn't like it one bit. Rylee tensed beside Amar, and he patted her knee under the table as if to reassure her that all would be fine. "Yes, sir. It was."

"And Jeremy lost the horse to you in a poker game," Isaac stated more than questioned.

"That's correct." Amar looked him directly in the eye. She liked that about Amar, that he wouldn't back away from a fight with Jeremy *or* her father.

"So you admit that you took the boy's horse? No doubt to impress my daughter."

"No, sir. I won it fair and square. He shouldn't have gambled with something so precious to him. But I do admit that I used it as leverage to gain Rylee's attention, but that only angered your daughter and I almost lost my chance with her."

"Didn't seem like you learned your lesson," Caleb finally spoke after remaining quiet for most of the evening, "because Rylee returned from the Derby brokenhearted. What do you have to say for yourself?"

Amar turned in Caleb's direction. "As I've explained to Rylee, my father suffered a massive stroke in my homeland of Nasir." Puzzled looks surrounded him at the table, and Amar clarified, "Near Dubai. I was unable to get word to Rylee, so she left Louisville thinking I'd abandoned her, but that was far from the case." He turned to Rylee. "I couldn't wait to get back to the States to see her."

"Sounds very romantic," Caleb said, "but Rylee lives here in Tucson and Bishop Enterprises is in ..." He let his sentence dangle, "How do you suppose on making a relationship with my sister work?"

Amar chuckled softly. "Well, it's a little early to say, but I'm sure *Rylee and I*," he emphasized the words, "will figure it out."

"Well then," Rylee said, rising to her feet and pushing her chair back, "if the Spanish Inquisition is over, I'd like to take a walk. Amar, care to join me?" She looked down at Amar, still seated, daring him to disagree with her.

"Sounds like a great idea," Amar said, rising to his feet. "Isaac, Madelyn." He nodded to her parents before turning to her siblings. "You all have a good evening."

Amar grasped her hand, and they quickly walked out of the dining room. Once they were out, Rylee released the huge sigh of relief she'd been holding in. "Thank God that's over."

"That really wasn't so bad," Amar replied, glancing at her as they walked down the corridor toward the front entrance. He'd expected her family to grill him much worse than they had.

"You don't say?"

Amar laughed as he opened the front door and allowed her to precede him out. "I would imagine if I'd had a sister, my brothers and I would be the same way."

Rylee glanced up at the dark sky as Amar joined her side.

"Your family cares about you, Rylee. How could I be upset by that? I wish mine cared more about me."

Rylee turned and looked up at him, but Amar was staring into the dark night. He seemed a million miles away.

"Was it hard being back in Dubai?"

He slowly walked to the porch steps and then took a seat. When she joined him, he took her hand and helped her down onto the steps until they were hip to hip. They sat in silence looking up at the stars before Amar said, "They didn't want me there."

"Your family?"

He nodded, and when he turned to her she could see an unspoken pain glowing in his eyes. "The only person happy to see me was my younger brother."

"What about your father? *He* must have been happy that you traveled so far to see him in his condition."

"I suppose," Amar said, shrugging. "He and I ... we've been at odds for so long, I don't think we know how to be father and son."

Rylee reached for his hand and squeezed it. "You going there meant a lot to him. I'm sure of it."

"I dunno. Maybe."

Rylee was sorry that she'd brought up such a painful subject. She could see that it was a sore spot for Amar, and she wanted to bring the light back into his eyes.

She turned his face to hers and lightly caressed his strong cheek. "Well, in case I didn't say it before, I'm glad you're here," she whispered.

"Me too," he murmured, and tenderly kissed her lips.

"How about we go upstairs?" she suggested.

Amar glanced toward the house. "Are you sure about that? I wouldn't want your father and brothers to come after me with a shotgun for stealing your innocence."

"Don't you worry about them," Rylee said, standing up. "Let's make tonight about you and me."

Instead of going to her wing of the house as Amar imagined they would, Rylee walked him out onto a pebbled path to the family's guesthouse. She produced a key which she'd tucked in her bosom to unlock the door. There was very little light in the room other than the moonlight coming through the curtains, but Amar could still make out Rylee's slender curves as she moved around the kitchen.

"Can I help?" he asked.

"I've got it," she said, searching several drawers before pulling out a handful of votive candles and a lighter. She lit each, placing them strategically throughout the small house before stopping at the master bedroom. She sat on the edge of the bed and held her hands out to Amar, and he eagerly came toward her.

He bent down, resting his nose against her hair. He could smell the lavender shampoo she'd used as he drunk her fragrance in. She used the time to lift each of his feet and rid him of his socks and the country boots he'd bought on his way to the ranch earlier that day. Amar wanted to lose himself in more than her hair, but when he went to push her backward, she swatted him away and rose to her feet.

She began unbuttoning his shirt. When each clasp was undone, she slid the shirt from his shoulders, leaving him bare-chested to her admiring gaze. The buckle on the belt that held up his jeans was next. She looked up at him as she slid the belt from each loop and tossed it aside.

He liked this "woman in charge" and tried to give her a kiss, but she sidestepped him by tugging on his jeans zipper. Before he knew it, she was sliding them down his legs. He had no choice but to rise so he could step out of them and let her take the lead. He'd never seen her this way before, and it turned him on as evidenced by the super hard erection sticking out of his boxer briefs. She stroked him over the fabric, and Amar felt himself swell in response.

"Rylee ..."

She glanced up at him with deliberate purpose, and in one fell swoop rid him of his briefs until he was as naked as the day he was born. Then she dropped to her knees and took him deep into her mouth.

Amar gasped just as sheer joy encompassed him.

Rylee used her mouth to take him to great heights, pulling him in and out one moment and then sucking him long and hard the next. She teased the head of his penis with her tongue, making figure eights while her hands stroked his length, keeping him hard and yearning for a release. He didn't want to let go until he was inside her, but she was relentless in her quest.

"Rylee," he groaned, grabbing handfuls of her hair as he took her head and kept her bobbing up and down his shaft. It was such exquisite torture; he didn't want it to end. How could she know what he needed when he didn't know himself? But somehow, she did.

So when she glanced up at him and gave him a look that told him it was okay, he gave himself over to her. He trembled, clutching her shoulders, and came inside her mouth. She accepted all of him with no hesitation. When she was done, Rylee licked her lips, and he got hard all over again. He wanted to please her as she'd done him, show her that he could be as selfless as she'd just been with him.

He lifted her to her feet and without losing her gaze, he slid the long, flowing skirt she'd been wearing down her shapely hips. It fell in a pile at her feet, and she stepped out of it. The peasant shirt she wore soon accompanied it on the floor. Rylee looked up at him with such naked desire in her eyes; it took all of Amar's willpower to take things slow.

He bent down and placed tiny love pecks on her shoulders and neck, all the while reaching behind her to unhook the satin bra she'd been wearing. He stopped kissing her long enough to slide the bra from her arms and toss it so he could admire her breasts.

He molded and shaped them with his hands. He watched her eyes flutter open and closed as he teased her nipples with his thumbs. When he lowered his head to have a taste of one dark chocolate nipple, her head flew backward, and she held his head as he loved each nipple with quick flicks of his tongue until they became hard pebbles. Finally, he lowered her nearly naked body onto the bed so he could worship her whole, how she was meant to be worshipped.

He teased one nipple between his teeth, taking love bites before opening his mouth and taking her full breasts inside.

"Oh," she moaned as he suckled her breast, molding the other with his free hand. When he moved to the other breast, he could feel Rylee undulating against his lower half. He knew what she wanted, what she needed, but he wasn't about to give it to her, at least not yet.

His hands trailed down her abdomen and stomach, coming to play at her belly button before going lower. When he reached the bikini briefs she wore, he slipped a finger inside and felt the soft hairs of her mound pulsating against him. His erection swelled, but he ignored it and surged further until his finger found her. He slowly inched in further and further, one beat at a time, as his mouth continued to pleasure her breasts.

"Oh, God!" Rylee moaned as his finger hit her clitoris. He teased it over and over, and she began to writhe and moan louder on the bed. "Amar ..."

"Yes, baby."

"I want you ...," she murmured. "Now!"

"Just a little while longer, baby," he whispered, leaving her breasts and placing tender kisses on her stomach until he came to her thighs. "I want to love you like you loved me."

He slid her panties from her trembling thighs and seconds later, darted his tongue inside her womanhood. Rylee jerked upward off the bed. His head rose. "Easy love, I've got you." His hands held her thighs in place as his mouth and wet tongue went back to work. He licked and teased her, firmer and faster until she was soaking wet with her juices, and when she could take no more, he removed himself long enough to put on a condom, place her legs over his shoulders and slide inside her.

"Amar!" Rylee yelled as a feeling of completeness and rightness went through her with his penis fully inside her.

She bit his earlobe, and he groaned his pleasure, plunging deeper. She rocked her hips upward to meet his thrust, her entire lower body tightening around him.

Amar didn't let up. He pumped hard, and Rylee let out appreciative groans. "Oh, yes, Amar. I've missed this." There was nothing gentle about his lovemaking, and she didn't want it that way. She wanted it a little rough and wicked.

"So, so have I," Amar groaned as she dug her hands into his butt, urging him on. "But we have to slow down baby — I want to draw this out." His hands gently stroked her back, but instead of slowing her down, it made her hot and lusty.

"We have all night," Rylee said, looking up at him as her internal muscles contracted around him. "Take me!"

Amar shifted as he slid his hand lower, where they were joined, and found her aching clitoris. He stroked it. Rylee thought about how perfectly they fit together, how he knew just where to touch her to set her on fire. "Yes, Amar. Right there ... just ... just like that. Oh, God, yes!"

Amar's thrusts became more aggressive, and Rylee moved her legs so she could wrap them around his waist and lock her ankles around him.

"Jesus, Rylee, you have no idea what you're doing to me," Amar groaned as he gave one final thrust.

"Oh, yes I do." Rylee rose up to meet his plundering manhood as sensation after thrilling sensation took them both over the edge to bliss.

The next morning, Rylee and Amar were sneaking up the stairs of the main house when they ran into Caleb. He was bare-chested and wearing running shorts. He eyed the two of them in last night's outfits.

"I guess I'm not the only one that just had a workout," he said as he jogged down the stairs.

Rylee blushed as she and Amar headed up. Once they made it to her bedroom and she'd locked the door, they fell onto her bed. They'd gotten very little sleep the night before. Having been away from each other for nearly a week, they hadn't been able to keep their hands off each other and had stayed up half the night making love in a variety of interesting positions. Rylee hadn't known she could be so adventurous or nimble, but Amar brought out the sexual animal in her.

"So," Amar said, turning over on his side to face her, "your whole family lives here on the ranch?"

She nodded.

"Have you ever thought about leaving?"

"Never been a reason to consider it," Rylee answered honestly. "And I love it here. I love all the open space, the outdoors and, of course, all the animals. I get to take care of the horses and lots of others."

"Sounds like you're in your ideal world."

Rylee looked at him. She wasn't sure what he was trying to get at. "Are you asking me if I would consider leaving?"

Amar paused for several minutes before saying, "Yeah, I guess I am."

Rylee shrugged. "For the right person I would, but they would have to understand that I'm not giving up my work. I'm a veterinarian. I'm not content being a wife and a mother. That's my father's image of who I should be, not mine."

Amar sat up at the critical tone in Rylee's voice. "Sounds like you've had to deal with this topic before."

"I have," Rylee said. "My father thought I would be like my mom, content to tend to hearth and home. It's why he wanted me with Jeremy, because that's the future he envisioned for me. Imagine his surprise when his daughter scoffed at debutante parties, opting to be in the great outdoors with her brothers and the animals. It was the cause of a lot of strife in the house."

150

"Your father seems to have accepted your choices now."

"He didn't have much of an option," Rylee said and jumped up from the bed. "C'mon, we should get ready for breakfast as I have a lot of work to do and I suspect my brothers have something in store for you."

Chapter 13

RYLEE IS RIGHT, THOUGHT AMAR. During breakfast with the family, Amar indicated that he wanted to stay on the ranch for a few days to spend time with Rylee and, of course, get to know the Hart family.

Isaac Hart had scoffed, but Madelyn had been gracious and extended an invitation for as long as he'd wanted it. The Hart brothers, however, had made fun of Amar and wondered if he could handle himself on a horse much less as a ranch hand. Amar had never backed down from a fight, and he planned on showing them just what he was made of after he checked in with Sharif.

"How's everything at Bishop Enterprises?" Amar asked after he'd stepped away from the dining room and stood in the foyer.

"Everything is in order," Sharif answered.

"And father? Any change?"

"I called Tariq earlier today, and he was a bit agitated that news had broken of his illness as the King did not want to appear weak. However, they've settled him down now, and Khalid is meeting with several heads of nearby states."

"Well, sounds like Khalid has everything under control," Amar said. Not that it should surprise him — Khalid had been training for this moment his entire life.

"How's Golden Oaks?" Sharif asked.

"If you're asking about Rylee, she's fine. Once I was able to explain what happened, she understood that I had to leave quickly to get to Father."

"And?"

"And what?"

"Are you coming back to Palo Alto?"

"No, not just yet," Amar said. He hadn't yet discovered what it was about Rylee that was so different from every other woman he'd ever been with and why he was powerless to leave her. Until he did, he had to stay. Perhaps if he just spent a few more days here, he could get her out of his system and move on. Or at least that's what he told himself.

"Alright." Sharif picked up on what Amar wasn't saying. "Let me know when you're ready to return, and I'll send the jet."

"Thank you, Sharif." Amar hung up. When he turned around, the Hart brothers were staring at him.

"Gentlemen." He nodded.

"Are you ready to work?" Noah asked. "Because we start our days early around here, and we're way behind schedule, so let's go." He began heading toward the front door.

Amar glanced at the dining room. "What about Rylee?"

"You'll meet up with her later," said Caleb as he put one arm around Amar's shoulder and led him out the door.

Amar knew what the Hart brothers were up to. They'd wanted to see if he was a genteel businessman who wouldn't know what to do with a horse or steer, but they'd soon found out that he was no wimp. He'd surprised Caleb, Noah and the ranch foreman that not only was he an expert horseman and knew how to suit up a horse, but that he was also a darn good cattle wrangler. Cattle might be different from the sheep in Nasir, but they were pretty darn close. He'd wrangled several wayward cattle that afternoon, earning the respect of the brothers Hart.

"Wow!" Caleb said as he removed his cowboy hat and wiped the sweat underneath with the bandana around his neck. "You're a pretty darn good cattleman, Amar Bishop." He reached for his canteen from his saddle and took a generous swallow. "Who would have thought?"

Amar smiled as he jumped down off the stallion Noah had given him to ride. This horse had been such a handful just a year ago when Noah had gotten Max, but Amar had ridden him quite easily. They didn't understand that he was used to much feistier Arabians. "In my world," Amar said, "the son of a king learns to ride young."

"Your world?" Caleb noted. "I'd heard you were of mixed heritage and had some relation to an Arab sheikh. Is that right?"

"It is so," Amar said as he took the canteen from Caleb and sipped. He wanted to show him he wasn't above being like everyone else, even after he'd made such a comment. "My father is a sheikh and runs a small country called Nasir, but my mother was African-American."

"Sounds like a story there," Noah said, joining the duo and taking the canteen from Amar for a swallow.

"Ah," Amar sighed. He'd told the story more times than he could remember, but it was never as important as this one because he wanted Rylee's family to like and respect him. "My father was a young man who laid eyes on a beautiful woman. One thing led to another, and she ended up pregnant with me. The only problem was, he was already betrothed to another."

"So what happened?" Caleb asked with open curiosity.

Amar shrugged. "What do you think? He married the other girl, and my mother had me. Except ..."

Noah spoke up. "Except what?"

"He could never forget the beautiful mahogany-skinned woman he'd met, and he certainly couldn't let his son, his first-born son, be raised any kind of way. He continued his affair with my mother for a number of years while ensuring I had the very best in life. It wasn't until my mother met my stepfather and remarried did the affair end, though I doubted it ever ended in my mother's heart."

"Sounds tragic," Caleb commented, and at Amar's withering look, he corrected himself. "I'm sorry. That sounded callous. I meant tragic in that your father never got to live life on his own terms but had to bow to the will of others."

"And Lord knows my brother hates that," Noah said. "Heaven forbid he actually does as expected of him."

Caleb rolled his eyes at Noah. "Hey, it's served me well, hasn't it? I'm happy with my life. But what about you, Amar? Are you happy? It sounds like you've led a life of privilege, completely different from Rylee. Why would you even be interested in our" — he pointed to Noah — "sister?"

"I'm with Caleb on this," Noah said. "What are your intentions toward Rylee?"

Amar looked back and forth at the two tall and commanding men. He appreciated that they were looking after their sister, but he also wouldn't be intimidated. "As I said at dinner last night, it's still too early to tell what Rylee and I are to each other, but I do know that I want to find out. Rylee is beautiful, smart, funny and passionate. She's unlike any woman I've ever known, and I want to see where this goes."

"You mean you just want to sex up my sister until the itch goes away?" Caleb asked, taking a step toward him.

"There's no need to be crass," Noah said, putting an arm in front of Caleb to hold him back. "We're all grown men here."

"I'm sorry you're taking it that way, Caleb," Amar said, "but I'm here because I want to be. I came back to the

States to see Rylee the day my father was released from the hospital after his heart attack. I came back because I care. If that's not good enough for you, I don't know what else to tell you."

"I guess that's going to have to be good enough for now," Noah replied. "And Caleb and I appreciate you being a man about it."

"Speak for yourself." Caleb pushed past Noah to go back to his horse, and he quickly jumped astride it. "Time will tell if you're good enough for my sister." He gave his horse a little kick and galloped off.

Amar turned to Noah. "Is he always that much of a hot-head?"

Noah laughed. "Always."

The week with Amar was idyllic for Rylee. He spent most of his days with her brothers in the field, but would sometimes stop in the stables or at the petting farm or wherever Rylee happened to be to check in on her or have lunch with her.

The nights were even more wonderful. They spent them in her room, his room or in the guest quarters, making the most of their time together, exploring each other's bodies or staying up to the wee hours of the morning just talking. She knew it would come to an end one day, but she hadn't expected his last day to be so eventful.

Everyone was gathered in the living room, as was the custom before dinner, having beer, cocktails, or in her father's case, whiskey, when the doorbell rang.

Rylee hadn't been expecting anyone, and she certainly wasn't prepared for Jeremy to come bounding in. He stopped dead in his tracks when he surveyed the room and saw Amar sitting next to her. All conversation immediately ceased at the unexpected visitor. Rylee could feel Amar tense up beside her as he sat on the arm of the couch where she and her parents were.

Chynna looked across the room at her with questioning eyes. She had no idea why Jeremy had come. If she had, she would have never agreed to have him stop by.

Her mother was the first to react. She was never one to lose her manners. "Jeremy," she said, opening her arms toward him as he stood frozen at the doorway, "what a pleasant surprise."

"Mama Hart." Jeremy accepted her hug even though shock and anger registered across his face at the sight of an interloper, who appeared to be embraced by his second family. "I didn't know you had company," he said as he walked into the room.

"You know you're always welcome here, boy." Her father rose from the sofa and gave him a big bear hug. *"Always."* He patted Jeremy's back.

Rylee noted his emphasis on the word *always* as if Amar's hospitality in his home might be temporary.

"Would you like a drink?" her father asked.

"I think he needs one," Caleb said from his usual perch by the mantel. "I'll make it." He rushed toward the wet bar and began throwing ice cubes into a tumbler.

"Jeremy, I believe you know Amar Bishop," Madelyn Hart offered, inclining her head toward Amar, who immediately rose to his feet.

"Yes, we've met," Jeremy said through clenched teeth before turning his gaze to Rylee. If she could blink and remove herself from this awkward position, she would. The way he looked at her with such hurt tore at her heart. "Rylee, how are you?"

"I'm great," Rylee eked out.

Caleb walked over and handed Jeremy a glass of whiskey.

"I can tell. You look happier than the last time I saw you." Jeremy accepted the glass from Caleb and gulped it. He turned his gaze away from Rylee and placed it back on her father. "I'm sorry to come by without calling, but my father wanted me to give you some paperwork on the steers you were buying from us." Jeremy reached behind him in his jeans pocket and produced an envelope. "I guess next time I'll call first."

"Thanks," Isaac Hart said, taking the package. "Why don't we look these over right now?"

"Dinner is served," Peggy suddenly announced from the doorway.

"Maybe not just yet then," Isaac said. "How about some dinner, son?" He grabbed Jeremy by the shoulder and began walking him out of the room.

Rylee turned to her mother and gave her a look. Her mother shrugged and rose to follow her husband. Noah, Chynna and Caleb couldn't escape quick enough, leaving Rylee and Amar alone.

Rylee turned to Amar. She could see he was seething at her father's blatant disregard for his feelings in asking Jeremy to join them for dinner. "I'm sorry."

"It's not your fault," he said with a frown. "This is your family's home, and they are welcome to invite whomever they choose, no matter how much I disagree."

"We can leave," Rylee offered. "Go out to dinner?"

Amar shook his head. "I wouldn't give him the satisfaction." He reached for Rylee's hand and nearly dragged her to her feet. "Let's go."

Dinner was an uncomfortable affair, probably worse than Amar's first evening at the ranch. Everyone was on pins and needles waiting for a fight to break out between Amar and Jeremy. But neither man rose to challenge the other. Instead, they chose the ultimate face-off to see who could stare down whom.

Rylee doubted it was a coincidence that Caleb happened to sit next to her, leaving Jeremy to sit next to Noah and Chynna. Her brother loved to stir the pot, and having both men stare each other down was just too hard for him to resist.

"How's Kenya doing?" Rylee asked, desperate to lighten the mood. She'd heard that Chynna's twin had been cast in yet another big movie role.

"Couldn't be better. She begins filming in Carter Wright's new movie soon," Chynna answered.

"Your sister, Kenya," Amar asked, "She played Yvette in his other film and won the Oscar, right? She was brilliant."

Chynna smiled, beaming with pride. "Yes, she did."

"Weren't you supposed to play that role?" Amar sipped his wine.

"I was, but I'm a much better singer than I am an actress. Thank God Kenya stepped in."

"Where are you off to next?" Rylee asked, thankful a conversation had started.

"I'm starting the European leg of my next tour and will be hitting London, Paris, Amsterdam and Brussels. I want to finish up before I'm into my second trimester."

"And you?" Jeremy asked, looking at Amar as he spoke. "Where are you off to now that Bishop Enterprises has expanded into the UK and is considering buying some hi-tech companies on the other side of the Atlantic?"

Rylee turned to Amar and her brow shot up in surprise. In all of their long in-depth conversations, he'd mentioned nothing about going to Europe, and she had no idea what that would mean for their budding romance.

Amar glared at Jeremy from across the table. He knew what the man was after. He wanted to cause trouble for him and Rylee, and he was off to a good start. Rylee was already giving him the doe-eyed look from his side as if he'd betrayed her by not telling her about his potential business move. The deal was still in the works, and the ink wasn't even dry on it. How could Jeremy have known?

Amar also noticed that Rylee's parents and her brothers wanted to know the answer to Jeremy's question. He had been completely upfront with them about his intentions toward Rylee, but now Jeremy was making him seem disingenuous, as if he planned to abandon Rylee just as soon as the deal was finished.

"Nothing is set in stone," Amar said. "We're still fine-tuning the details."

"So you won't be staying in Tucson?" Jeremy pressed, cocking his head to one side.

"My plans, whatever they may be, are between Rylee and me," Amar said directly to Jeremy.

The two men stared at each other for several long seconds before Jeremy wiped his mouth with his napkin and rose from the table. "Mama Hart, thank you for dinner as always, but I really must be going. Isaac, we can conclude our business another time when it's just family and when guests aren't in town. And Rylee, I'm sure we'll be seeing each other since you'll have a lot of free time on your hands soon."

Jeremy flipped his cowboy hat to the women and turned on his heel to leave.

Amar suddenly rose from the table, his dark eyes ablaze with fury, and nearly knocked the chair behind him to the floor. It was Caleb's quick hand that caught it before the chair crashed. Amar would not tolerate being disrespected, least of all by Jeremy, a lesser man and one who didn't hold a candle to him. He was ready to go outside and teach him a lesson he wouldn't forget.

"Easy now." Noah rose from the other side of the table.

The smug look on Jeremy's face from the doorway was all Amar needed to settle down. He hated that he'd let the bastard get under his skin. Slowly, he sat back in his chair, refusing to look at Rylee as he reached for his wine glass and took a sip.

"Now that was a powder keg situation," Caleb said once Jeremy left.

"Oh, shut up, Caleb," the Hart family said in unison.

Chapter 14

"I'M SORRY ABOUT DINNER," RYLEE said as she and Amar prepared for bed later that evening in her bedroom. She'd just finished washing her face and brushing her teeth, and Amar was still as quiet as he'd been since dinner had ended.

Everyone had recognized the evening was a bust and had retired to their separate corners. Rylee's parents had gone to sit out on the porch swing while Noah and Chynna went for a moonlit walk. And Caleb, well Lord knows where Caleb had gone, probably off to some woman's room.

Amar had undressed and slipped into his night clothes without a word. Rylee had never seen him this way before. His eyes were icy and unresponsive as he sat on her bed in his silk pajama bottoms with no shirt as he doodled on his iPad.

"It's fine," he finally commented in response to her statement about dinner, but he didn't look at her.

"I highly doubt it's fine," Rylee spat and stormed over to the balcony. She swung open the French doors and looked out over the starry night. She didn't know who she was more upset at — Jeremy for coming over uninvited and trying to start a fight, or Amar for almost letting it happen.

A few moments later, she heard footsteps behind her and noticed Amar had joined her on the balcony. His massive arms circled her waist as he pulled her close. "I'm sorry," he whispered, kissing her neck.

"Sorry?" Rylee asked, spinning around to face him. "It wasn't my fault Jeremy came here. *I* didn't ask him to stay."

"No, you didn't," Amar replied stonily and pushed away. "But your father did. Clearly, he thinks Jeremy, a good ol' boy, is the better choice for you." He tugged up his pajama bottoms in a mocking fashion.

"Don't you dare mock our simple country lifestyle," Rylee said. "We work hard for every luxury we have here."

"And I haven't?" Amar said.

"That's not what I said."

"You didn't have to. Your whole family," Amar said, pointing through the open door, "thinks I'm some rich playboy playing cowboy. They don't take me seriously as a suitor for you."

"Who cares what they think?"

"I do!" Amar pounded his chest with his fist. "I want them to think *I'm* the man for you, not some Neanderthal who gambles away the best thing that ever happened to him. And I'm not just talking about the horse."

Rylee's expression softened, and she slid back next to him. "The only people's opinions that matter are mine and yours."

"That's easy for you to say, Rylee. You've never been told you're not good enough, that you're less than. I've felt that way my entire life. I don't want to feel that way with you or your family."

Rylee touched his cheek. She could see the anguish in those murky depths. "You're good enough for me," she said, brushing her lips across his.

"Are you sure about that?" Amar asked, looking down at her. He wasn't sure why he was feeling so insecure, but he was and needed reassurance. He kissed her back, keeping it light. "'Cause Jeremy isn't giving up on you. I saw it in his eyes tonight, the way he looked at you with such hunger. I wanted to punch him in the face."

Rylee smiled. "I'm sure, because I don't want Jeremy." Her arms curved around his neck, and she drew his head toward hers. "I only want you," she said seconds before her tongue invaded his mouth.

She coaxed a response from him as she deepened the kiss and pressed against him, pushing him backward against stucco. Every stroke of her tongue caused his penis to swell and a shudder to run up his spine, even now when he was upset. But he wasn't upset with Rylee. In a short time, she'd become everything to him.

He shifted his stance so he could put one thigh between her legs. He could feel her heat emanating from the flimsy negligee she wore. He wanted it off her. Now.

He hooked a thumb under the strap of the negligee and bared her shoulder to him, nibbling tiny kisses down her shoulders and neck until the strap slid lower and revealed a breast. He leaned forward to take it in his mouth and sucked hard; she arched toward him, and he accepted her weight.

Her eyes were closed as she tipped her head back and offered herself to him. He took her, sucking her other breast with equal fervor. When he completed his ministrations, he moved upward so he could kiss her hard and run his fingers through her hair. Then he darted his tongue inside her mouth. She returned his ardor by gripping his butt and pushing the pajama bottoms he wore down, freeing his erect penis against her.

Amar lifted Rylee's negligee, and his hands went to make work of the little scrap of fabric she called panties, but he found she wasn't wearing any.

His brow rose. "Naughty girl."

"Only for you. Only for you."

Amar hoisted Rylee in his arms, lifted her legs around his hips until his penis was at the apex of her womanhood and then plunged inside. He shuddered into her warmth.

"Oh, God, Amar, this feels ..." Rylee didn't know how to describe it. Wonderful. Unbearable. Delicious. Thrilling. The sensation of Amar's hot, sweaty chest on her heaving bosom with him deep inside her was heady. She wrapped her arms around his neck and captured his mouth in a hungry kiss. Her body had a mind of its own and began to move frantically up and down on his penis. "Harder. Faster," she urged.

He slammed her back against the stucco and surged further inside her with power and heat and lust. In. Out. In. Out. Everything within her began to tighten as Amar devoured her mouth. Lust and heat fused together, and her breath began to hitch.

"Amar!" His mouth muffled her scream as her back arched and the full force of her climax hit her. Slowly, Amar pulled out, lowering her to her feet. Her legs felt like noodles and before she knew what was happening, Amar was carrying her to her bed, pushing back the comforter and laying her down.

She glanced up at him through pleasure-sated eyes. "You didn't come."

"I couldn't, **habibti**," Amar said, "We were not protected, and even then we took a risk."

"What does **habibti** mean?"

"My love," Amar responded through heavy-lidded eyelashes. "It's a term of endearment. Occasionally my Arabic comes out when I least expect it."

"About the protection ... I wasn't thinking." Rylee began to sit up. She hadn't even though about the fact that they'd just had sex without a condom. She'd been so caught up in the incredible moment of being with Amar with no emotional filters that she'd simply forgotten.

"No apologies," Amar said, squeezing her nose as he looked at her. "We are both responsible. In that moment, I wanted you just as much as you wanted me. That just means you're going to have to make it up to me to ensure I come."

"Is that so?"

"Oh, yes," Amar said, lying back on the pillows. He reached for a condom on her nightstand and slid it onto his still-erect member. He pulled Rylee atop him. "Here's your opportunity to make it up to me."

She made it up to him all night long.

"You guys did it on the balcony?" Camryn asked the following day on the telephone when Rylee called to dish about the hot sexual encounter she'd shared with Amar.

"Girl, yes, and can I tell you, it was hot, hot, hot." Rylee fanned herself with her free hand.

"Omigod!" Camryn put her fist in her mouth to keep from screaming at work. She didn't want the other reporters at the newspaper to hear her. "I imagine it must have been. Hell, I'm surprised your family didn't hear the screams from the opposite wing."

"Amar muffled them with his kisses," Rylee whispered, glancing around her on the front porch to make sure no one was listening. She'd come outside with her coffee later that morning for some privacy.

"You sexy diva, you," Camryn said. "So, what's next for you two? Do I hear wedding bells?"

"Wedding bells?" Rylee asked in horror. "It's too soon for that kind of talk, Camryn." The thought had crossed her mind during his stay, but she'd tried to push down those images. "We've only known each other a couple of weeks."

"That may be so, but didn't your parents fall in love at first sight?" When Rylee remained silent, Camryn continued, "And Noah and Chynna? They fell in love during her stay on the ranch too. Tell me you can't see you and Amar together."

"That's the problem, Camryn." Rylee let out a sigh. "I can. I can see a future with Amar, but he's not known for sticking it out for the long haul. Heck, his own magazines have done articles about him as the interminable playboy. About the only thing he holds on to are his companies, but women? Not even."

"Who's to say you can't be the exception, not the rule?"

"I don't know, Cam. We're so different. And from different worlds, how would we make that work? I mean Amar lives in Palo Alto, and I live here."

"So? There are ranches in California."

"True. But what about his lineage? His father is a sheikh."

"Your father is a hard-working rancher, so what? It doesn't make Amar better than you. Only unique."

"Wow! When you put it like that, it makes it seem like I'm not proud of my dad and what he and mom have achieved, and I am."

"Listen, Rylee, that's not what I'm saying. Hear this — you can come up with a myriad of reasons why it won't work between the two of you. No one ever said this love thing was easy, but look at Noah and Chynna. She's a superstar for Christ's sake, but she still comes home to Tucson to be with Noah, because she *loves* him. Surely if both of them are willing to make it work, you two can make a go of it."

"You really think so?"

"I know so."

Amar had been listening to Rylee from the front doorway. Rylee had no idea that he'd overheard her entire conversation with Camryn. He hadn't meant to eavesdrop,

168

but when he'd heard his name, he hadn't been able to resist. Not only had he learned just how much Rylee had enjoyed their passionate encounter on the balcony, he'd heard what she wasn't telling him, which was that she feared their relationship would end.

And he had his playboy reputation to thank for her uneasiness. He wished he could say it wasn't true, hadn't been true up until now, but it was. He'd run away from every relationship that turned serious. If a woman got too clingy, too needy, wanted too much, he showed her the door. But Rylee was different. She had been from the start.

He'd felt a peace and serenity with her that he hadn't known existed, that he had been searching for his entire life. She was his harbor in the storm of life. Her family, on the other hand, was a little more difficult. Amar knew he'd won over Madelyn with her sweet, yet classy disposition. Noah, he'd earned his respect by his willingness to work hard in the field from sunup to sundown. Amar made it a point to eat and stay with all the ranch hands until the day was over.

Rylee's father, Isaac, and her brother Caleb were another matter altogether. Amar recognized Caleb for the sly fox he was. Caleb was a ladies man, so he recognized one when he saw one. And to his credit, a couple of weeks ago, Caleb would have been right about Amar's love 'em and leave 'em reputation, but the moment he'd set eyes on Rylee, Amar hadn't wanted or so much as looked at another woman. Amar knew that with a little time and resilience, Caleb would come around his way.

Her father, however, would be a tough nut to crack, and that's what made it worse, because her father's respect was what Amar wanted the most. He supposed it had something to do with his own relationship with the Sheikh. He yearned for a father figure, for someone to believe in him, to respect him. But Isaac Hart had his heart set on Jeremy Wright. Jeremy was not the man for Rylee.

Not only did he not possess the charisma or personality, but he didn't have that fire in his belly that a man would need to keep up with a woman like Rylee.

Amar was that man. He hadn't yet figured out how to make a long-distance relationship work between them. Didn't even know if that was the route they would go. The one thing he did know was he didn't want to spend his nights without Rylee by his side.

Amar's cell phone rang in his jeans pocket, and he fished it out without looking at the display. "Hello," he asked, trying to catch the call.

"Amar?"

It was Tariq. This was the second call he'd received from his brother, and something told him it wasn't good news. He moved away from the front door and began to pace the foyer entrance.

"What's happened?"

"It's father. He-he's taken ... a turn for the worse," Tariq responded with a choked voice. "Had another heart attack last night. The doctor's—"

Amar didn't let him finish his sentence. "I'm on my way."

"Hurry, Amar. There isn't much time."

Amar ended the call and took the stairs to Rylee's suite two at a time. He called Sharif to get the jet — which he'd kept grounded at Tucson International — fueled and ready. It would take a couple of hours to get the plane and flight plan good-to-go, but that would be enough time for Amar to pack and get to the airport and return the SUV he'd rented.

He burst through the door of Rylee's bedroom and searched frantically for his suitcase. After the first few nights in different rooms, he and Rylee had long since given up the pretense of separate bedrooms and had begun to sleep in hers.

He found his suitcase in a nearby corner where the maid must have put it when she came to tidy Rylee's room. He rushed over and opened the double doors to her closet and immediately began snatching clothes off the hanger and throwing them inside the suitcase, no thought to care or wrinkles. He had to get home. He was so busy throwing clothes into the suitcase and running back and forth from the bedroom to the bathroom that he didn't notice Rylee come in until she was standing right in front of him.

"Amar?" She looked at him questioningly as he tossed his toiletry bag into his luggage. "What's going on?"

Amar glanced up, barely seeing her. "It's my father. He's had a massive heart attack. They don't give him much time. I have to go."

"I'm so sorry." Rylee rushed to him and tried to hug him, but he disengaged her arms and went back to his task. "Is he okay?" she asked, confused, staring at him.

Amar shook his head, not looking up. "Don't know." He brushed past her to walk to the nightstand and grabbed his iPad. He began stuffing it and several file folders he'd been reviewing into his briefcase.

"What can I do?" Feeling helpless, Rylee watched him rush around the room frantically.

At her question, Amar glanced up. "There's nothing you can do, baby. I wish there were." He zipped up his suitcase, grabbed his briefcase and began heading toward her bedroom door.

"Wait!" Rylee grabbed his arm. "You're going alone? I mean—"

"What? What is it?" Amar yelled through a cloudy haze of anxiety and grief. He couldn't think straight. Time was running out. He had to get to Nasir. He had to see the Sheikh one last time.

"Nothing," Rylee responded, "nothing. You just go."

"I'll call you when I land," Amar said and rushed out the door.

Tears had filled Rylee's eyes when Amar brushed past her and out of her bedroom. She hadn't known what to do to comfort him over his father's imminent passing, but she certainly hadn't expected him to shut her out so thoroughly. He'd acted as if she were invisible or barely existed as he'd stuffed his belongings into his luggage.

She'd thought their time together had meant more to him. She'd thought in his time of need that he would lean on her, maybe even want her to come with him. She'd never expected him to turn as cold as ice.

She threw herself on her bed and began sobbing.

Several minutes later, she felt a reassuring rub on her back as someone let her release all her agony at Amar's abrupt departure.

"It's okay," Chynna whispered. "Whatever happened, it's going to be okay."

"How can you say that?" Rylee asked, glancing up at Chynna, her eyes brimming with tears. "Amar's gone."

"Gone? Why? What could have happened to change things so drastically between you?"

"It's not us," Rylee said, sitting up on the bed. "At least not directly. His father suffered another heart attack, and this one's bad. They don't think he's going to make it."

"Omigod!" Chynna's hand flew to her mouth.

"I know, right?" Rylee nodded. "It's terrible. And you would think Amar would want the woman he's been spending time with the last couple of weeks with him, but did he ask me to go with him? No! Instead, he just pushed me away."

"Cut him a little slack," Chynna said. "He's under terrible duress right now, Rylee. Losing a parent isn't easy. I know."

Rylee glanced up and saw a sadness wash over Chynna. For a moment she'd been so caught up in her own grief that she'd forgotten that Chynna and Kenya had lost their mother not too long ago.

"I'm sorry, Chynna. I was being selfish."

Chynna sniffed. "It's okay." She patted Rylee's arm. "But you have to know that Amar is beside himself and not thinking clearly. You need to think clearly for the both of you."

"I don't understand." Rylee's brow crinkled in a frown.

"I mean, if you want to go with Amar to his home country to be there for him in his time of need, then you need to pack a bag and follow him."

"But he didn't ask me."

"Should he have to?" Chynna challenged with her arms folded across her growing bosom.

Rylee thought about Chynna's question. Amar was in the middle of a life-altering experience and she couldn't expect him to think rationally, but she could be the clear-minded one. "I'm going with him," Rylee said, rushing toward her closet. "You're right," she said, looking back at Chynna. "I have to go to him. Show him that I will stand by him no matter what. Show him I have his back in the toughest of times."

A broad smile spread across Chynna's face. "There's my girl. Go get your man!"

Rylee had precious little time to pack. She threw what she could into her suitcase as Amar had, including shoes, purses, toiletries and her makeup, all the while using her Bluetooth to speak to Sharif to find out where she could find Amar. He'd been shocked to hear from her since their last meeting had been far from pleasant, but he agreed to help her.

Noah on the other hand hadn't been too happy to drive her at a breakneck pace to the airport. As much as he'd begrudgingly begun to warm up to Amar, he wasn't on board with her decision. "I don't like this, sis. I don't like this one bit. You're going off to some strange country we know nothing about. What if something happens to you over there? Mom and Dad would never forgive me."

"Nothing's going to happen to me," Rylee replied. "Amar will take care of me."

"Are you sure about that? He just up and left the ranch without you."

"Wouldn't you drop everything if something happened to Mom and Dad?"

"Of course I would, but I would take Chynna with me."

"Even during the early stages, when you'd just found out she'd lied to you about who she was?" Rylee's brow rose as she invoked the memory of Chynna pretending to be her twin and lying to Noah about her real name. "I know you're worried, but I got this."

"Alright, sis," Noah said as he slid the pickup truck into a nearby parking space at the departure terminal and turned off the engine. "Promise me you'll take care of yourself."

"I will." Rylee leaned over and planted a wallop of a kiss on his cheek. Seconds later, her passenger door flung open, and she'd grabbed her suitcase from the back compartment and ran for the terminal.

Amar paced the small floor of the Learjet as he waited for clearance so they could take off. The pilot had informed him there had been a delay from air traffic control. Amar couldn't afford delays; he had to get to Dubai. The trip would already take him nearly a day, and he wasn't sure that his father had that much time. There was so much left unsaid between them. Would he get the chance to say his peace? Or would fate intervene and take his father as it had tragically taken his mother?

He was sure his family would think him heartless for having left in the first place. They would say his place was by the Sheikh's side, but Amar didn't, couldn't, regret his decision to come back to the States and be with Rylee. If he hadn't, he would have never known that Rylee could be *the one.* The one woman he was meant to spend the rest of his life with.

He knew some believed him to be unfeeling and heartless, but they were wrong. Deep down he was a romantic and believed in soulmates. How else to explain that a few weeks ago he'd been going about his everyday life seeing the world in black and white. Then he met Rylee. Suddenly the world was in Technicolor. There was a kick in his step, and a current shot through him every time he was around her.

And it wasn't just lust either. Lust he could explain away. What they had was chemistry ... and something more. He'd gotten to know her, and she had every quality he could want: She was sexy. Beautiful. Smart. Funny. Caring. Giving. And he'd enjoyed every minute with her on her family ranch and would have continued had it not been for Tariq's call. Only one question remained: *Can this be love?*

He got his answer when the door to the plane swung open and Rylee came rushing into the cabin.

Chapter 15

"AMAR!" RYLEE THREW HERSELF INTO his muscled arms. He caught her, nearly falling backward onto the seat, but he righted himself. His shocked expression was priceless.

"Rylee? What are you doing here?"

Rylee smiled as he slowly released her and looked at him. "I'm going with you."

"You are?"

Rylee nodded. "I know it might seem presumptuous of me as you didn't ask me to come, but I felt like you needed me just as I needed to be here." She wasn't sure he'd heard her because he'd stared at her as if she'd suddenly sprouted a horn on top of her head. "Did you hear me?"

"Yes," Amar said, nodding, "and I couldn't be happier."

"Really?"

"Of course. The moment I learned about my father, all I could think about was getting to Nasir. It never occurred to me that you would be willing to leave your family to come with me."

Rylee reached for his hands and stared into his dark eyes. "Then you still have a lot to learn about me," she replied, "because I'm loyal, and I will be there when someone I—" She caught herself from nearly saying *love* because she wasn't quite ready to say that word. So she rephrased it: "I will be there for someone I care about."

"And you consider me on that list?"

Rylee answered him: She wrapped her arms around his neck and gave him a slow, lingering kiss.

"You have no idea what this means to me," Amar whispered, pulling her closer.

On the plane ride from Tucson to New York's JFK airport, Rylee and Amar talked nonstop about anything other than how he was truly feeling about the fact he could lose his father. She figured it was a coping mechanism, and she wouldn't push him until he was ready to face the facts.

She would, however, remember the nearly thirteen-hour flight from JFK to Dubai and subsequent hour flight to Nasir as she'd only slept off and on. The accommodations on the private liner were comfortable, including a king-sized bed in the back of the cabin, but she'd tossed and turned worrying about what to expect in the country and how Amar's family would treat her. If he felt like an outcast, how would she fit in?

She managed a shower in the tiny stall provided in the miniscule restroom, and it perked her up somewhat before landing. When she emerged, Amar had a pot of coffee waiting for her. Rylee sat beside him on the couch and buckled herself in.

"I'm sorry it's not much," Amar said as he poured her a cup, "but it was all I could manage with the limited facilities."

Rylee half-smiled. "It's fine." She accepted the steaming mug and took a generous sip.

"You normally don't drink it black," Amar commented.

Rylee's brow crinkled. She hadn't realized he'd been paying such close attention to her habits. "I, uh, need something a little stronger this morning."

"You did not sleep well," Amar stated.

"Neither did you."

"There is much to think about."

Rylee nodded. "Is there anything I can do?"

"Actually, there is." Amar reached toward a box that Rylee hadn't noticed sitting on the table in front of them. He sat it on his lap and opened it, lifting out a hijab. The veil was a colorful pink print made of silk. "I will need you to wear this. It is custom in Nasir for women."

Rylee accepted the veil. She'd anticipated that she might need to dress differently and had packed some modest slacks, tops and a few loose-fitting shift dresses. She didn't want to embarrass Amar or have people looking down at her as a Western woman. "Thank you. I'll put it on."

This time, Amar half-smiled. "Thank you," he said, stroking her cheek. "I need you to understand that Nasir is not like Dubai. It's still knee deep in old traditions, and women are not permitted the same luxuries as in America. You must stay close to me at all times."

"And should I be seen and not heard too?" Rylee scoffed. As soon as she said the words, she wished she could take them back because Amar seemed mortally offended by her comment and glared at her. "I'm sorry," she said. "I was trying to lighten the mood."

"This is serious, Rylee. And you need to hear me. You must realize that you're in a different country now. You can't say things like that, even in jest. It would be considered disrespectful and frowned upon. Do you understand?"

"Yes."

"Good." He reached for her hand and squeezed it gently. "Then follow my lead."

The plane landed thirty minutes later, pretty much in the middle of a desert, and Rylee knew that Amar had been right. As they'd flown from Dubai and she looked through the window, she could see them moving farther and farther away from Western civilization. Eventually, an old city had materialized in the middle of the desert, straight out of a movie.

Rylee had never seen anything like it. She must have had a wide-eyed look on her face because Amar asked, "Overwhelming?" He took her hand as he helped her down the staircase to the tarmac.

"A little," Rylee said.

By this point, Amar was wearing a dishdāshah, a traditional ankle-length garment with long sleeves, much like a robe Rylee had seen Arab men wear. But she'd never seen Amar in this vein, and it was unsettling.

She was wearing the hijab as requested and was glad of it. Amar had been right when he'd said she'd be out of her element. A dark SUV was waiting for them along with what appeared to be two bodyguards surveying the landscape. Rylee wondered whether they were in danger as the driver got out of the car and began loading their suitcases into the back of the SUV under the watchful eyes of the guards.

"It's just a precaution." Amar must have read her thoughts when he saw her eyeing the guards suspiciously.

"Against what?" she asked.

"With father on his deathbed, some might see me as a threat."

"But you're not in the line of succession."

"Very true, which is why it's just a precaution. Come." Amar opened the passenger door. "It's a short ride to the palace."

Palace? Rylee thought. She felt like Dorothy in *The Wizard of Oz*. She was a long way from Kansas.

Rylee slid inside the SUV, and Amar joined her.

When the driver was finished loading their bags, he and the bodyguards jumped inside the vehicle and they all took off toward the palace.

As they drove through the city, Amar pointed out several places of interest, but nothing he said could squash the butterflies flying around in Rylee's stomach. She was about to meet Amar's family, and the thought terrified her.

When they arrived to the estate, large wooden doors opened and Rylee nearly lost her breath as the palace came into view. Nothing could have prepared her for the sheer luxury of it all. The SUV stopped, her passenger door swung open, and the bodyguard who'd been sitting in the front seat helped her out.

"Thank you," she said. He didn't speak. He merely nodded.

Before Amar could come around for her, a tall dishdāshah-clad olive-toned man with straight jet-black hair opened the palace doors and came rushing toward them. "Amar, I'm so glad you're here."

He greeted Amar with a warm hug, and Rylee instantly knew he had to be his brother Tariq. They shared the same facial features though not the same hair. Amar pulled away and grabbed Tariq's shoulders, which were just as broad as his. "Father?"

"He's still holding on," Tariq answered. "I think long enough so you could get here."

"How sentimental of you, Tariq," another man said from behind. He wasn't quite as tall as Tariq and Amar, but he had the same dark hair and olive complexion as Tariq, yet unlike Tariq's warm brown eyes, his were cold and distant. Rylee was sure he had to be Khalid, the middle brother and next in line to be King.

"Don't start, Khalid," Tariq warned.

"I'm not starting anything," Khalid replied. "Father's favorite is here, and he can die in peace."

"Of course you would think so," Amar replied, rolling his eyes. "I need to go to him, but first, I'd like you both to meet Rylee." Amar turned and reached for Rylee's hand.

She tentatively accepted and moved toward the tense group.

"This is Rylee Hart."

"You brought your mistress here to the palace when Father's on his deathbed? You can't be without her for a few days?" Khalid asked. "I should have known that you wouldn't show common decency."

Amar let go of Rylee's hand and stepped toward his brother. Rylee didn't like the dangerous look in his eyes. He looked ready to murder Khalid on the spot. "Rylee is not my mistress. She's my girlfriend."

"Your *girlfriend*?" Khalid and Tariq said aloud as if the thought was utterly ridiculous. *Has Amar never introduced a woman to his family before?* Rylee wondered.

"Yes," Amar stated, "my girlfriend. And you would do well to remember that and treat her with the same courtesies as I extend to your wife, you got that?" He poked his index finger into Khalid's chest.

Khalid rolled his eyes. "As you wish. I doubt she'll last long anyway, as you're known for not keeping the same bed partner for more than a second." He turned on his heel and walked back inside the palace.

Rylee blanched. Khalid's words cut her to the quick as he'd intended, and Amar quickly turned around to face her.

"I'm sorry about that," he said, taking her hands and brushing his lips across them. "Khalid and I don't get along."

"Th-that's an understatement," Rylee said, finding her voice. She refused to show just how hurt she'd been by Khalid's words.

"Let's go inside," Tariq interrupted them, "so you can freshen up and go see Father."

Tariq led them through the marble hallway filled with what Rylee could only imagine were priceless artifacts and works of art. The palace was like something out of a movie or fairytale, and she marveled at the crown mouldings made of gold and the two-story columns. Tariq led them up a marble staircase to the second floor of the palace and then down a long corridor before stopping at a door.

He swung it open, and Rylee's mouth dropped at the lush décor. It housed a large canopy bed swathed with lavish silks. Fine draperies hung from the windows. "This is your suite," Tariq said. "I will send up one of the ladies to assist you with your unpacking while Amar and I go see Father."

"Thank you." Rylee half-smiled.

"I'll be back soon," Amar said from the door as Tariq closed it behind them, leaving Rylee alone with her thoughts.

Rylee was unsure of what to do first. Should she unpack, or should she look around? She chose the latter and used her time alone to peruse the suite of rooms, because that's exactly what it was. The suite included their sleeping quarters, a study, and a large bathroom with a rainfall shower and sunken tub that could easily fit half a dozen people and a living area with a balcony the size of her bedroom back at Golden Oaks. She stepped out into the warm, muggy air and took a deep breath to steady her shaky nerves as she surveyed the desert.

She glanced toward the door and thought of Amar. He was no doubt about to say goodbye to his father, a man with whom he shared a complicated history. He would need someone to lean on during this emotional time, but Khalid's earlier comment had her wondering if she'd made the right decision to come here.

The fact that Amar had called her his girlfriend, even though they'd never discussed exactly what they were to each other, was promising. But the flip side of the coin was that he needed a soft place to land and once it was over, he'd be on to his next conquest. Rylee wasn't sure she could take that. Amar had come to mean something to her, and she had strong feelings for him that she wasn't ready to say out loud — feelings that began with the letter "L".

"You brought a woman with you?" Tariq commented as he and Amar walked swiftly down the palace corridors. "I must admit I'm shocked by this, Amar."

"I didn't invite her," Amar replied as they turned the corner and began walking toward the Sheikh's wing of the palace. "She came to the airport and met me, but I have to tell you, when she came through the jet's doors, I wished I had because I'd never been happier to see anyone in my entire life."

"Sounds like you really like this woman."

"It's more than *like*," Amar said just as they reached the Sheikh's door, which was flanked on both sides by two bodyguards. They nodded to Tariq and Amar before allowing them in.

Amar walked inside the partially darkened room and saw Saffron sitting in a chair by his father's bedside. His once-vibrant, commanding father lay still on a custom-built bed.

Saffron rose when they approached.

"How is he?" Amar asked.

When he got closer, he could see she'd been crying and held a handkerchief in her hand.

"He's been anxious and restless," she murmured. "I think he's been waiting for you, Amar. He couldn't go without seeing you one final time." She began to sob and then rushed out of the room.

"Is that you, son?" his father's voice weakly called.

Amar rushed over to the bed and looked down. The Sheikh had aged two times over since Amar's previous trip to see him in the hospital. "Yes, it's me," Amar said. "I'm here."

"I'll give you two some time alone," Tariq whispered.

Amar glanced up and nodded his thanks before glancing back down at his father. "Are you in any pain? Do you need anything?"

"N-no," the Sheikh replied. "Just you."

"Why me?" Amar didn't understand. They'd never shared a strong father-son connection.

"There's so much to say ...," his father responded, and Amar could only nod in quiet agreement. "I-I've never been a good father to you. Wasn't the father I should have been."

"We don't have to rehash this," Amar said. "You should save your strength."

"I saved it for this moment," his father eked out and reached for Amar's hand, "to tell you that I did you a great disservice. To tell you I'm sorry for how I treated you and your mother. I loved her. I always did and always will."

Amar didn't want to feel anything, but he could feel tears threatening. He refused to be weak, even in this moment.

"Why are you saying this now?"

"Because I need you to know," his father whispered, "that she was the *love of my life*, and so were you."

Amar frowned. "What? What did you just say?" He was confused.

His father motioned Amar closer so he could hear him. Amar leaned forward.

"I didn't know how to love because my father had never shown it to me as his father had never shown him it to him. I tried to show you by giving you the best in life."

"Material possessions never meant anything to me, Father. But you never got that. All I ever wanted was your love and your affection."

"And I couldn't give it. Not with my entire heart, because I knew if I did, I would walk away from everything, from the kingdom, from my responsibilities. And I couldn't do it. I'd been groomed for this life."

"So you chose wealth and power over me and Mother?" Amar stepped away from the bed. Hearing this now was *too* much and *too* late.

"I know," his father murmured, "and I'm ashamed by my actions. It's why it's always been so hard for me to have you around. You were a constant reminder of my shortcomings, of my cowardice."

"And what do you want me to do with this information now?" Amar asked, turning back around to face the man he both loved and hated.

"Forgive me, son." His father reached his hand out to Amar. "Forgive me for my failures as a father."

"You have no idea what you're asking of me." Amar had spent his entire life hating him, all the while wishing that his father had loved him as he did Khalid and Tariq. Now he was saying he loved him, had always loved him, but could Amar believe him?

"I do know what I'm asking, but you're a better man than I."

"Why should I believe anything you've said? You've never shown me one ounce of compassion, of love." Amar shook his head, wrestling with his mind, his conscience, his *soul*.

"Of love?" his father asked. He tried to sit up but couldn't muster the strength, so Amar came back over to help him sit against the pillows. When he did, his father held on to his arm and wouldn't let him go.

"I do love you, Amar. Believe that. *I love you.* Grant me this dying wish, and I promise you will see that I have always loved you."

Amar sat back, momentarily baffled as he stared into his father's dark eyes that mirrored his own. *What is he talking about? I will soon see what?*

His father touched his cheek. "I love you, son."

His words broke through Amar, and Amar said the words he'd never dare utter: "I love you too." A small smile crossed his father's features and with a heavy sigh, he sank into the pillows just as Amar said, "I forgive you."

Several minutes later, Amar found the rest of the family downstairs, and as soon as they saw his face, *they knew.*

"He's gone," Khalid stated rather than asked.

Amar nodded.

Saffron wailed and Freya, Khalid's wife, rushed over to sit with her while Tariq put his head in his hands and wept.

"Then Tariq was right. He was waiting on you," Khalid replied somberly.

Amar didn't say a word. He walked over to the wet bar and poured himself a Scotch, neat. He lifted the tumbler to his lips and let the fiery liquid burn in his throat.

"Arrangements will need to be made," he heard Khalid say. "I'll start tending to them."

And without a word, Khalid walked out of the room. It had to be the first time Khalid hadn't picked a fight with him, and Amar was grateful.

He'd never expected his father to reveal so much in his final moments, and it had shaken Amar to his very core. He needed time to make sense of all he'd heard and all he'd said, but as he looked around the room and took in the grief, he knew now was not it. He may not be next in line as King, but he was the oldest and could help with their grief.

He put down the Scotch and walked over to sit beside Tariq, who crumbled in his arms. "It's okay, brother," Amar said, hugging him tightly. "It's going to be okay."

Rylee thought she would busy herself with unpacking while Amar spoke with his father, but no sooner than she'd gotten started, a knock sounded on her door. Two women were on the other side.

"I am Karam," one of the women stated. She was tall, slender, had a dark-olive complexion and wore a simple hijab over her dress. "And this is Basheera." The other woman was petite and similarly attired. "She doesn't speak good English, so I will speak on our behalf." When Karam saw Rylee's open suitcase on the bed, she colored. "We will assist you with anything you need during your stay. You need not unpack."

Rylee smiled. "Why, thank you, but it's really not necessary. I can unpack myself."

"No," Karam said. "You are Amar's mistress. We must take care of you."

"Mistress?" There was that word again. It made her feel sleazy.

She must have looked uneasy, because Karam came to her. "I have offended you and I'm sorry, but you and Amar are lovers, are you not?"

Rylee nodded reluctantly. It was strange having her relationship acknowledged so commonly.

"We will ensure you are ready for him when he returns. He will need you," Karam advised. "We will draw a bath for you and bring you some hot tea and a sweet platter of baklava, basbousa and mugasgas. I imagine you must be hungry."

"I could eat a bite."

"Good. You rest on the bed while Basheera and I tidy."

Rylee hadn't wanted to, but she doubted they would have taken no for an answer. They made quick work of putting away her belongings, and Rylee used the time to call home. She'd made quick calls to the family back at the ranch during each of her legs at JFK in New York and Dubai, but she needed to tell them she'd landed safely. She glanced at her watch. Amar had told her there was approximately a thirteen-hour time difference between here and Arizona, so it would be five AM in Tucson. She only knew one person who would be up at this hour.

"Hello?" Noah answered on the other end of the line.

"Noah." Rylee was so happy to hear his voice.

"Rylee? Is that you?"

She could hear his relief. "Yes, it's me."

"Do you have any idea what time it is?"

"Yeah. I knew only one person who would be up at this hour," Rylee replied. "You."

Noah chuckled and poured himself a cup of coffee from the pot that had been set to brew by Peggy the night before. "That's true. How are you? How are they treating you over there? Do I need to come over there and kick some prince's ass?"

Rylee laughed. "No, you don't. Everything's fine. We made it to Nasir about an hour ago. Amar's with his father now."

"Did he make it in time?"

"Yeah," Rylee nodded. "Thank God. I would have felt so guilty if he'd come back to the States for me and his father had died before he'd had a chance to say goodbye."

"It wouldn't have been your fault."

"I know, but I'm glad all the same."

"How long do you think you'll be staying?"

"Not long. A few days, I would think. Amar and his family aren't close."

"Sounds like it's not a bed of roses."

"You could say that again. His family is as cold as ice, Noah. No wonder he likes spending time with our family."

"Well, he would be lucky if you chose him to be a part of it," Noah replied.

"You never know."

"Are you saying you might get hitched to that playboy?"

"I thought you liked Amar."

"I respect Amar, but that doesn't mean I think he's good enough for my baby sister."

"Would anyone be?"

Noah laughed heartily. "No, I don't suppose they would. You keep in touch, ya hear. And you don't let those smug sons of bitches act like they are any better than you. Promise me."

"I promise." A smile spread across Rylee's lips as she hung up. A hearty dose of family was exactly what she needed to get through the next couple of days in this place.

Karam came toward her. "Your bath is ready." She led Rylee to a soaking hot tub. It smelled of shea, coconut and jojoba.

"Thank you." Rylee went to unbutton her shirt, but neither of the women moved a muscle. "I can take it from here, thank you."

Karam nodded and headed toward the door with Basheera. "We are nearby if you need us."

"Thank you, Karam."

Rylee soaked in the tub, sipped tea and ate a few desserts before toweling off and slipping into a plush cashmere robe Karam had left for her. She had just enough energy to lotion her skin before falling backward onto the pillows and taking a nap.

The sound of a door opening and shutting woke her, and she sat up with a start. She must have slept longer than she thought because the room was dark with only moonlight creasing in from the balcony drapes. She could, however, make out Amar's figure as he drew near to her on the bed.

His shoulders were hunched over, and she knew in that moment that his father had passed away. He arrived beside her and sat down. She wasn't sure what to do, but she didn't have to do anything because Amar reached for her and pulled her into his arms. He hugged her to him tightly.

"I'm sorry, Amar," she crooned in his ear. "I'm so sorry."

She felt him shudder, and they hugged each other for what seemed like an eternity before she felt a pull on the robe she was wearing and a rush of cool air hit her. Amar's hands slid around her, and he lowered her backward against the pillows.

Rylee looked up at him. She didn't know what to say. What could she say in a moment like this that wouldn't seem trite and insignificant? So she didn't speak. Instead she offered herself to him as a salve to his pain. She circled her arms around his neck and pulled him down on top of her. She felt his desire swell, and he kissed her with a crazed passion she'd never seen before. He was hungry for her and sucked, tasted and savored every inch of her mouth as if he couldn't get enough of her. She knew he wanted to forget the pain, and she was a willing participant.

Amar didn't speak. He just opened her robe farther so his hands could caress her curves while he kissed and nuzzled the nape of her neck. He slid them down the slope of her breasts, cupping and molding her orbs. He squeezed her nipples, but his hands didn't stop. They traveled lower to her abdomen and stomach before coming to her thighs. He greedily pushed them apart with one hand so his fingers could find her.

He slid two fingers inside her, teasingly. Each touch stirred Rylee and intoxicated her, making her feel guilty that she could experience pleasure in this moment. Her womanhood's swollen lips opened like a flower to his thrusting fingers, and she began to throb. She was on fire.

She wanted his tongue. As if sensing her desire, he lowered himself on the bed and pulled her toward him until his mouth was at her womanhood. She felt his breath on her clitoris as he squeezed her buttocks and dove in. He tongued, licked, and sucked her until she hummed. She tried jerking to free herself, but his tongue just moved deeper inside her, flicking her clitoris as he savored her sex with his tongue and fingers.

Rylee was overwhelmed, and she closed her eyes as her body began to twitch when a powerful orgasm rocked her. As the spasms shook her entire being, she looked up to see Amar hurriedly unzipping his jeans and pushing them to his ankles and ripping off his dishdāshah. She felt his weight as he joined her on the bed. His powerful thighs spread hers apart, and she felt the tip of his erection at her slick center seconds before he thrust inside her.

She let out an encouraging moan as he dove deeper. "Oh ..."

Amar took her boldly, with confidence and skill. He penetrated her over and over, moving his hips like he was dancing a beat from the Islands.

"Oh ...," she moaned as he pumped her hard and relentlessly. She cried out as her pleasure intensified, stroke after stroke. Rylee used her pelvis and squeezed her ankles around his butt to take him even further. She knew he needed this release and she would give it to him. She was his. Tonight. Tomorrow. Forever if he wanted her. She gripped his behind, and Amar let out a curse and shuddered as his orgasm exploded inside her.

Chapter 16

T HE NEXT MORNING WHEN RYLEE awoke in a tangle of damp sheets, she found Amar was already up and sitting on the sofa in the living area, staring off into space. She wondered what he was thinking about. What had transpired between him and his father before he'd passed? Even after they'd made love last night, Amar had said nothing. He'd just held her.

She sat up, not caring that the sheet had fallen away and that she was bare-chested. "Good morning."

Amar glanced up and saw her. "Good morning." He rose and walked over to her. "How are you?"

"I'm fine."

"Are you sure?" he asked, staring into her eyes. "I was a little out of my mind last night and was a bit rough with you."

"You weren't rough. A bit determined, yes, but not rough."

He nodded and sat down beside her. "I, uh, didn't use a condom last night, so if you're pregnant ..."

Rylee put her fingers to her lips. "We'll figure it out," she finished. As much as she should be concerned about their unprotected sex, she wasn't. Even though they had only spent a few weeks together, Rylee knew that whatever happened, Amar would stand beside her.

"I won't be my father."

"I know." She looked into his eyes. He seemed to want to say more, to tell her what had transpired between them, but he didn't.

"Good." Amar rose and began pacing the floor. "Because I wouldn't want you to think that I would abandon you."

"Amar!" Rylee rose from the bed, uncaring of her nakedness, and grabbed his hand. "It's okay. Whatever happens, we'll figure it out. Let's not think about that right now, okay? You have enough on your plate. Is there anything I can do?"

Amar glanced down at her and smiled, just now realizing that she wasn't wearing a stitch of clothing. He bent down for the discarded robe from last night and wrapped it around her. "No, and there's not much *I* can do either. Khalid pretty much has everything handled, except for some business matters."

"Alright." Rylee slipped her hand into each arm of the robe. "What should I do then?"

"Get dressed," Amar said, wickedly glancing at one breast as she closed her robe. "We'll have breakfast downstairs."

Amar wished he would have stayed in the guest quarters for breakfast, as his and Rylee's appearance a half hour later in the formal dining room was met with hostility, except from Tariq.

"Good morning," Rylee said when they walked into the room.

"Good morning, Rylee." Tariq offered a blank smile.

"How can you say it's a good morning when our father is dead?" Khalid scolded.

Rylee blanched, and Amar immediately went on the defensive. He could see Rylee wanted to leave. "Khalid, for

Christ's sake, it's a pleasantry. Can't you act the least bit hospitable?"

Khalid started to say something, but at the murderous look on Amar's face, thought better of it.

Amar guided Rylee to two open seats at the table. Rylee was silent at his side. He felt terrible for the way Khalid had treated her, but he wasn't sorry she was here. She'd been a godsend. His father was dead, and the only thing he'd wanted to do was curl up in a corner and block out the entire world.

But last night, when he'd walked in and seen her bathed in moonlight, she'd been like a balm to his tortured soul and he'd sunk into her lushness. She'd freely offered herself to him even though she'd known he was using her to block out the pain. Rylee Hart was an amazing, selfless woman. He'd never met anyone like her and doubted he would ever again.

He loved her. And when this was all over, he would tell her so. He would tell her that he'd fallen in love with her and wanted to spend the rest of his life waking up with her. He wouldn't be a fool like his father and let the love of his life slip through his fingers for money or power.

"Amar?"

Amar glanced up. "Yes?"

"We were discussing the service and who would give the eulogy," Tariq said.

"It should be me," Khalid said. "I knew him best. Plus, it'll reassure the people of Nasir that I'm in control and they've nothing to fear from outside factions."

"Control of what?" Ibrahim Haddad, their father's lawyer, said from the doorway.

Khalid frowned at him. "Of Nasir. What else? I'm next in line to be King, and the people need to know that there's someone at the helm."

"That might be a bit premature," Ibrahim responded.

"What do you mean?" Khalid said with a dark tone.

"He doesn't mean anything," Amar responded. "Why are you hostile to everyone that comes in the room? You're not the only one who lost Father."

"Are you saying *you* did?" Khalid scoffed. "Like hell! Where have you been the last three decades? Not by father's side, that's for damn sure."

"In case I have to remind you, he was my father too!" Amar replied. "Long before he was yours. C'mon, Rylee." He pulled Rylee's chair back. "I think we'll eat elsewhere." He grabbed her by the hand and led her out of the room.

Once they were no longer within earshot, Amar stopped midstride in the hall and apologized. "I'm sorry, baby. I shouldn't have allowed you to come here into this den of vipers. If it wasn't for Tariq, I wouldn't even be here. I said my peace to Father. I should leave now."

Rylee touched his arm. "You told me your family was harsh, but I never imagined it was this bad." She glanced back at the dining room. "I'm just going to have to develop a thicker skin while we're here, because you can't leave until after the service. And what about your father's will? I imagine he has one, yes? Don't you want to see if he left you anything?"

Amar paused for a moment, remembering what his father had said. *Grant me this dying wish, and I promise you will see that I have always loved you.* Would the will hold any clues to his father's mystery promise? "Okay. Okay. But as soon as the will is read, we're out of here."

A Muslim service was new to Rylee. They'd bathed Amar's father's body and shrouded it in a linen cloth. Then members of the cabinet and other heads of state gathered to offer their collective prayers at the palace and view the deceased before he would be paraded through the streets by carriage so the Nasirian people could say their goodbyes.

Amar was quiet and distant, and Rylee couldn't tell what he was thinking. Rylee didn't understand much of the traditions and wanted to ask questions, but she hadn't dared. She was thankful when Karam and Basheera had arrived at her door early that morning to prep her. She'd expected lavish silks and robes, but instead their custom was to avoid decorative clothing and jewelry. Instead they'd put her in a traditional Nasirian dress and hijab.

Amar, Rylee and Sharif sat silently in a carriage as they rode behind the one carrying Amar's father through the streets. After ensuring Bishop Enterprises's business was addressed, Sharif had flown out from Palo Alto to Nasir. Neither he, Rylee, nor his boss spoke a word. Thousands stood along the sidelines eager to see the Sheikh and the Royal Family. Rylee noticed how Amar was treated. He was in the last of the carriages as if he were an afterthought. He generously shook hands with several folks as they walked past, and they seemed to know of him regardless of the fact that he was not considered part of the Royal Family. Rylee wanted to comfort him or say something, but he was introspective, so she merely squeezed his hand.

After the royal processional, the Sheikh was buried. Amar reached for Rylee's hand at that moment, and she was happy for this sign that he still remembered she was there. They walked hand in hand to the burial site and stood silently together while Khalid and other family members gave prayers; Amar was not one of them.

Hours later, they all retired to the palace and Rylee stood at Amar's side as more dignitaries stopped by to pay their respects. The pomp and circumstance that went with each greeting and announcement of royalty made her head spin, but she smiled when spoken to and uttered polite pleasantries. The only person she knew was Sharif and even he was preoccupied with several friends.

Khalid, however, was in his element. He fit right in with the other royals, and for the first time since Rylee had met him, he seemed happy.

She left the gathering for a moment and went for a walk outside in the garden. It was the first time she'd had to herself all day.

She felt someone behind her and looked up to see Amar. "Are you alright?" he asked. "When I looked up and didn't see you at my side, I panicked."

"What did you think happened?"

Amar shrugged. "I don't know. But I told you to stay by my side, yes?"

"You did, but I needed some air. It's a little suffocating in there with all those egos."

"Kind of how you thought about me once upon a time, yes?" Amar laughed, glancing back at the palace. It was the first time Rylee had heard that laugh since they left Tucson.

"Oh, you still have an ego," Rylee said, smiling. "It's just been put on the backburner."

He grinned broadly and then turned somber again. "Won't be too much longer now. Tomorrow, we'll read the will and then we can head back to the States, and I can put this place behind me."

"Will you ever come back?" Rylee asked, staring up at him.

"Doubt it," Amar said. "I know my place, and this isn't it. Tariq can always come to the States. But there's one thing I do know." He swung her into his arms.

"And what's that?"

"That I couldn't have done this without you." Amar circled his arms around her middle. "And that I can't thank you enough for coming here with me." He bent down and placed a feather-light kiss on her lips.

"You're welcome."

The next morning, Amar and Rylee gathered with the rest of the Mahmud family in the palace for the reading of the will.

Ibrahim sat at the late Sheikh's large cherry-wood desk and began reading the bequests. Most of them were typical and gave away, to members of the Sheikh's family and cabinet, land, jewels, artifacts and other works of art the Sheikh had collected over the years.

It wasn't until Ibrahim got to the last few items that the shit began hitting the proverbial fan.

"I, King Abdul al' Mahmud, do bequeath equal shares of Mahmud Oil to my sons, Khalid and Tariq, with ten percent held in trust until my first grandson is born. Since Amar has amassed his own empire, I know he has no interest in the oil business."

Amar could see Khalid's gleam of amusement that his father had cut him out of the oil empire, but Amar was alright. He had no interest in oil, and it was as it should be.

Rylee squeezed his hand.

"I, King Abdul al' Mahmud, do bequeath all horses, including my prized Arabians in Nasir and Kentucky, to my first-born son, Amar, since we share a common love of all things equestrian."

Rylee beamed by Amar's side. "That's wonderful!"

"And very generous," Khalid hissed. "Did you just say *all* horses? *I've* been running the stables for years here in Nasir, and he gives him" — he pointed to Amar — "all of them. It's just not right."

"It was your father's wish," Ibrahim replied.

"Are there any more wishes?" Khalid asked, then answered his own question, "I believe that about wraps it up." He rose to leave, but Ibrahim interrupted him.

"Please sit down, Khalid. I'm not done."

"What else could there be?"

"I have a royal decree that I must read," the barrister replied.

Khalid sat up straight. "Well, then get to it."

Amar could see Khalid's chest puff out. He couldn't wait to hear announced to the world that his father had named him King.

"I, King Abdul al' Mahmud, do decree that next King of Nasir is my eldest son, Amar al' Mahmud."

Stunned silence fell across the room, and all eyes turned to Amar. His mouth fell open. He, like everyone else, had assumed the decree would announce Khalid as the next ruler of Nasir. He hadn't expected for his father to defy royal succession rules and appoint him, his bastard son, as King.

Silence soon turned into chaos.

"This can't be done," Queen Saffron screamed and jumped to her feet. "He can't do this!"

"He can, and he did," the barrister replied.

"No!" the Queen said. "I married him with the guarantee that *my son*, not his bastard" — she pointed to Amar — "would be the rightful heir to the throne!"

Khalid's blood boiled, and he rose in a huff. "This is a travesty, and I will fight it."

"I'm sorry, but the King signed this document, and it's legal and binding."

"Like hell it is," Khalid said. "I" — he pounded his chest — "have trained for this my entire life. I have given my blood, sweat and tears for this country, and I will not let a bastard come and rule. What did you do, Amar? Did you make him sign a deathbed decree?" Khalid charged toward him.

Amar rose, prepared to battle with Khalid, but the barrister's words stopped Khalid in his tracks. "That's not true. This decree was written several years ago."

"What?" Amar was stunned. He didn't know what to make of any of this.

"Your father was of sound mind and body when he wrote this decree. Amar," he said, reaching inside his portfolio and removed an envelope, "he wanted you to read this."

Amar's head was spinning. *Me as King of Nasir?* All he knew was that he couldn't breathe and he needed to get out of there. He snatched the letter and raced out of the room.

Rylee sat in the study, flabbergasted by Amar's father's declaration. Everyone had left the room, leaving her alone with the barrister as he packed up.

"Are you alright, miss?" Ibrahim asked.

Rylee blinked, trying to bring him back into focus. "Uh, yes, I'm fine."

Rylee watched him put several files in his briefcase before she asked the question on the tip of her tongue. "What now?"

"I don't understand."

"For Amar? What now?"

"Well, the royal decree makes him King of Nasir. He can do what he sees fit."

"What does that entail?"

"I suppose you're wondering what that means for you?"

Rylee nodded.

"Amar will be tasked with running this kingdom. He'll be required to lead a country of hundreds of thousands and make important decisions on finance, commerce, laws and more. It's not an easy task, especially since he hasn't been groomed for it."

"You think he will fail?"

"The people of this country have a long memory. They haven't forgotten that his father went off to America when he was engaged to Saffron and got an African-American woman with child. It nearly cost him his marriage to Saffron. The only reason she agreed to take him back after the infidelity was with the proviso that her son be King. I warned Abdul not to make this decree, but he was determined."

"Do you know why?"

"The why is in the letter Amar has in his very hands right now."

That's what Rylee was afraid of.

Amar had taken off for the stables the second he received the letter. His only thought: He had to get away. It didn't take him long to saddle up his favorite Arabian and take off for the desert. He raced the horse for miles before he finally got winded, especially with the sand kicking up. He stopped to catch his breath at a nearby tent where several herdsmen were shepherding sheep and camels. What was he running from? From his fate?

How could he have known that his father would royal decree him as King of Nasir? It was ludicrous. He didn't care what Ibrahim said. The man must have been out of his mind.

Amar jumped down from the horse and spoke several broken words of Arabic from the summers he'd spent in Nasir and from forced Arabic lessons before the Sheikh had ended his visits. He'd lost the skill after little use of the language, but managed a few words now.

The herdsmen seemed to understand and offered him respite in one of their tents.

Amar nodded his thanks and sought refuge inside it. The tent was sparsely decorated with some sleeping bags, pillows and minor food provisions. But Amar didn't care. He sat down cross-legged on the pillows and pulled the letter Ibrahim had given him from his britches' pocket. He gingerly opened it.

My dearest Amar,

If you're reading this letter then you know that I have used the royal decree to name you King of Nasir. My decision might come as a shock to you, but secretly I have always known you would make a great king. What you lack in knowledge of the country's ways, you have in determination and fortitude. Your strong will impressed me from the moment you were a baby and stood up on your own at ten months.

Your brother Khalid, although capable, is too hungry. He wants it too much, which is why I think he needs this reality check to humble him and make him a better man. I too used to be like Khalid, ruled by title and privilege. That's until I went away to America at twenty-one and met Camilla, a beautiful professor. I'd never seen someone so stunning in my country, and I was swept away, so much so that I wanted to turn my back on my native home. And when she told me she was pregnant with you, I nearly did. But my father sent his men after me, forcing me home, reminding me of my obligation to Saffron and the promise he'd made to her family. So, I was a coward and chose duty over love.

That decision was the single biggest regret of my life. Not having a relationship with you was the other. To choose duty required me to give you and your mother up. And the only way I knew to do so was to keep you at arm's length. I allowed myself a month each summer to remember the love we'd shared and to bask in your adoration, because that's how you used to look at me when you were little. But as the years passed, the adoration was replaced with ice and hostility for a love denied. I couldn't bear it, which is why I made your visits shorter and shorter until I terminated them altogether.

The decree was the only way I knew how to show you just how much you meant to me. To show you that I loved you and that I was never ashamed to call you my son. To show you that you made me proud when you started your own company, Bishop Enterprises, with no help from me. To show you I respected the man you'd become, despite me. I know this decree is a consolation and is perhaps a little too late, but please know that you always had my love and my heart.

Your father,
Abdul al' Mahmud

Amar dropped the letter to the ground, and, with his head in his hands, began to cry. He couldn't remember the last time he'd cried. And then it came to him.

It was the summer of his ninth year. He'd been so happy to come to Nasir. He hoped that by showing his father what an excellent horseman he'd become, the King would be proud of him. But instead, he'd overheard Khalid whispering with another boy that Amar was a bastard and that he would never amount to anything.

Amar had wanted to cry, but instead he let his anger fuel him and he'd vowed to never cry again, to never let anyone cause him that kind of pain. Until now. His father had broken him. He'd finally shown him unequivocally that he loved him as much if not more than his brothers, because he had been willing to defy duty and country to make him King. He was validating Amar the only way he knew how.

The problem was, Amar had never wanted validation. All he'd ever wanted was his father's love and now he had it, but at what cost? Was he willing to give up everything, Rylee included, to prove to his father and the people of Nasir that he was somebody?

Chapter 17

ARLY THE NEXT MORNING, RYLEE paced her and Amar's palace suite. She glanced at the clock. It was five AM and still dark, but she hadn't slept. Amar hadn't come back to the palace after the reading of the will, and she hadn't been able to go downstairs for supper. How could she when all of his family were vipers and would be throwing daggers at her for Amar's assumed betrayal? So she'd stayed in her room, asking Karam to bring her a bowl of soup because her stomach was jittery.

Where could Amar be? When will he come back? Will he ever come back? For me? He'd promised not to leave her side while she was here, but he had. He'd left her all alone without any allies.

The door to her suite suddenly burst open, and Khalid came stumbling in. "Ah, here's my brother's mistress," he slurred as he stepped into the room.

From where she was standing, Rylee could smell the liquor on his breath, and she didn't like the leer he was giving her as she stood in her nightgown and robe. "What do you want, Khalid?"

"I want that no-count brother of mine," he hissed, circling around her.

"Well, he isn't here," Rylee replied, watching his every move. Khalid was exactly the type Amar had warned her

205

about. She doubted he respected women or their opinions very much.

"That's obvious," Khalid replied. "How long do you think he's going to stay your lover now that he has this whole kingdom" — he spread his arms wide while still holding on to the liquor bottle — "of women at his beck and call. Do you know how many women he can get now that he's King? They will fall to his feet." He motioned to the floor. "And let's not forget that Amar must marry and produce a male heir. To appease the people and cabinet, he'll have to choose a wife from Nasir. And you," he said, pointing to her, "will be a thing of the past."

"I don't have to listen to this," Rylee said and headed toward the open door. "You should leave!"

She'd barely reached the door when Khalid rushed over and slammed it shut. "Who do you think you're talking to?" He pushed her backward and when he did, Rylee's head slammed against the door. "I may not be King, but I'm the Prince of Nasir and you'll show me respect."

The blow was slight, and Rylee recovered long enough to defend herself. She'd been around bullies before and pushed Khalid right back. "That may be so, but I'm not one of your subjects. You can't treat me—" She never got the words out because Khalid backhanded her, and Rylee went sprawling to the floor.

She looked up at him, holding her cheek.

"Oh, God!" Khalid said, dropping to his knees. "I'm sorry. I shouldn't have ..." But he didn't get to finish his sentence because suddenly Amar was in the room hauling Khalid to his feet. Rylee saw Amar's fist connect with Khalid's jaw, sending him careening to the floor.

"How dare you touch my woman?" Amar yelled, lunging for him.

"I'm sorry," Khalid said, fear in his eyes. "It was an accident. I never meant to hurt her."

"You think so." Amar grabbed him by the collar and landed another punch.

"Amar, no!" Rylee screamed, but Amar didn't seem to hear her. He just hit Khalid again.

"Go on!" Khalid said, holding his bloody lip. "Hit me!" When Amar paused, Khalid sucker-punched him, landing a good jab at his right jaw.

"Stop it!" Rylee yelled at both men, but neither one of them heard her. They were too caught up in their own hurt.

"Hit me again!" Khalid taunted, putting his fist together and circling Amar. "You know you want to."

"Damn you!" Amar raised his fist again, and Rylee tried grabbing his arm, but he was too strong and the effort she spent trying to ward him off allowed Khalid to jab him in his abdomen. Amar went stumbling forward as did Rylee. That's when she knew she had to go get help.

She rushed out of the suite. She found Tariq running down the hall toward her in his pajamas and a robe. He must have heard the noise and commotion.

"Stop him!" Rylee said, pointing to their suite.

"I will, Rylee." Tariq touched her arm. "I promise." He rushed inside the room.

Rylee stared at the door. She couldn't go back in there. She hated to see brother against brother. What kind of life was this? She had to get away from the madness. She needed to go back home. It was clear that her presence was only a hindrance to Amar. Soon he would be asked to take a wife not of his choosing. Better she leave now and avoid the heartbreak than have him send her away later.

Rylee looked at the door. Her heart told her to stay, to be there for Amar if and when he needed her, but her head told her she had to go for her own self-preservation. Rylee made a split-second decision and ran down the hall.

She knocked on Sharif's door. It took several minutes, but eventually he appeared, looking slightly disheveled as he fumbled to put on his glasses. When he'd brought her into focus, he said, "Ms. Hart." His voice hitched, and he glanced down the hall to make sure no one was listening. She could only assume it was completely inappropriate for her to show up to his door unannounced in the wee hours of the morning. "Can I help you?" he asked.

"Yes, Sharif."

"Why do you hate me so much?" Amar asked, looking down at Khalid's face, a glowering mask of rage. When Amar had come back to the palace, he'd been in a peaceful state of mind. He'd made peace with his father's decree. That's until he saw his brother lording over Rylee, and she was holding her cheek. *I should have never left her alone.*

"Hate you?" Khalid laughed and blood splattered onto his shirt. "I don't hate you, Amar. I envy you." He tried to rise to his feet but couldn't. "Don't you get it? You were Father's favorite. Even though you were gone, you weren't forgotten. He loved you more than any of us. Isn't that right, Tariq?"

Amar looked to the door and saw his youngest brother staring at them in horror.

"Tell him," Khalid said, stumbling to his feet. "Tell him, Tariq. Tell him how Father talked about him all the time — Amar this, and Amar that." He gestured wildly with his hands. "Tell him how we could never live up to the great Amar. And now this!"

"I never wanted this!" Amar yelled back at him.

"You didn't have to," Khalid said, "because apparently it was always yours to begin with. Father was just humoring me and allowing me to keep your seat warm."

"That's not true," Tariq replied, rushing to Khalid's side. "He must have had a change of heart. He had to have his reasons."

"His reasons?" Khalid laughed bitterly, pushing Tariq away. "That's bull, Tariq, and you know it."

"It's not," Amar said. "You were always the golden boy, Khalid. Father made you in his image."

"Because he'd lost *you!*" Khalid shouted. "And what did it get me?" He pounded his fist with his chest. "A slap in the face. I spent my entire life trying to please that man."

"And you did," Tariq responded. "Father looked to you to lead this family."

"Ha, what a joke." Khalid laughed bitterly. He made an attempt to sit on the bed but ended up sliding down the edge and fell on his bottom.

Amar stifled a laugh but kept a straight face. He heard a helicopter flying overhead and wondered who would presume to arrive at the palace at such an ungodly hour, but he ignored it and said, "It doesn't have to be a joke."

"What are you talking about?" Khalid asked.

"I'm telling you that nothing has to change," Amar replied. "You can still be King."

"After I've dragged our father's name through the mud?" Khalid asked from the floor. "Ruined his legacy." He shook his head. "As much as I want to, I can't do that. I won't give his enemies the satisfaction."

"Not after," Amar said. "Now!"

"I don't understand." Khalid peered at Amar in confusion.

"Neither do I," Tariq commented, turning to his brother. "What do you mean?"

Amar kneeled until he was eye to eye with Khalid. "I never wanted to be King, and I don't want it now."

"What do you mean you don't want to be King?" Khalid couldn't believe the words that were coming out of Amar's mouth.

Amar rose to his feet and turned to Tariq. "I never wanted any of this. I didn't ask for it, and I don't want it. The only thing I *ever* wanted was my father's love, and now I know that I'd had it all along. I could care less that he decreed me the monarchy. You can have this bloody kingdom and every brick and mortar that comes with it. I want *my life back in America*."

Khalid stared back at him, dumbfounded, and Tariq appeared speechless. Amar continued, "Though he loved me, Father was a coward. Rather than tell me his feelings, he took the easy way out and told me in a letter." He pulled the envelope from his pants and held it up. "A letter, a goddamn letter! The two of you," he said, pointing to his brothers as a stray tear fell down his cheek, "he showed the two of you love all of your lives, but *me*, I was the outcast. I was treated like a leopard and all because of his duty. Well, you can have your duty, Khalid, and all the privileges that come with it. I just hope you wield your power better than he did. I hope you're able to show your son that you love him and not wait until your deathbed confessional."

Khalid slowly rose to his feet, staring at Amar all the while. "You're serious, aren't you? You don't want to be King?"

"No, I don't," Amar stated emphatically. "So we can burn that decree as if it never existed."

"But it was Father's wish," Tariq said quietly.

"And I'm exercising mine," Amar replied. "I am happy to know that Father really *did* love me, but I don't belong here any more than I did as a child. The only thing I want is to leave here and move on with my life with Rylee. Speaking of which, where did she go?" He hadn't seen Rylee since his altercation with Khalid had begun.

Amar walked to the suite door and looked both ways down the hall. It was empty, save for several bodyguards who'd no doubt been dispatched in case one of the brothers murdered the other.

"I don't know," Tariq answered. "The last time I saw her, she was running down the hall for help."

"You really mean this?" Khalid asked, switching the subject back to the kingship as he looked at Amar. "Because you know once you do, there's no turning back."

"I'm a man of my word."

"Then let's shake on it." Khalid offered his hand.

"You were born for this, Khalid," Amar replied as he and Khalid joined hands. "Embrace it. Just promise me one thing."

"What's that?"

"That you'll be a good king, a fair king."

"I can promise you that," Khalid replied, and for the first time, he reached out to hug his brother.

Chapter 18

"THANK YOU SO MUCH, CHYNNA," Rylee said into her cell phone many hours later after she had arrived in London. Chynna had just returned to Tucson from one of her tour stops and had assured Rylee over the phone that her jet was available to fly from Arizona to New York to pick her up and bring her back home once she arrived in the States.

Riley's exit from Nasir had been unplanned, and she'd been ill-prepared. It had taken some convincing, but she'd finally gotten Sharif to agree to help her, and thanks to him and Karam, while the brothers were arguing she had snuck back into her suite to retrieve her purse and her overnight bag. She barely had time to change clothes and get her belongings before she'd hopped on the helicopter and flown out of Dubai.

A day later, when she finally landed in New York and turned on her phone, it instantly started beeping to tell her of missed voicemails and texts. She didn't have to read or listen to know who they were from. She was sure Amar was upset with her, but she had had to leave abruptly because she didn't want Amar to prevent her departure.

She had refused to wait in Nasir like some lovesick teenager and have him show her the door. She cared about him too much, *loved* him too much. She let out a long, tortured sigh. She really loved him. There was no question about that now. It was an indisputable fact. She loved Amar.

She loved his sexiness. His intelligence. His wit. She even loved his arrogance. It kind of went with his persona that made him uniquely Amar and uniquely hers. But was he? They'd never made any commitments to one another. And now that he was decreed King of Nasir, they never would. Khalid and Ibrahim had told her that Amar had a duty as King. He would have to marry someone of Nasirian descent, and Rylee would be left out in the cold.

She had to accept her fate. Yet again, she'd fallen in love with someone she couldn't have. Why hadn't she learned her lesson the first time with Shelton? She supposed some lessons you didn't learn you were destined to repeat.

But why does it hurt so bad? Rylee felt like her heart was literally being split in two, one half she'd left in Nasir with Amar and the other she was bringing back with her to Tucson. Perhaps Jeremy had been right. Perhaps she'd made a mistake falling for Amar. Or was Caleb right and she should be happy to have loved and lost than never to have loved at all?

Rylee's head was spinning. All she knew was that she'd lost the man she loved, and she didn't know if she would ever recover.

The previous day, Rylee's surprise departure had thrown Amar into a crazed daze.

"What do you mean she's gone, Sharif?" his voice had risen several octaves. After his long talk with his brothers, he'd gone in search of Rylee to apologize to her for not only leaving her alone at the palace as he'd grappled with his father's bequest, but also because he'd wanted to apologize for the scene she'd witnessed. He hadn't, however, expected for his trusted friend and advisor to tell him that he'd helped facilitate Rylee leaving Nasir, *leaving him.* "You should have never let her go."

"I'm sorry, Your Highness," Sharif had said and bowed. "I meant no disrespect, but she'd vowed she would leave, in her words, *'one way or another.'* "

"Get up, Sharif," Amar had said, grabbing Sharif by the arm and lifting him to his feet. "I'm not *Your Highness.*"

"But the decree?"

"Is null and void," Amar had replied. "I appreciate the sentiment behind it, but I'm no more interested in being King than I am in walking on the moon."

"So what happens now?"

"Khalid will be King as he should be, but I don't care about any of that right now," Amar had huffed as he paced the floor back and forth. "I want to know why you agreed to help Rylee leave here without speaking to me first?"

"I didn't want any harm to come to Ms. Hart if she found her own transportation outside the palace. You know how stubborn she can be. You would have my head if something happened to her, so I called the pilot and asked him to take her to Dubai."

Amar had known Sharif was right. Rylee could be as stubborn as a mule, especially if she believed something to be true. "And where was she going then?"

"Presumably, after several connections, home to Tucson?" Sharif had offered.

"Damn!" Rylee had left thinking Amar was some brute beast, thinking that becoming King *would change him, had changed him.* He had to tell her that he didn't want any of it. He had to tell her that he wanted her and only her. He had to tell her ... *he loved her.*

"I'm so glad you're back home, sis," Caleb said, hugging Rylee after she'd exited the airport terminal and found him waiting for her with the pickup truck.

"I'm glad to be home," Rylee replied.

"What was Noah thinking, allowing you to go out there?" He threw her belongings into the back of the truck before coming around to open her door.

"Noah couldn't have stopped me," Rylee said, sliding inside. "Once I got it in my head that I was going with Amar, nothing and no one could have stopped me."

"I could have." Caleb closed the door behind her. He walked in front of the pickup to the driver side and climbed in. "It was reckless going to a foreign country, Rylee. You must see that now." He turned on the engine and kicked the truck into gear.

"I wasn't thinking of that." Rylee defended her actions. "I went there to be with Amar. His father was dying. I *had* to go."

"And what happened?" Caleb asked, glancing at her as he drove. "It blew up in your face."

"Not in the way you think," Rylee said. "Amar didn't cause any of this."

"Then why did you leave?"

"I left on my own accord. It was my choice to leave."

"But why?"

"There was a tough decision ahead of Amar between duty and his family and me. Rather than have him struggle, I made it easy for him, and I left."

"You took the choice out of his hands?" Caleb surmised. "Do you think that was fair?" The truck came to an abrupt halt at a stoplight, and Caleb turned to glare at her. "You didn't give him the chance to choose you. How do you know he wouldn't have?"

Rylee stared at him before answering, "I don't."

Caleb shook his head in frustration. "If I were him, I'd be ready to spit nails."

"I'm sure he is," Rylee said. "But I stand behind what I did. I made the right choice."

"Are you sure about that?" Caleb asked. "Because from the looks of it, you were over the moon for that prince, yet you're willing to throw that all away. Can you live with that decision?"

"I have to," Rylee stated with conviction. "I want Amar to be happy, even if that isn't with me."

"That's pretty selfless," Caleb responded, keeping his eye on the road. "I doubt I could do the same if I were in your shoes. But then again, I respect my big sister. You're an amazing woman."

Rylee reached across and touched his arm. "Thank you, Caleb. That means a lot."

"You're welcome. But what happens when Amar comes looking for you? Because you know he will. In the little time I got to know him, he doesn't strike me as the type to take this lying down."

"He won't," Rylee said. "He'll be too busy, and if he does, I won't be here."

"Where are you going?"

"Chynna and Kenya offered to let me tag along on their twinie weekend back to the Canyon Ranch Resort. As soon as we get back, I'm heading there for a few days to try and get my head on straight."

"I hope you're able to make peace with yourself."

"I'm certainly going to try."

Rylee didn't waste any time packing her bags again once they returned to the ranch. Her mother wasn't happy to see her leave so soon after she'd just got her back, but Rylee needed time and space. Some walks alone at the resort might be exactly what the doctor ordered. After a long hot shower, within an hour she had repacked and was on her way to the spa in her Toyota RAV4.

She didn't anticipate that Amar would come for her, but in case he did, she couldn't be at home. She needed to get away and really evaluate their relationship. Amar might try to talk her into coming back to Nasir or even into a casual sex setup, and she wasn't sure she was strong enough to resist him. Would any relationship with Amar be better than nothing at all?

It could, but she wouldn't, couldn't be like his mother - waiting for Amar to come to the States to appease his fleshy urges. No, she had to be strong, because deep down she knew what she wanted. She wanted commitment, a real one in which they would vow their eternal love to one another. She would settle for nothing less than his entire heart.

She arrived at the spa twenty minutes later and drove the tree-lined street to the private villa. Chynna and Kenya had stayed there previously when Chynna had been trying to escape the paparazzi. It's where Chynna and her sister had concocted their elaborate plan to switch places over a year ago. Rylee didn't need to hatch any crazy schemes, but she did need some shoulders to lean on and ears to listen, and she found them in her sister-in-law and her sister-in-law's twin.

Kenya opened the door to their villa just as Rylee was pulling her suitcase out of the back of the SUV. "Here, let me help you with that," Kenya said, rushing toward her.

Sometimes it was so weird for Rylee to see Chynna's face on someone else. Chynna and Kenya had both been gifted with great DNA and svelte bodies — that was until Chynna's recent baby bump. And now, Kenya had cut her hair into a stylish bob.

"Kenya!" Rylee smiled when she approached and greeted her with a hug.

"Good to see you, Rylee. I would say you're looking well," Kenya replied, taking Rylee's toiletry bag out of her hands, "which you usually are, save for those dark circles under your eyes. Did you get any sleep on the flights?"

"Not much," Rylee replied, hauling her suitcase out and closing the trunk. She followed Kenya up the stone steps to the villa.

"Rylee!" Chynna gushed, running toward her when she walked in. "So happy you could join us."

"Thanks for the invite," Rylee responded as she glanced around and really saw the nicely decorated villa for the first time. She'd been inside once, when she'd come to help Chynna pack her bags after she'd crashed her jeep at Golden Oaks and first met Noah. It was funny that it seemed a lifetime ago after the last few weeks spent with Amar.

"I think you need some serenity more than us," Chynna replied, grabbing Rylee's arm and walking her toward the sofa. They both sat down. "Why don't you tell us all about it?"

"Over a bottle of wine," Kenya added, setting Rylee's toiletry bag on the floor in the foyer. "I came prepared this time." Kenya had remembered that the spa was dry and brought her own supplies.

"That sounds great," Rylee said. "It's been a long day."

"No problem," Kenya said. She'd already uncorked a bottle with the wine opener and had left it breathing on the counter. She walked over to the cupboards, grabbed two wine goblets and began pouring one for her and Rylee. Chynna would have to have sparkling cider.

"I'm surprised Mama Madelyn didn't make you try and stay," Chynna replied. "They missed you terribly. You'd think Amar had gone and kidnapped you the way they carried on about the way you'd left on a whim. I couldn't bear to tell them that I" —

she touched her chest — "was the one who encouraged you to go after Amar."

"And you were right," Rylee said. "I don't regret that. I would certainly hope he would have done the same for me, if someone in my family were on their deathbed."

"How did it go?" Kenya handed Rylee a glass of wine. She returned to the kitchen and poured her twin some cider.

"It was a somber time, as is to be expected," Rylee replied, "but the hostility was so prevalent with Amar's family, you could cut the tension with a knife. It was worse than I'd imagined."

"Did that extend to you?" Chynna accepted the glass of cider from her twin as Kenya sat opposite her.

"You better believe it," Rylee said. She took a sip of her wine and put it on the coffee table. "And I was made aware that I was not a wanted guest and that they all saw me as nothing more than a body that kept Amar's bed warm. I could never live there in that culture, where women are second-class citizens."

"Sounds like it was eye-opening," Kenya commented.

"It was." Rylee stifled a yawn.

"You should go get a bath and relax. We can talk more later," Chynna said, "if you're up for it."

"That's an excellent idea," Rylee said, rising from the sofa. She reached for her wine goblet and took it with her. "Maybe while I'm in there, I'll figure out my new lease on life."

She doubted it would be that simple. She doubted anything would be simple again, because now that she knew what love looked like, it wouldn't be easy to go back to her former life.

Chapter 19

"I'M REALLY SORRY, SIR," SHARIF said in the limo on their way to Bishop Enterprises.

"Enough, Sharif," Amar said as he fixed his tie on the custom designer suit he wore. He didn't feel Sharif needed to apologize again for letting Rylee get on that helicopter when he knew Sharif had been a good friend by watching out for her. He would get her back in due time.

If Amar had his choice, he would go directly to Tucson and toss her into his car and bring her back with him to California, but he couldn't. Some critical business deal at Bishop Enterprises required his attention in Palo Alto. He had to make a pit stop in his hometown before finding Rylee. He had a real bone to pick with Ms. Hart. Thanks to the press getting wind of his father's death, rumors were flying around that he would be stepping down as CEO of Bishop Enterprises.

Did everyone, including Rylee, think him so fickle that he would drop his entire life at the drop of a hat, all on his father's last whim? Well, they were wrong.

When the limo stopped and the driver opened the door, Amar climbed out, buttoned his suit jacket and sauntered into the building with Sharif close behind him.

"Good morning, Mr. Bishop," a receptionist greeted him.

He smiled. "Good morning." Amar stared at the signage, "B.E.," behind her. He'd built the company from the ground up, and he'd be damned if he let anything destroy it. He had called an emergency board meeting and would Skype in several key stockholders. Since his company had gone public a couple of years ago, he had to keep them in the loop on any major decisions, though Amar had retained fifty-one percent of the stock. He couldn't bear giving up complete control, no matter how fat it might make his pockets.

The meeting was nearly convened when Amar sauntered in.

"Good morning, everyone."

All conversation ceased as they looked in Amar's direction. Most were shocked that he was there. He had been somewhat absent at B.E. of late from day-to-day operations, but he was still their leader.

"I'm here today to squash the rumors that I will be stepping down as president and CEO of Bishop Enterprises," Amar stated, looking around the room. "I'm as committed as ever to the success of this company, for myself and for all of you." He looked at the investors on the multiple screens. "In fact, we are on the cusp of some new innovations. Sharif, show them what we have."

Over the next hour, Amar expounded on the next acquisitions that would come under their multimedia conglomerate in the United Kingdom as well as some innovations in the works. When the meeting concluded, several businessmen and women walked over to greet Amar.

"Glad you're staying on, Amar."

"Knew you wouldn't leave us to run a small country," another said, laughing.

Amar smiled. That man didn't know how right he was, and his father hadn't been entirely wrong. He may not be a king, but he was definitely leader material.

After the room had cleared and it was just Amar and Sharif, Amar turned to his dear friend. "I'm leaving you here in charge as I have business to attend to."

"Would that business be Rylee Hart?"

Amar smiled. Sharif was nothing if not observant. Amar nodded.

"What are you going to do?" Sharif asked. "What are you going to say?"

"I'm going to tell her what I should have told her a week ago — that I love her, and I don't want to live without her."

Sharif grinned broadly. "Smart man." He was glad to hear Amar finally admit what he'd known from day one, which was that Rylee Hart had stolen his heart. "Go get her."

"I'm going to do just that."

Rylee was confused. She was starting to have doubts if she should have left Amar. She missed him. Not just the passion, which flew off the charts, but she missed their fun. She missed the quiet moments when they'd sat out on the porch just talking or when they'd gone horseback riding at Golden Oaks. It had been a time of self-discovery.

From the moment they'd met, there had been sparks. Sparks she'd tried to deny, but even Jeremy had seen it. It was undeniable. And when they'd made love, Rylee had experienced a bliss she hadn't known possible, and it was all because of him. Then he'd gone and she'd been devastated, but there again, she'd been wrong. He'd come back for her, determined to show her and her family that he was *worthy* of her, and he'd nearly succeeded but then his father's condition had worsened.

She'd doubted him again, because he hadn't asked her to join him, but the joy on his face when he'd seen her on that plane told her she'd made the right decision. But even she couldn't heal the rift between him and his family. The scars went too deep, were too painful. And so when faced with the opportunity of honoring his father's last decree to be King of Nasir, he would do what was necessary. How could he not?

Rylee couldn't see the situation ending any differently, but now she had her doubts.

"Rylee?"

She looked up to find Chynna had joined her on the hiking path.

"I'm sorry to disturb you. I know you wanted to be alone, but I also thought you might want to talk," Chynna said. "And if not, I'm here just to keep you company."

"It's okay," said Rylee, patting the large tree branch where she sat. "Come join me."

"You seemed deep in thought."

"I was. I was second-guessing myself, was wondering if I made the right decision."

"And what did you come up with?"

"I haven't," Rylee said, turning to her. "I just know this — I love him, Chynna." She finally said the words out loud. "I love him." She shrugged. "And I left without telling him how I feel. I left because I was afraid he would ask me to leave, and I couldn't bear the thought of losing him. But I don't know if I did the right thing. If I told him how I felt, would it have made a difference?"

"Funny about hindsight, right?" Chynna laughed bitterly, "Things look much clearer when you're away from the situation."

"I guess I will never know," Rylee said.

"Where is she?" Amar yelled. He jumped down from the horse he'd borrowed from the Golden Oaks stables to ride out to the pasture, where he confronted Noah and Caleb, who were working with the cattle that afternoon.

As soon as he'd left Sharif, Amar had returned to his jet and set a course for Tucson. He and Rylee needed to talk. He could only assume she'd left in some misguided attempt of giving him his freedom so he could rule Nasir. He didn't need it. Or want it. He only wanted Rylee, and he was here to tell her that. But when he'd arrived and gone to the main house, he'd learned from the housekeeper that Rylee wasn't there and had gone away for a few days. Mr. and Mrs. Hart were out visiting guests, so Amar had no choice but to find Rylee's brothers and convince them that he needed to see her.

Noah and Caleb looked up from the cow they'd been wrangling free from a wire fence.

"What the hell do you want?" Caleb asked.

"I asked you where Rylee was," Amar stated. He was in no mood for Caleb's theatrics. He'd had enough from his own brothers the last week.

"And I asked you what the hell do you want?" Caleb rose from the ground where he'd been holding the steer and stood to his full six foot three to Amar's six-foot-four stature. Caleb's chest was puffed up as if he were ready for a battle.

"Easy now," Noah said. He motioned to one of the other ranch hands to take over. Once the ranch hand did, Noah joined Caleb and presented a united front to Amar.

Amar took a deep breath and reminded himself that getting into a fight with Rylee's family would be counterproductive. He needed their help and the only way he would get it was if he was straightforward and honest about his reason for being there. "I want to speak to Rylee. She left my home country of Nasir unexpectedly without even speaking to me, and we have some unfinished business."

"Rylee called me and my wife distraught about whatever happened in your *home country*," Noah replied. "I don't want or need to know what happened over there." Noah waved his hand around. "That's between you and Rylee. What I *do* know is that I won't have you coming back to cause my sister any more hurt. You've done enough."

"That's fair," Amar responded, "and I respect that, but I'm not here to hurt Rylee. I hope my presence will show her that I'm in it for the long haul."

"Meaning?" Caleb asked, folding his arms.

"I love Rylee," Amar admitted without hesitation. "I think I have since we first met, but I never told her. And I want to tell her now. I need to tell her that I want to start a life with her." He watched Caleb's brow rise in surprise. "If she's willing," he added.

"Well, you should have led with that," Caleb replied, smiling.

Noah chuckled. "I'm with Caleb on this one. Listen, Amar. We only want what's best for Rylee, and if she chooses you then we won't stand in her way. We just want you to do right by her, ya hear?" He offered Amar his hand.

Amar accepted and shook it fervently. "I hear. So, where the heck is she?"

Rylee and Chynna returned to the cabin nearly a half hour later. They didn't recognize the car in front of the villa and went in to see who their guest was. Chynna entered first, but Rylee paused in the entryway to remove her mud-covered hiking boots.

Kenya rose from the sofa with a huge smile. "You're back," she said.

"Yeah, Rylee went for a hike," Chynna replied, "and I joined her."

"Wow! Who would have thought it? As I recall, you never liked hiking before, sis," Kenya said.

"That's until my hike led me to Noah," Chynna replied. "So whose car is outside?"

"Do we have a guest?" Rylee asked, walking into the living room.

Amar exited the powder room to her left, and Rylee sucked in a deep breath at the sight of him. "Amar?"

His eyes locked with hers. "Rylee."

Kenya and Chynna glanced at the two lovebirds and, using their twin telepathy, they didn't speak a word and quickly left the living room.

"Omigod, I am so glad he's here," Rylee heard Chynna whisper on her way up the stairs with Kenya.

"Wh-what are you doing here?" Rylee asked nervously, glancing around. "Shouldn't you be back in Nasir?"

Amar shook his head. "My place is here. With you."

"It is?"

His brow furrowed. "Yes." He walked toward her, but she took a step backward. She wasn't afraid of him, but perhaps she was afraid of herself and what she might do if she were too close to him. Would she spring herself into his arms and beg him to forgive her for ever leaving him?

"Can we sit and talk?" He motioned to the sofa.

She didn't answer, but joined him by sitting in the big armchair across from the sofa. She didn't know why Amar was here, and she was too afraid to hope of what it could mean. She would just have to hear him out. She sat in silence and waited.

He cleared his throat.

Amar didn't know it was going to be this hard revealing his true feelings to Rylee. He'd already said he loved her to Sharif, even her brothers. So why was it so hard to tell the person he loved that he cared for her? Maybe because he'd never told a woman that.

Rylee was the first. And the only.

There would never be another woman for him, hadn't been since he'd laid eyes on her. He'd been hungry for her the moment they'd met, and now was no different. When she'd walked in with Chynna wearing those skimpy leggings, a flyaway cardigan and that snug tank top, which he knew housed small, but pert breasts, he'd wanted to ravish her on sight.

Instead he summoned his courage and began pouring out his heart. "I'm sorry you had to see my brother and I behave that way in Nasir the day you left."

"That was hard to see," Rylee said. "I'd never seen you behave like that before."

"That's because you and your family are so close," Amar responded. "I've never had that."

Rylee nodded. "I know, and I got to see for myself the abuse you must have endured as a child over the years. It must have been so hard for you, Amar, growing up like that, without—"

"Without love?" he offered, looking into Rylee's eyes.

"Yes, without love."

"It was," he replied. "I never knew my father loved me until the barrister handed me that letter."

Rylee wondered how someone could, in a few short words, spill a lifetime of regret. "What did it say?"

"That he loved my mother. Always had. That he chose duty over love, over me. And it was the single biggest regret of his life. It said that he was leaving the country to me as proof of his love. By defying the succession rules, he wanted to show me that he loved and respected me. But you know what?"

"What?"

"It was a little too late," Amar replied. "I needed to hear the words in that letter long before he died. Not after. Hearing it should have given me solace, but instead it made me angry." He rose to his feet and moved closer to Rylee. "It made me so angry that he didn't have the guts to tell me himself. He thought he *showed me* by giving me the best in life."

"And all you wanted was him."

Amar nodded. How was it that Rylee seemed to know him so well in such a short time? She was truly his soulmate. "I needed time to process it all, and I'm sorry it took me all night. When I got back, I wanted to tell you that as much as I appreciated the grand gesture, I didn't want to be King of Nasir. I never did. I just wanted to be looked at as his son and not a bastard. I came back to the palace to tell Khalid that the kingdom was his. But when I got to the suite and saw that Khalid had hit you—"

"It was an accident," Rylee said, interrupting him.

"I know, but I didn't know that at the time, and all I could see was all the years of love that Khalid had that I didn't, and I lost it for a minute."

"It frightened me, seeing you like that." She'd been so scared of the hatred in his eyes that she'd almost, almost wondered if he was the right man for her, but deep down she knew the answer.

"I'm sorry about that, baby," Amar said as he kneeled in front of the chair to face her. "But I was a ball of raw nerves, and seeing you hurt just set me off."

The room was silent for a moment as Rylee processed everything Amar had just said. *He didn't want to be King. What does that mean?* "So, what happened when I left?"

Amar rose back to his feet. "You mean after we stopped beating each other to a bloody pulp?"

Rylee half-smiled.

"We called a cease-fire, and I told Khalid that I didn't want to be King. I burned that royal decree as if it had never been written."

Rylee's eyes grew large. "You did?"

Amar laughed. "I did. Khalid was stunned. He'd always been jealous of me because he knew I was the rightful heir and he thought I wanted to be King. But instead, I handed him the keys to the kingdom and told him to do with it as he saw fit."

"He must have been floored."

"To say the least," said Amar as he rested his arm on the fireplace mantel. "I told Khalid that he was groomed for greatness and to be a good king, and then I went to look for you. Imagine my surprise," he said, turning around to face her, "when Sharif told me he helped you escape Nasir. I wasn't just speechless, I was furious."

"Please tell me you didn't fire Sharif. He was merely trying to help me. And I didn't make it easy for him. I threatened to leave on my own."

Amar sighed. "I didn't, and he told me you forced his hand. Anyway I came back to the States as soon as I could to find you."

More silence. Who should speak? Should it be her? No, he'd come for her, so she wanted to hear what he'd come to say. She prayed that it was what she was wishing and hoping for. "And?"

"And, that part of my life is over, Rylee. That's not to say I won't see my brother Tariq, maybe even visit Khalid one day, but I'm ready for the next phase of my life. And that part is with you."

A lone tear trickled down Rylee's cheek.

Amar came back to her chair and bent down so that the two of them were at eye level. He grasped one of her hands.

"I love you, Rylee. I have from the start, and I know I was long-winded just now, but I wanted you to understand, to see that I had to face a lot of baggage to get to this moment, but I'm here. And ... and I'm hoping that you feel the same way about me that I feel about you."

Rylee's free hand reached out and stroked Amar's cheek as another fresh tear trickled down her face.

"Please don't cry," Amar responded. He hated to see her do that.

"They're tears of joy," Rylee whispered, "because I love you too, Amar."

"You do?"

Rylee nodded. "And I'm sorry I left you in Nasir. I was scared that you might be like your father and choose duty over me. I was afraid you might not love me. I'm so sorry I let my fears get in the way, because I regretted it the minute I got back."

"Oh, baby." Amar leaned in, grabbed both sides of her face with his hands, and kissed her. It was light and soft and sweet and oh so right. "I don't care about any of that now. I only care that you love me as much as I love you."

"And I do," Rylee said, pulling away so she could look into his eyes. "I really do."

"I don't deserve you," Amar said, hugging her tightly.

"Yes, you do," Rylee said. "You deserve love just like the rest of us, if not more so, because it was always denied to you."

"I will spend the rest of my life showing you just how much I love you."

"What?" Rylee couldn't believe what she was hearing, and she pulled away to look at Amar. *The rest of his life?*

"You heard right. I'm asking you to marry me, Rylee Hart. I'm madly, deeply, crazy in love with you, and I want you to be my wife and the mother of my children. Say yes."

"Yes." Rylee circled her arms around Amar's neck and sealed her lips to his. "Yes, I'll marry you. A hundred times, yes."

An insurmountable passion flared between the two of them. Rylee just wanted to be with Amar and feel his mouth and hands on her. His kisses became hotter, fierier and more urgent. His tongue pressed forward in her mouth and mated with hers, exploring every nook and cranny. The two of them ignited a fire.

They forgot where they were until they heard two loud coughs. They sprung apart, and Rylee glanced up to see Chynna and Kenya at the door of the villa with their suitcases at their feet.

A grin stretched across Chynna's face when she said, "We're, uh" — she motioned to Kenya at her side — "going to go back to the ranch and leave you two lovebirds here, alone. Looks like you might need this place more than us." She winked at Rylee as she and Kenya headed out the door. "The villa is yours for the weekend."

Rylee blushed. "Thank you."

When the door closed behind the twins, Amar tucked his arm underneath Rylee's bottom, lifted her into his arms and carried her up the stairs. "Which room?" he groaned.

Rylee motioned to the bedroom at the far end of the hall.

Amar kicked it open with his heel and then slammed it shut. He lowered Rylee onto the bed and began removing his clothes as fast as he could. His shoes were first, followed by his tie and shirt.

Rylee didn't wait for Amar to undress her. She quickly tore off the cardigan and hauled the tank and sports bra she'd been wearing over her head until her breasts were bared. She heard a sharp intake of breath and looked up to find Amar watching her undress. He'd stopped and was still wearing his trousers.

"Don't stop," Rylee said as she sat on her knees. "I want to see all of you. And you can see all of me." In one fell swoop, she lowered down her thighs the leggings and bikini panties she'd been wearing. She kicked them off and then slid backward completely naked on the duvet toward the pillows and beckoned him with her index finger.

His eyes roamed over her body appreciatively, and they blazed a path from her breasts to her triangle patch. Amar quickly made mincemeat of his trousers and boxer shorts, and they followed the same path as the rest of his clothes, piled high on the floor, so he could join her naked on the bed. His entire body covered hers, and Rylee felt his hard arousal pulsing against her thigh. His tongue traced the outline of her lips and of their own accord, her lips parted, allowing him entry.

A shudder of desire swept through Rylee, and she responded by meeting his tongue and stroking it intimately with hers. Amar groaned but didn't break the kiss. Instead, the kiss just intensified, going on and on and on, until eventually they broke free for air.

Amar paid homage to her breasts by tasting, sucking, licking, biting and devouring them. Rylee reveled that this man was hers. All hers.

His mouth returned to Rylee's lips while his fingers skimmed her breasts, stomach and navel before claiming the area between her legs. His fingers stroked, probed and caressed her, making her wet with need. She wanted all of him and couldn't wait until they were joined together as one.

"Amar, please."

"Please what?"

"Make love to me."

"Oh, I will," Amar said. "I can't wait, but first I want this." His fingers pushed deeper inside her, and his mouth left hers to trail a path of hot kisses to her earlobe. He licked and teased her ear while his expert fingers teased her clitoris. He seemed to relish the moans and involuntary purrs that escaped her lips.

Amar could take it no longer. He had to be inside her. His erection guided him to his destination, and he leaned down to capture Rylee's lips. He stroked her tongue with his while her muscles encompassed all of him. She lifted her legs and wrapped them around his waist, bringing him even deeper inside.

"Rylee," Amar groaned as she began writhing underneath him. "You're not playing fair."

"I know," she murmured.

Amar grabbed her wrists playfully and pulled them above her head. He began riding her with an urgency that bordered on obsession. Rylee was his and would always be. He heard her whimpering sounds of pleasure as he pumped away. They were on a journey that Amar hadn't taken with any other woman. Rylee had branded him and made him hers.

"Amar!" Rylee let out a shuddering breath, and he felt her milking him, clenching all around him, but he wasn't there yet.

He gave several more quick thrusts and let out a huge guttural groan from not only sexual gratification but love that washed over him, claiming his body and his mind. In that moment, Amar felt at peace and knew he loved this woman and would never get enough of her.

Epilogue

"**W**HAT DO YOU THINK ABOUT a double wedding?" Rylee asked her family as they all gathered at the Golden Oaks Ranch for dinner two months later. She and Amar had just come back from a two-week vacation off the coast of France to visit Amar's brother Tariq.

"With who?" her mother asked.

"With us," Kenya James and her fiancé, music mogul Lucas Kingston, replied as they walked into the living room. Kenya was looking stylishly chic in her new haircut, summer dress and some slingback mules, while Lucas was dressed casually in trousers and a royal-blue shirt that accentuated his dark features, from his complexion to his midnight eyes.

"Really?" Chynna asked, excitedly running her hands through her hair. "Oh, I can't wait. This is going to be twice as much fun."

"Yes," Rylee said, nodding as she fingered the six-carat solitaire engagement ring Amar had given her. It still surprised her that she would soon be Mrs. Amar Bishop. So much had happened in such a short amount of time: their courtship, their engagement and now their impending marriage. "Amar and I are ready to tie the knot, and Kenya and I got to talking, and with her and Lucas's wedding coming up in a few months, it seemed like a win-win."

"Gird your loins, Kenya and Rylee, you're going to be in for a bumpy ride," Noah commented from Chynna's side as he rubbed her expanding six-month middle. "You two getting married on the same day — it's going to be grand."

"You don't mind sharing your big day, Lucas?" Caleb asked the mogul as he played his usual role of bartender and prepared Lucas a drink.

"The more the merrier," Lucas replied. "I can't wait to make Kenya my wife." He glanced over at his amazing fiancée with adoration. "And if Rylee and Amar want to join the festivities, why the heck not?"

"Wow!" Caleb said. "There's just a little too much love and romance in the air here. I'm going to have to escape before I catch what's going around." He handed Lucas his drink.

"Just wait, little brother. You're next," Rylee said.

"I'm not the marrying kind," Caleb replied.

"You think so now," Amar said, pulling Rylee toward him, settling his arm comfortably around her waist, "but wait until you meet *the one*." He looked down at her adoringly. "Then you'll see — because once you do, you'll have no choice but to embrace the power of love."

Amar bent down and planted a full kiss on Rylee's lips in front of her family. He didn't care about showing anyone and everyone that he and Rylee had a love for the ages.

Acknowledgements

My fans have been wonderfully supportive of my writing career the last decade. It's because of them that I keep striving to hone my craft and create great stories filled with drama, love and passion.

A huge thank you to Alina Vale, DVM, I couldn't have done it without you. Thank you for all your insight, tips and helpful contacts.

Thank you to Dr. Denise Mose for her info on the Kentucky Derby. Wish I could have made it there with you in 2014. Maybe next year!

To my cheerleader of going rogue on ebooks and staying the course: Kiara Ashanti.

And in the words of Sprint, I thank my framily (friends and family) for all their support: Austin, Asilee, Kimberly and Cassandra Mitchell; Lateisha Sawyer, Tonya Conway, Therolyn Rodgers and Dimitra Astwood, Tiffany Griffin Bhushan Sukrham. Last but not least, a big kiss to my love, Freddie Blackman, you keep me grounded.

About the Author

Y AHRAH ST. JOHN BECAME A writer at the age of twelve when she wrote her first novella after secretly reading a Harlequin romance. She's the proud author of forty-three books with Kimani Romance and Harlequin Desire plus her own indie books.

When she's not at home crafting one of her steamy romances with compelling heroes and feisty heroines with a dash of family drama, she is gourmet cooking or traveling the globe seeking out her next adventure. For more info:

www.yahrahstjohn.com

Other Books by Yahrah St. John

One Magic Moment
Dare to Love
Never Say Never
Risky Business of Love
Playing for Keeps – Orphan Series
This Time for Real – Orphan Series
If You So Desire– Orphan Series
Two to Tango– Orphan Series
Need You Now – Adams Cosmetic Series
Lost Without You– Adams Cosmetic Series
Formula for Passion– Adams Cosmetic Series
Dirty Laundry
Delicious Destiny – Drayson Series
A Chance With You
Entangled Hearts
Entangled Hearts 2
Untamed Hearts
Restless Hearts
Heat Wave of Desire– Millionaire Mogul Series
Can't Get Enough
Cappuccino Kisses – Drayson Series
Taming Her Tycoon – Knights of LA Series
Chasing Hearts
Miami After Hours – Millionaire Mogul Series
Secrets of the A-List
Taming Her Billionaire – Knights of LA Series
Unchained Hearts
His San Diego Sweetheart – Millionaire Mogul Series

Captivated Hearts
At the Ceo's Pleasure – The Stewart Heirs
His Marriage Demand – The Stewart Heirs
Red Carpet Redemption – The Stewart Heirs
Secrets of a Fake Fiancée – The Stewart Heirs
Insatiable Hunger – Dynasty Seven Sins
Claimed by the Hero – The Mitchell Brothers
Two Hot Kisses – New Year Bae Solutions
Consequences of Passion – The Lockett's of Tuxedo Park
Winning Back His Wife – The Lockett's of Tuxedo Park
*Blind Date with the Spare Heir – The
Lockett's of Tuxedo Park*
Seducing the Seal – The Mitchell Brothers
Holiday Playbook – The Lockett's of Tuxedo Park
A Game Between Friends – The Lockett's of Tuxedo Park
Vacation Crush – Texas Cattleman's Ranchers & Rivals

Coming Soon
Guarding His Princess – The Mitchell Brothers
Her Best Friend's Brother - Six Gems

Made in United States
Orlando, FL
17 September 2022

22530258R10137